Real readers love Emma Hornby's page-turning, absorbing sagas:

'I was **hooked** from the very first page. A gripping story'

'Got me reading **till the wee hours of the morning**'

'I love books based on the lives and communities in WW2 and
this book had it all . . . Cannot wait for the next one'

'So many **fantastic characters, and twists and turns galore.**
Couldn't put the book down'

'An emotional rollercoaster of a read. **I loved** it'

'A **fantastic** read with lots of surprises and moments
that **make the hairs on the back of your neck stand on end.**
Can't wait to read the next book from this talented author'

'Twists, surprises, sadness and happiness all
intermingled in a **riveting** story'

'Emma Hornby's books **just keep getting better
and better.** Honest, gritty, lovely characters'

'Emma is a **wonderful storyteller** and
I can't wait for the next one!'

'Similar to Rosie Goodwin and Dilly Court,
Emma Hornby **tells a brilliant story** that will keep
you guessing with twists and turns. **Pure talent**'

www.penguin.co.uk

Also by Emma Hornby

A SHILLING FOR A WIFE
MANCHESTER MOLL
THE ORPHANS OF ARDWICK
A MOTHER'S DILEMMA
A DAUGHTER'S PRICE
THE MAID'S DISGRACE
A MOTHER'S BETRAYAL
THE CHIMNEY SWEEP'S SISTER

Worktown Girls at War
HER WARTIME SECRET
A DAUGHTER'S WAR

A SISTER'S FIGHT

Emma Hornby

PENGUIN BOOKS

TRANSWORLD PUBLISHERS
Penguin Random House, One Embassy Gardens,
8 Viaduct Gardens, London SW11 7BW
www.penguin.co.uk

Transworld is part of the Penguin Random House group of companies
whose addresses can be found at global.penguinrandomhouse.com

First published in Great Britain in 2024 by Bantam
an imprint of Transworld Publishers
Penguin paperback edition published 2024

A CIP catalogue record for this book
is available from the British Library.

ISBN
9781804993545

Typeset in 12/16pt ITC New Baskerville Std by Manipal Technologies Limited.
Printed and bound in Great Britain by Clays Ltd, Elcograf S.p.A.

The authorized representative in the EEA is Penguin Random House Ireland,
Morrison Chambers, 32 Nassau Street, Dublin D02 YH68.

Penguin Random House is committed to a sustainable
future for our business, our readers and our planet. This book is made from
Forest Stewardship Council® certified paper.

For TOB

And my ABC, always x

Lord help the mister, who comes between me
and my sister . . .

'Sisters' by *Irving Berlin*

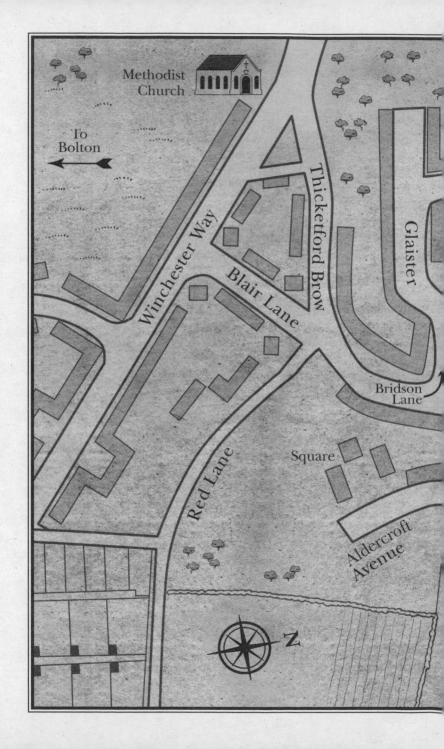

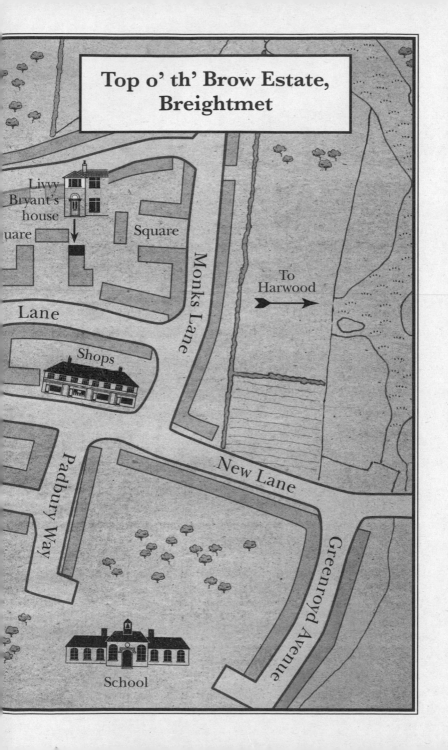

Chapter One

Bolton, Lancashire
July 1943

'JOAN, DO THESE lines look straight to you, lass?' Twisting about on the spot, Livvy Bryant tried to get a good view of her calves. The eyebrow pencil she'd used to draw on the imitation seams clamped between her teeth, she frowned. 'I've re-done them half a dozen times as it is – they're not still wonky, are they?'

Keeping one ear on the wireless, evidently loath to miss a second of the half-hour programme *Ivy Benson and Her Girls Band* playing on the Home Service station, the younger woman scrutinised her sister's legs through the fire's muted glow. 'They look all right to me,' she offered up at last, before lifting the mug she had her hands wrapped around and taking a sip of her Rowntree's cocoa.

'You're sure? Only I've a big night on tonight and want to make a good impression.'

'Big night? Doing what?' Joan eyed her curiously, and Livvy bit her lip.

'Oh, it's not so important really,' she said with what she hoped was a light laugh, trying desperately to backtrack – damn her tongue. The last thing she wanted was for this pure and innocent lass here to get a sniff of what she was really up to. 'Right, well, I'd best be off. Vera will only get a cob on if I keep her waiting.'

Before making for the door, Livvy took a last look at herself in the scallop-rimmed mirror suspended by its bronze chain above the mantelpiece and allowed herself a bunched-lipped smile. As always, she was pleased with her appearance. Not that she was swollen-headed, like, far from it; she would have been the first to protest had anyone passed remark. No, she was simply aware that she cut an attractive figure when she made the effort – what was wrong with that? Nothing, so far as she was concerned. She took pains to look nice and the results spoke for themselves. She planned on making the most of it before her looks began to fade, and to hell with any-one who disapproved.

As if on cue, a comment from the kitchen doorway broke her train of thought and she turned to roll her eyes at the aged man as he shuffled into the living room: 'Oh, don't start, Grandad . . .'

'All dolled up like a dog's dinner,' Morris Tattersall repeated, unperturbed. 'Anyroad, that's enough titivating, surely to Christ – shift yonself from there. I want to catch a warm and you're blocking out all the heat.'

Sidestepping from the fire, Livvy folded her arms. 'You'll be all right, the two of you, whilst I'm out? You'll get yourselves to the shelter, aye, if need be?' she pressed, eyeing them in turn before bringing her gaze to rest on her sister. 'Joan, you'll make sure he goes, won't you, lass?'

'I do posscss a tongue of my own, you know, jabbering about me like I were an imbecile or summat,' Morris grumbled before Joan could answer. He fished out the newspaper from beneath the sofa cushion and shook it out. 'Nagging bleedin' wenches at every turn, that's what. Thought I'd known the last of all that when your grandmother had gone. But no, here I am again, forced to listen to them what have no rights telling me what to do, doing just that—'

'Eeh, shurrup moaning, will you!' Livvy cried. However, there was merriment in her eyes. 'By 'eck, you don't half go on, you know – you're worse than a ruddy woman.'

'Well, I don't like the rotten thing, do I? Ruined

my garden, it did, erecting that. Killed all my best flowers – known around these here parts afore the war for my blooms, I were.'

The poor fellow had a point there, Livvy was forced to concede. Like the majority of the males on the estate, his little front and back patches had at one time been his pride and joy. Neighbours would exchange flower and plant cuttings as well as advice, and happily so, the general consensus being that if one man grew slapdash, it impacted on them all. Just one untidy plot spoiled the overall look of the whole street. The result had been some very pretty gardens. Hitler's ears had surely been burning ever since, the amount of disgruntled green-fingered folk that railed against him still to the heavens.

These days, Morris got his hands dirty tending instead to the few vegetables he'd planted both in the ground and on the roof of the shelter. It was the same the country over. From parks and football pitches to railway embankments – anywhere that the land could be given over to growing food and culti-vated into allotments, it was done. After all, it was, as the population had had drummed into them from the start, every bit as vital to the war effort as any other battle.

'Did I ever let my plot run to weeds? Nay, I did not.' His carping droned on. 'Did a single sorrel stalk or dandelion survive peeping its head over the parapet on my grass? Nay, it didn't! Dirty great monstrosity, that bunker, it's nowt else. And it stinks.'

'So do you,' Livvy shot back, rapidly growing bored with it now. 'So you should feel right at home in there.'

'Don't you get fresh with me. Less of your sauce!'

'Anyroad, I'm not standing about here all the night through arguing the toss with you. If the siren goes, you do as you fancy. So long as I know our Joan's safe. Go to the shelter, don't go to the shelter, *you* can just please yourself.'

Truth be told, it was highly improbable that her grandfather would be put to the test in making a choice. Close on a full year had passed since the warbling wail of the air-raid warning had filled the skies of their town. The night of 23 August it had been, to be exact – Joan's fifteenth birthday. They had had to continue the celebrations squashed together like sardines playing snap in the Anderson. The all-clear had sounded less than half an hour later, if she remembered rightly, and without incident, as was normally the case in their part of the country – Bolton had little to speak of that posed a threat or that the enemy wished to destroy with their bombs – which of course was something to be thankful for.

Still, you never could tell what was around the corner, could you? Slippery devils, those Germans were.

5

Livvy always made sure to drive home the dark fact when leaving her family for the evening.

'Stubborn owd swine,' she muttered on her way to the door. Pausing by Morris's chair, she stooped and dropped a kiss on to his lined brow.

'You smell like a whore's handbag.'

'Ta, Grandad.'

'Daft as a brush, you are – 'tain't a compliment. 'Ere, remember, it's my birthday the morrow!' he added to her retreating back. 'What am I getting?'

'A black eye, you bugger, if you're not careful,' Livvy said on a laugh. She threw a wink to her grinning sister and left the house.

Her home for the past five years, number twenty-two Glaister Lane, was one of ten abodes situated in a compact, horseshoe square – the block heels of her black suede, peep-toe shoes made an authoritative sound as she passed purposely through, and she was soon turning towards the tram stop. As ever, as she drew level she was sure to keep her gaze from straying in the direction of Red Lane . . .

The council housing estate of Top o'th' Brow, nestled in the open and leafy heart of Breightmet, some three miles from the centre of Bolton proper, was a relatively new build. Livvy loved living here. Certainly, the neat and modern dwellings and well-kempt streets that it boasted far surpassed the terrible conditions of the tumbledown slums in which she'd been raised.

She'd known love and security from her decent, hard-working mam and dad in abundance, that was true enough, but little in the way of even the most basics of comfort, and especially during the terrible years of the last decade. In fact, looking back now, it was a miracle to her how they had managed it in the midst of a great depression and the country on its knees.

Originating in the United States as the 1920s were drawing to a close, the economic slump had rapidly spread its catastrophic touch around the globe. Falls in world trade and profits soon plunged Britain into devastating straits, leaving millions unemployed. This was felt predominantly so in mining and industrial areas – the north of England in particular.

Destitution was rife. Diseases born of vitamin deficiency and poor diets, such as rickets and scurvy, spiked, and for the malnourished, reliance on soup kitchens became the norm – Livvy recalled it all too well. Inevitably, this gave rise to unrest, prompting protests such as the Jarrow Marches, when hundreds of working-class men whose families were starving trekked almost three hundred miles, from Newcastle to London, in a desperate yet unsuccessful bid to appeal to the government concerning their plight.

Here had been no different. A centre of the textile

industry, Lancashire relied heavily on export, and their cotton town of Bolton had suffered appalling hardship.

Recovery was painful and slow, and still the nation wasn't fully healed. However, the Bryants had been amongst the blessed few who managed to scrape through those terrible years. This was owed in no small part to the fact that Livvy's parents had mercifully held on to their jobs. God had certainly been smiling down on them. Things could have easily been so very different.

She and Joan wouldn't ever go back to that life of grinding want – this she'd vowed from the first day they moved in with their grandparents following their parents' deaths. And never would she finish up as her dear mother had: worn down with worry and old before her time.

There would be no marriage in the future for Livvy Bryant, no husband and children shackling her to a hearth-and-home prison and holding her back – this she frequently told herself she was adamant on. Life was for the living, and by God she intended on enjoying every damn second of it.

A sandy-coated, gangly-legged dog appeared over the lip of the hill she'd just descended, and she watched it idly as she leaned, her back against the tram stop post. Bar the animal, the street was deserted, glory be.

The plain truth was, few of her fellow residents liked her.

Black looks – and when anyone did deem to speak to her, which wasn't often, coarse remarks – from folk hereabouts was the daily norm, owing to what she chose to do for a living. Not that Livvy ever let her feelings at their open animosity towards her show. Let them think what they liked. They didn't know her, not really, not deep down. To hell with their perfect lives and their judgement . . .

The tram turned the corner and she stepped forward a few paces with a sigh of relief. A quick scan through the windows showed her that several occupants were preparing to disembark – she moved aside, arms folded, and kept her gaze averted, loath to make eye contact. Yet her aloofness had little effect. She experienced the disapproval nonetheless, heard the sniffs and 'harrumphs' from the women, and felt the daggers from their glares as they stared her up and down.

'No better than she ought to be . . .'

'I bet I can guess where she's off to, an' all.'

'Shameless, that's what.'

'Aye – hussy.'

Chin held high, shoulders back, Livvy ignored them completely and walked smartly towards the tram. However, her dignified front wasn't to last. She'd barely time to lift a foot and climb aboard when something warm and wet ran the length of her calves in rapid succession. With a small squeak, she turned in confusion – then cried out in horror. It was the dog she'd spotted shortly before, and it was licking exuberantly at the gravy salt she'd painted on to her legs in lieu of stockings. Titters started up from the bystanders – mortified, Livvy kicked out at it. The dog dodged and, exacerbating her embarrassment yet further, her shoe flew off. It spun several times through the air before bouncing to a stop on the opposite side of the pavement.

'Mutt!' she yelled, hobbling to retrieve the footwear amid hoots of laughter, her cheeks ablaze. She snatched it up, cursing beneath her breath to see the scuff marks scoring the material, and rammed it back in place.

'You getting on or what?' the clippie called out. Her cheeks were wet with mirth.

No, I frigging well ain't, Livvy was close to snapping back. *Sod your tram and sod you. Sod you all!* However, that blasted hound was still skulking about nearby. If she attempted the journey through neighbouring Tonge Moor and on to the centre of town by foot, then it and its horrible tongue would likely follow her all the way. It had got a taste for her now, was eyeing her with definite verve . . . Banking down her pride, she nodded. Then, sticking her nose in the air, she stalked past the smirking women from earlier, up the steps and down the aisle before dropping gratefully on to a seat.

A thorough check of her legs when they had set off had her groaning inwardly. The flawless colouring of earlier was now streaked and patchy, and the pencil seams were smudged. She looked a sight, all right. What's more, the evenings now stayed lighter for a while yet; the hour wasn't even seven, so no chance of her hiding the state of her pins under the cover of darkness. All she could do was pray that Vera came up trumps for her with the nylons she'd promised. Damn this clothing rationing; she was that fed up with it.

By the time she reached the corners of Higher Bridge Street and St George's Road and caught sight of the domed, tiled edifice of her destination, her mood had improved somewhat. There was a new band performing at the Astoria Palais de Danse – or plain old Palais, as it was known locally – tonight. It should prove an enjoyable, not to mention lucrative night . . . Then she spotted her friend standing outside – and in her hand she was waving two rectangular packages: stockings! – and Livvy swiftly forgot all about the stinging spitefulness she'd endured at Top o'th' Brow. *Oh, thank the Lord!* Grinning, she hurried to catch Vera up.

'All right?'

'All the better for seeing you, love,' Livvy

11

responded, pulling the woman to her in a quick hug. 'Eeh, can you believe the mess of me; I look ruddy well.'

Taking stock of Livvy's legs, Vera pulled a face. 'What happened to you?'

She regaled the woman with the animal's antics. 'It ain't funny, you know,' she finished over Vera's guffaws. 'I wanted the ground to open wide and swallow me up, felt a first-rate idiot.'

'Well, ne'er mind about that now. Let's get inside and have ourselves a gradely evening, eh?' Her gaze sparked with purpose. 'I've seen some reet handsome blokes go in, you know, whilst I were waiting for you. Tonight's going to be a good 'un.'

Livvy didn't need telling twice: 'Well, what are we waiting for?'

After a quick detour down a back entryway, which afforded privacy and allowed Livvy, after spitting on her hanky and scrubbing clean her legs the best she could, to slip into a pair of the new stockings, they hurried back for the main street and the Palais.

Linking arms, they climbed the three wide steps between the white stone pillars. Inside, Glenn Miller's 'In the Mood' was playing. As was usual for dance halls, the premises was unlicensed to sell alcoholic beverages, however the thrilling trumpet, trombone and saxophone arrangement, which was so popular amongst all ages, was intoxicating enough – the women shared a smile and, after depositing their coats in the cloakroom and dropping their tickets into their handbags for safekeeping, went to collect themselves a drink. They found an empty table and, as they sat sipping their lemonades, scoured the room.

The crowd was predominantly young. Couples doing the foxtrot dotted the sprung dance floor, however the preponderance of people present were single. They sat or stood milling in small, same-sex groups, eyeing up the talent from a discreet distance, the object of the night for most concerned to find a partner. Uncomplicated, innocent – far removed from the main objective of Livvy and Vera's presence here tonight.

Most of the men were in uniform. Those not in active service for whatever reason and dressed in civvies would come back of the queue to their half-god hero counterparts in the eyes of the majority of the girls, the friends knew. Deflated, confidence dented, the sorry sods would prove easy pickings later for seasoned pros like Livvy and Vera.

A small crowd of soldiers, evidently on short home leave and keen on a good time, caught their attention across the room. A couple of them flashed smiles and waved. The women gave one another a raised eyebrow and a nod and rose from their seats.

'All right, lads?' Livvy bestowed her brightest smile on each man in turn. 'By, you're a sight for sore eyes.'

The men smiled back, involuntarily forming a semicircle around the attractive pair.

'D'you want to dance?' the tallest of the party asked Livvy, whilst the man at his left moved to take Vera's hand.

'We're not here to skip the light fandango, lad,' Livvy told him. Her tone was now low and seductive. 'You see, my pal here and me, we're not like other lasses here this evening. You don't need to waste your time on wooing us the night long, buying us drinks or making small talk during the interval, and all for a quick shy kiss at the end of it all – if you're lucky. No. Oh no, not with us.'

They looked perplexed for a moment as they absorbed her words. Then, slowly, their faces cleared in understanding. One or two laughed awkwardly, a few more whispered into each others' ears and grinned.

'But . . . You're both . . .'

'Bonny?' Livvy finished for the man who had asked her to take a turn on the dance floor. 'Aye, we are good-looking, you're right.' Normally, other women who plied a similar trade were washed out and much older; desperate, poor cows. War widows, a lot of them; or for those whose menfolk were still clinging on to life on the battlefield, struggling to make ends

14

meet alone and feed a huddle of children at home on a paltry dependant's army pension. So, his surprise was understandable. 'What's more,' she went on, leaning in to let him catch a brief feel of her full breasts pressing against his chest and allow a waft of her floral perfume to send his senses spinning, '*we* don't say yes to just anyone. We're able to pick and choose who we spend a bit of time with, if you get my meaning.'

Nodding, he licked his lips. He got it, all right.

'Course, what's been mentioned is also reflected in the price, you understand, and so I hope you've got deep pockets.'

His nod was immediate. He snaked an arm around her waist.

'Well?' Now it was Vera's turn. Her sweeping black lashes fanned her cheeks as she blinked up at her own suitor. 'And what says you, handsome?'

'Let's get out of here,' was his husky response.

The foursome broke off from the gathering and left the hall. Outside, Livvy and Vera turned to the men. All smiles were gone. Now that their wiles had worked and their clients were secured, the clinical matter of money was at the forefront of their minds – they got straight down to business. Time was precious and these fellows would be far from their only customers this night.

'Right, lads. Here's the deal.' Livvy faced them,

hands on hips. 'We ain't your average tarts, ain't the sort what go in for a knee trembler in t' back alleys, as I'm sure some like to think. Vera here has a few rooms over a café a few streets away, so you're sure of a bit of comfort. Course, this too affects the price. All right?'

The men glanced to one another, and for the first time their expressions showed uncertainty. It was clear they were worried whether they could afford it. 'How much?'

The friends shared a smile. Some of the more professional women, if they still retained a decent face and figure, could manage to squeeze ten shillings. Naturally, it depended on the individual client and what women surmised they could pay. Some were charged more if it was reckoned the client could supply it. Livvy and Vera, on the other hand, could afford to be choosy and never, under any circumstances, would they be swayed on the price. The sum was fixed – like it or lump it. Of course, they were under no illusions that they wouldn't always hold all the cards, that one day they too would be past their best. However, that day wasn't now, and not only did they themselves know it but men did as well.

'As you yourselfs agreed,' Vera replied, 'we're a cut above your average doxy. If it's a two-shilling slap and tickle you're after, then you've come to the wrong place . . .'

'How much?'

'We don't lift our skirts for less than a pound.'

'A pound!'

'Listen here, it's true to say that others will do it forra lot less. Bloomin' 'eck, some women give it away forra free drink – and aye, it's a dose of cock rot you'll finish up with for your tightfistedness with them, an' all, let me tell you.'

'Eeh, lads, trust me when I say it'll be worth it,' Livvy assured them, giving each a soft, sultry wink. 'It'll be summat to think on when you go back to the madness – summat to see youse through the rest of this war even, believe me. So what d'you say?'

'You know what, you're right.' Her fellow thrust out his chest and nodded. 'God only knows what'll happen when we return to action – what says you, Bob?' he added, turning to his pal. 'We could cop it, you know it as well as me, and that'll be that. I plan on enjoying every precious minute whilst I can. You in?'

'I'm in,' said Bob with a grin.

'Come on, fellas, this way.'

'By, I'm fagged.' Smothering a yawn, Livvy stretched languidly.

Vera took a last drag of her cigarette, stubbed it out in the tin ashtray and rose to her feet before saying, 'Aye well, no rest for the wicked – come on, girl. Back to it.'

'He were bloody handsome, him. And by, for all his inexperience, he knew his way about once he got into his stride. Aye, I enjoyed that.'

Vera let out a harrumph. 'Well, he did better than that Bob then; the bugger couldn't get the horn.'

'No!' Turning over and pulling herself to her knees, Livvy laughed. 'I reckon you must be losing your touch.'

'As *if.*' Vera made a play of swatting at her friend's head in mock offence. 'Perish the thought! No, he were just nervous is all. I soon got him going.'

'Poor buggers.' Livvy bent and felt beneath the sagging two-seater sofa for her shoes. 'I hope they make it out of battle in one piece.'

'Who's to say? Right, now, come on you, get a shimmy on. There's brass to be made.'

The new band was in full swing when they arrived back at the Palais. Again, they ordered two lemonades and, as all the seats were occupied, went this time to loiter by the stage. Sipping their drinks, they tapped their feet to the beat. It wasn't long before two men standing nearby had sidled across to join their company . . .

Four more punters later, Livvy was ready to call it a night. 'That's me, I reckon – I'm all in,' she told

Vera, kneading the small of her back with her fingertips when they had returned to the dance hall yet again. 'And my trotters are killing me.'

'All right.' The woman did a quick calculation. 'That's a round five pounds each we've earned this evening – that's not bad going, eh?'

'Aye – and 'ere, earned it we ruddy did, too!' Livvy finished with a repleted smile.

'How's about we collect our coats and nip along to the Fleece for a proper drink before heading home? I could do with one.'

'Me an' all,' Livvy was swift to agree. She crooked her arm for her friend to link. 'Stick your leg in, girl – and aye, you're buying!'

Bradshawgate was but an arrow's flight away. Nonetheless, by now the skies were inky dark, the blackout in full force, and it took them twice as long, squinting and holding on to each other for safety, to get there. Trips and tumbles were all too often the norm in wartime Britain once night-time fell – a bashed face or twisted ankle would be detrimental to business and something the women wished to avoid at all costs, so they were taking no chances.

A series of whoops and shouts went up when they entered the pub. This was their local haunt and the regulars knew 'the ladies of the Fleece' well – and quite a number of them more than. Livvy and Vera returned the licentious greetings with good humour.

'The usual, lovies?' the buxom barmaid, Gwen, called warmly over the hubbub – as usual, the place was jam packed. A sound sort, she'd never once discriminated against the women's lifestyle choice, unlike the majority of their sex. Although alcohol wasn't officially 'on t' ration' it had increased in price, and certain beverages, spirits in particular and especially whisky, oftentimes saw bouts of unobtainability. Nonetheless, the common choice of tipple – beer – was generally in plentiful supply. The women nodded gratefully.

Livvy was swigging back the last of her drink minutes later and preparing to leave when a voice drawled in her ear, the speaker's hot breath fanning her cheek unpleasantly; she squirmed, pulling a face, and craned her neck around to face them. 'What?'

'I said, honey, can I buy you another?'

She'd have surmised the American serviceman to be in his late twenties. Fresh-faced with muted blond hair, he was good-looking enough in a lithe sort of way, she supposed, but not exactly her cup of tea. She shook her head. 'No ta. I'm just off.'

'But . . . It's Independence Day this weekend.'

'That means nowt to me, lad!'

'Come on, I'm celebrating. Just one.'

'Look, I said no. Thanks, but no thanks.'

He blinked as if unaccustomed to being snubbed, miffed that she'd had the audacity to refuse him. 'I don't offer twice, you know,' he finished after some moments, his chin going up in dented male pride.

Her top lip peaking in half incredulity, half sneer – this one was full of himself, all right – Livvy looked him up and down. If there was one trait she could not abide in a man, it was arrogance. 'Well, ain't that a good job, for my answer would be the same, and I'm not in the habit of repeating myself. Now, if you don't mind . . .' She edged past him and reached for her handbag on the table. 'I'll be seeing you, Vera.'

'You'll be all right making your way in t' dark? I can walk with you if you want?'

'No, don't worry, I'll manage.'

'Goodnight, God bless, then, lass. See you tomorrow at seven.'

Livvy had made it to the door when a hand shot out over her shoulder before she could open it. It was the GI – he pressed the flat of his palm against the wood, halting her exit, and grinned. She rolled her eyes.

'Look you, I'm tired and in no mood for this. Shift yourself, will you, before you make me miss the last bus—'

'Sure, you're a hard nut to crack,' he interjected, cocking his head. 'Okay, okay, if you really don't have time for a drink then how about I escort you to the bus stop? A pretty little thing like you, out alone at night . . . I won't hear of it.'

'No.' Livvy was losing patience fast and the effort to remain polite was rapidly waning. Something about him set her teeth on edge; the sooner he got the message, the better. 'Ta all the same.'

'Oh, come on, just let me—'

'I said no – for Christ's sake!' she cried at last. 'Go and bother some other bugger, can't you, and leave me in peace?'

His dark stare blazed with clear annoyance. He released a sharp laugh. 'Please yourself.'

'I will, too. Good night!'

''Ere, lad, I'll have a drink with you. Come on, come over here and keep me company,' Livvy was in time to hear Vera call before she hurried from the pub.

Outside, she glanced back once or twice as she passed up the street, but of the Yank there was no sign. Glory be, he hadn't got it into his head to tail her – Vera's proposition must have done the trick. Thank God for her friend – she must remember to thank her tomorrow. Eeh, what a night!

The house was quiet when she arrived – having successfully resisted looking towards Red Lane again en route. After taking her time to shut the door softly so as not to disturb the family, she slipped off her coat and hung it on a peg in the tiny hallway.

The fire had been banked down not so long ago – embers still glowed ochre in the grate. She jabbed at them with the poker, returned it to the companion set at the side of the hearth, and lowered herself into her grandfather's chair. Then finally making reality of what she'd been fantasising for hours, she kicked off her shoes and wiggled her throbbing toes with a delicious sigh.

A cup of tea was out of the question, although she could definitely have murdered a cup. Their ration had to be used sparingly, leaves were precious, and she wouldn't squander them on a pot just for herself. She shrugged. Rising once more, she picked up her shoes, yawned and stretched, then made her tiptoed way upstairs.

Although the house boasted three bedrooms, Livvy and Joan had always shared until very recently, when her sister had suddenly asked for a room of her own – Livvy smiled at the memory. The lass was growing up, desired her own space; although it must be said she did miss the younger woman when they parted ways, albeit she was only across the minuscule landing. And even a few weeks ago during Wings Week, part of a Wings for Victory savings campaign, Livvy had got another glimpse of her budding womanhood.

Joan had taken a trip into town to visit Victoria Square with her friend Doris, who dwelled on nearby Thicketford Brow, to see a Hudson Aircraft of RAF Coastal Command which had been installed on the town hall steps. Yet thoughts of the brave men protecting Britain from the perilous skies had been far from the minds of the girls upon their return. Whilst out, they had purchased a tube of tangee lipstick, and the pair had practised with it for an age in the mirror, applying and reapplying until they were satisfied with the results. Watching her sister had evoked in Livvy a mixture of both amusement and sadness.

In no time at all, the lass would be a woman. She'd meet a lad, then she'd fly the nest – just what would Livvy do without her? The thought was a scary and altogether miserable one. *Please God that whoever she gave her hand to was decent and treated her kindly. Let this blasted war be over before Joan got serious with someone. Please, please, let her know long and lasting happiness. Don't have her end up like me . . .*

Shaking her head to dispel the depressive musings, she made for the room facing and clicked shut the door.

It remained a marvel still, to Livvy, the bathroom. The fact they had the luxury of not only an indoor toilet but a proper tub – a mere pipe dream to many, who knew yet only the small and scratchy tin bath in the kitchen once a week, and a dark and dingy privy at the bottom of the backyard – was something she doubted she'd ever learn to take for granted. She undressed and piled her neatly folded clothing on the floor. Bending forward, she pressed in the bath plug and turned on the tap.

Hygiene products such as shampoo and soap had found themselves on the ration last year and remained in short supply – a fact that would have rankled if not for Vera's black-market sources. The woman was never without and could get her hands on practically anything. Furthermore, she always ensured that her friend didn't go without either – smiling now, Livvy liberally sprinkled rose-scented bath salts into the flow of water. Then, remembering the government guidelines and rolling her eyes, she hastened to turn off the tap – this due in the main to what her sister would have to say than anything else.

Coal was vital for the war effort and consequently, in order to conserve fuel, the nation had been instructed to limit their use of hot water. A staunch Joan, as with everything concerning doing one's bit, took the rule very seriously – woe betide she discovered it being flouted. She'd drawn a black line the depth of five inches – the recommended amount – inside the tub and insisted that the family adhered to it. Apparently, even the baths in Buckingham Palace now had them, though Livvy struggled to imagine the king huddled shivering in a shallow puddle like the rest of them! Of course, those in power couldn't realistically enforce it, see into homes, but it was in bad taste to disobey the issue and extremely un-patriotic.

As always, she gave herself a thorough all-over scrub and felt infinitely better afterwards, seeing the scummy water drain away with the dirt of her day. Her evening activities were washed away was how she saw it – once more, she was sanctified, cleansed. The sense left her comforted.

Plucking down her beige-and-brown dressing gown from the back of the door and wrapping it around herself, she stuffed her clothing from earlier under her arm and padded out to her bedroom. If she'd been tired before, the heat from the bath had anaesthetised her further. Her eyelids were like ton weights, but she forced herself to carry out her nightly beauty regime of applying cold cream to her face, brushing out her jet-black hair until it crackled and inserting dinky curlers. Finally, she dragged a cotton nightdress over her head and crawled into bed.

Within moments of meeting her pillow, sleep was upon her – she snuggled deeper beneath the bed-covers. Yet there was still one last task to complete before she could let slumber in, something she never shirked on, despite it hardly ever making a differ-ence. Nonetheless, she followed the ritual regardless – the mantra fell from her lips in a rapid whisper:

'Lord, please don't let me dream of Red Lane. *Don't* let me dream of him . . .'

Chapter Two

'RIGHT, WHERE'S MY presents?'

Pausing in her task of laying the table for breakfast, Livvy faced her grandfather, hands on hips. 'By gum, would you look at the state of him,' she said to Joan. 'It's like a lad of ten you're acting, giddy with excitement for your birthday treats! Have you just tumbled from your bed and straight down the stairs?'

Patting down his tousled grey hair and tucking into his trousers a shirt tail that was sticking out, Morris sniffed. 'Will that do thee? Do I pass your high and mighty standards, now? Blimey!'

'Come here, you pest.' Chuckling, Livvy readjusted his braces, all twisted in his haste to dress, and reattached them properly to the buttons at his waistband. 'There, that's better. Eeh, what are we going to do with you, eh?'

'Buggered if I know.'

She laughed again and planted a hearty kiss on his cheek. Joan rushed across and mimicked the action:

'Happy birthday, Grandad,' they chorused in unison.

He batted them away: 'Aye yes, ta very much, very ruddy nice – now, presents! Come on, cough up.'

'You can sit yourself down and get some grub inside you first,' Livvy told him with a nod to a mahogany chair. 'Go on. Joan lass, pour the birthday boy a cup of tea.'

Ignoring the old man's grumbling, the sisters busied themselves with the meal – Joan duly obliged and reached for the teapot whilst Livvy crossed to the fire to check on the bread speared on the toasting fork.

'This will keep us going until this afternoon and the birthday tea,' announced Livvy. 'Vera, my mate, saw me right with a few food bits so it should be a half-decent spread—'

'It's not black market, is it, this "stuff"?' Joan cut in to demand. 'I'll not be eating it if it is!'

'No, no,' she lied. Then, thinking on her feet: 'Vera's pally with a girl whose parents run a shop and they've let her have a few things, extras from under the counter, like, what they normally save for their favourite customers. Don't fret, lass.'

Placated, Joan nodded. 'Oh well, that's all right, then.'

'Aye. And 'ere, I've a pair of stockings upstairs for you off Vera as well.'

'Really? Eeh, ta ever so!'

Smiling, Livvy made back for the table and reached for the butter dish. Mindful as ever of the ration and stretching out their meagre allowance as far as was humanly possible, she coated her grandfather's toast in a thin scrape. 'We'd be lost without her, wouldn't we?'

'I want to be just like Vera.'

An ice chill ran the length of Livvy's spine – her smile melted instantly. 'What?'

'I said—'

'I heard what you said: what the hell did you mean by that?'

Joan, blue eyes wide, frowned in puzzlement. 'Just that I wish I worked on the hosiery section in a nice department store, and could get discounted stockings and the like, as Vera does. Why, Livvy? What did you think I meant?'

'Nowt, lass, nowt.' The older woman was full of contrition. For one harrowing moment there, the innocent comment had evoked terrible notions – she'd been assaulted with a vision of her pure sister getting up to the things that Vera and she did . . . Never, *never*, would Joan end up that way! 'Ignore me. I'm a grumpy sow this morn, that's all,' she soothed, fetching back to her lips the easy smile.

'Right, that's it, you've made me wait long enough.' Morris thumped the tabletop with the side of his fist. 'Grub and tea and mindless talk of your bloody friend – and aye, even the offer of a gift for our Joan! All pointless, pointless! It's *me* you should be worrying about, you know. It's *my* special day. Now hand them over!'

'You big bleedin' babby, you're nowt else . . . All right,' Livvy capitulated. 'Put him out of his misery, lass, will you,' she told her sister, motioning to the deep drawer of the sideboard where they had secreted his presents. 'We'll never hear the last of it, else.'

Rubbing his hands with glee, Morris watched as his youngest granddaughter hurried to do Livvy's bidding. 'Oooh!' he exclaimed when, tearing at the wrapping, he saw the new quality pipe with walnut bowl and half-pound tin of fine-cut shag tobacco. 'Just the ticket, that is – ta, lasses.'

''Ere, and just you look after this one, won't you?' she was swift to warn. He'd thrown his regular pipe at the wall last week in a fit of temper whilst listening to some bulletin about Adolf Hitler on the wireless, almost setting alight the peg rug in the process, and it hadn't smoked the same since. 'No playing silly beggars with that, all right?'

'I told you afore, weren't my fault: don't blame me, blame the Führer!'

Whilst Joan, seated beside her, struggled to smother a giggle, Livvy sighed and shook her head, then flicked her chin to the other package. 'Go on, open that, let's see if it fits.'

'Ay, like a second skin,' Morris confirmed, having unveiled the thick, dark grey woollen pullover and put it on. 'By, it's gradely – and reet warm. It's spoilt I am, aye.'

'You're worth it, I suppose,' Livvy told him with a wink, making him grin. 'Now, let's finish up here and then you can sit and relax in your chair and read the paper whilst me and Joan get everything sorted for your do. All right?'

Happy to comply with her wishes now he'd got his way, Morris agreed readily, and the trio settled down to enjoy breakfast.

The sisters got busy with their chores shortly afterwards. Firstly, there was the housework to see to. Guests were due later and Livvy would sooner die than have them think her a poor homemaker. Whatever else people might deem she had going against her, no one could accuse her of slatternliness.

The furniture was polished to a high sheen, the flames dancing merrily in the gleaming fireplace, and the glassware atop the cream embroidered table-cloth sparkling by the time the first knock sounded at the door. Joan went to answer it and returned seconds later with Ned, their grandfather's elder cousin and weekend drinking partner.

'Alreet, Morris?' Smoothing down his thick side-burn whiskers, he crossed the floor to where Morris sat neat and tidy now at Livvy's insistence, proudly sporting his new pullover and puffing on his pipe, and shook him by the hand. 'Best wishes, happy returns, and all that malarky.'

'Ta. Drink?'

'Aye, aye.'

Livvy did the honours. 'There you are, Ned. Take a pew there next to Grandad; don't stand on ceremony.'

'Is there owt else needs doing now, Livvy, or can I nip up and get changed?' Joan asked wearily. Her knitted turban had drooped, almost covering one eye – she looked all in.

'Aye, take that mucky pinny off. You've worked like a Trojan alongside me this morning to get everything arranged and I thank you for it. I'll come up with you.'

'Can I wear my lipstick, an' all?'

Smiling, Livvy nodded. 'Course you can. Let's get our skates on before the others arrive.'

When Livvy emerged from her bedroom a little later, she cut a very different figure from that of the previous night. Her face and lips were nude; she wore no make-up bar a light dusting of powder. Gone were the killer heels and alluring red rayon dress with black trimming and large central buttons. That was a uniform she reserved for work alone – during daytime hours, she could have passed for any one of your average lasses on the estate.

She'd teamed a light cotton blouse in pale blue and a brown box-pleated wool skirt with utilitarian lace-up brogues. Nor did her hair bounce freely in soft waves about her shoulders, and there wasn't a striking victory roll in sight. She'd fixed a few pin curls to the sides instead and gathered up the rest into a neat Gibson tuck at her nape. A navy cable-knit cardigan, which she'd collected on her way out, completed her outfit, and this she slid her arms through as she descended the stairs.

Joan had just joined her sister and the men in the living room, and replenished the glasses of the latter, when voices filtered through the open window from the garden path. At Livvy's nod, she went to admit the other guests.

'Madge,' the birthday boy said with a curt nod.

'Morris,' his wife replied every bit as clipped.

A heavy silence took hold of the air.

Celia and her nephew Clifford, who resided at number nineteen, facing the mouth of the square, stood hovering by the door. Keen to break the tension, Livvy hurried to welcome them inside, exclaiming, 'Come through, come through! Drink? Ham and tomato butty?'

'Here, and happy birthday.' Madge, built like a battleship with legs like barrage balloons, thrust a package into Morris's hands. 'It's new carpet slippers – your owd ones are falling apart.'

Another nod: 'Ta very much. Gradely, they are.'

'Drink, Grandma?' A smiling Joan guided Madge to a seat. 'Will you have summat to eat now or will you wait a while?'

'Now, lass, I'm fair clemmed – do us a plate up, will thee?'

As Madge and her friend Celia settled themselves down next to Morris and Ned and they began chatting amongst themselves, Livvy breathed a sigh of relief. Then, grinning, she motioned to Clifford and he followed her to the table, which had been pushed up against the far wall to allow the revellers more room.

'Thank God for that! I thought the pair were going to come to blows forra minute,' she said through the side of her mouth, chuckling. 'What are they like, eh?'

At a little over six foot, Clifford came head and shoulders above Livvy; he lowered himself on to a dining chair so that they were eye level. 'They love each other really.'

'Aye, and pigs might fly! They wouldn't be dwelling at opposite ends of the street in separate houses, would they, if that were the case?'

Running a hand through his sleek, dark Brylcreemed hair, he laughed softly. 'I reckon they enjoy the battling, you know, on t' quiet. They'd not be without each other, though.'

He had a point – she nodded concession. After yet another blazing row with her husband at the tail end of winter, Madge Tattersall had bundled up her possessions and stormed off to Celia's house.

The act was a weekly occurrence at least, had been so for more years than Livvy cared to count, but the final time had been different. Normally, Madge would vent her frustrations to her friend then return an hour or two later, calmer and willing to forgive and forget, and everything would go back to normal. However, that wasn't to be: Madge had informed her family that she wasn't coming home. She was sorry, but she just couldn't stay another minute beneath the same roof as 'that cantankerous owd sod' or she'd end up doing for him. Celia had offered her the spare back bedroom, and Madge had accepted. And nothing anyone could say or do would change her mind.

At first, the upheaval had come as a major shock. Couples separated, of course they did, but no one had really believed it conceivable of the Tattersalls, in spite of their tumultuous relationship, not for a moment. Morris had yelled and railed something chronic – just what the devil would folk think? – and, when that hadn't worked, had eventually resorted to apologising and asking his wife nicely to come home. However, she'd refused to be swayed.

A suffragette in her younger days and programmed

to stand up for herself and do what she deemed was right in the face of oppression, to see a cause through to the bitter end if it was for the greater good, coupled with a stubbornness and iron will that would have won her prizes if such competitions existed: there was no getting round her. She'd made her decision and was sticking to it. 'Sorry, but there it is,' had been her closing words on the matter. Along with his granddaughters, Morris had had no choice but to accept it.

Livvy and in particular Joan had been crushed. After losing their parents, a second chance at normal family life had been the balm needed to help along the healing process. Now, they had found themselves adrift again, home life unstable – the reality and the unpredictability of the future had caused more than one sleepless night for the sisters. And yet, as the days then weeks had rolled by, they came to see that their worries had been unnecessary ones, for something quite unexpected happened. Morris and Madge began to get along, and far better than they ever had before.

The change didn't come about overnight, but come it did. Livvy had soon noticed that when her grandma called in at number twenty-two, as she did at least once a day to tidy around or cook a meal for the family, the wedded pair were conversing amiably. Sometimes, they even laughed. In some different sense, normality had been restored, and with it a sense of comfort that just maybe a reconciliation wasn't a prospect altogether lost to them.

Of course, nothing in life is ever plain sailing and the couple still had their gripes, hence the frosty reception just now upon the guests' arrival. A recent petty spat had carried across several days – Madge, it must be said, was a champion at holding grudges. However, it seemed the dust had once more settled if the easy conversations going on now were anything to go by, glory be.

'So how've you been keeping, Livvy?' Clifford was asking now. Snapping back to the present, she let her shoulders rise and fall.

'Oh, you know me, lad. I'm all right, always am. And you?'

He nodded, smiled. 'Aye, not too bad. Listen, Livvy, I were wondering . . . well. If you've nowt on tonight whether we might—?'

'Oh, sorry, Clifford, I've plans already,' she blurted.

'Work?'

'That's right.' Turning away from him, she busied herself with the plates of food to avoid looking him in the eye.

As with Vera – Livvy had said that her friend was employed in respectable shop work – so far as her nearest and dearest were concerned, Livvy herself was, too, and earned her money as a barmaid in town. It allowed her to keep the unsociable hours that came with her actual trade without raising suspicion and, although she disliked the deception, no one had questioned her thus far. She accounted for her healthy income and the fact that Joan had no need to go out to work and could instead stay home and keep house, that her sister could provide for them with ease, by stating that drinkers were generous with tips when in their cups.

Whether they knew the rumours or not – folk aplenty around here had either guessed or seen her in action themselves, after all – Livvy couldn't say, although she doubted it. No one was brave enough to flap their tongue in Madge's earshot and risk a thick lip from a swipe of her beefy fist. Certainly Livvy hadn't probed her family for answers.

'I understand, it can't be helped.'

'Sorry.' Then, curiosity getting the better of her, she asked him, couldn't help it, 'Why, what had you in mind?'

'A bite to eat in town, mebbe a dance? But no matter – another time, eh?'

'Aye, lad. Perhaps.'

As ever where Clifford was concerned, her emotions were conflicted. He was sweet and kind, not to mention handsome. What's more, he was mad about her, and she was very fond of him. But there was no way she could . . . no. Not again. Never would she allow herself to try, to give her all, and for what? Just for it to be snatched away, like it had been with . . . *Don't think. Don't think.*

'Livvy?'

'Hm?' She shook her head. 'Sorry, what? I were in a world of my own then.'

'Are you all right?' Clifford half rose from his seat, his face creased in concern, and she realised she had tears in her eyes – she blinked them back furiously.

'Oh aye, aye. I reckon I'm coming down with the summer sniffles or summat – water something awful, they do, when I'm getting a cold. Anyway,' she went on quickly, keen to change the subject in case her wretched mind took it upon itself to stray to uncharted territory once more, 'what have you been up to? How's work treating you?'

A shadow of pain entered his eyes but was gone again in seconds – he mumbled something along the lines of everything being well then fell silent, and Livvy did likewise.

Though he hadn't divulged every detail, and Livvy, out of politeness despite her interest, hadn't pressed for them, she was aware that Clifford had registered as a conscientious objector in 1940.

He wasn't alone. Tens of thousands of British men and hundreds of women were of the same persuasion. Nonetheless, she doubted his decision was on religious grounds, as was normally the reasoning behind pacifism; so far as she knew, he was no zealot, nor even a regular churchgoer. The one thing she was sure of, however, was that whatever reason had prompted him to take the route he had was immeasurably important to him. This was no easy way out for him; a means to avoid his duty. Clifford was decent, upstanding and straight as a die; certainly, he was no coward.

He'd divulged to her only once his circumstances. It had been last year, shortly after he came to live with his aunt, and like Celia had quickly become a friend of the family. He and Livvy had been nattering at the front gate one afternoon when two young local lads marched past them along the street in full uniform, having been called up – Clifford had broken conversation with her to watch them. The expression of pure desolation on his face when, finally, he'd turned back to face her had shocked her; grasping his sleeve, she'd begged from him the matter.

Opening up to her his situation in hushed tones, he'd been keen to make clear his fierce condemnation of Hitler's regime, that he was by no means defending it or in support of Nazism; the very notion was abhorrent. He'd gone on to tell that he'd had to go through a tribunal headed by a civilian judge – something Livvy guessed had deeply affected him, by the way he spoke on it – which he'd been successful in convincing.

Pacifists of the Great War had endured a far rawer deal but had done much to shine a light on the topic and gain some rights. This time round, the governmental view was greatly more tolerant, and this Second World War generation of objectors were spared the hardship of their forefathers – namely incarceration.

Clifford's willingness to compromise and genuine desire to nonetheless help in some capacity with the war effort, to offer himself in a non-combatant aspect, had gone strongly in his favour. He'd been assigned instead work of national importance on the home front, coal mining, and toiled at a colliery in nearby Manchester. It was hard graft to be sure, but preferable to the alternative.

The public's opinion, however, was a wholly different area; Livvy was aware of this without him having to utter it. Conchies were vilified by many. Being cut off by their communities and treated as if they didn't exist, or otherwise relentlessly abused whenever they set foot out the door, was a grim reality for some. She'd heard herself the comments about him, caught snatches of derivative discussions in the shops. Tearing down a man they knew little to nothing about for gossip's sake. *Just as they did about her.* He was to an extent an outsider, assigned to the fringes of society like she was. Probably what drew her to him, she supposed.

Looking at Clifford now, Livvy felt alongside her usual buried feelings a rush of camaraderie, a deeper closeness that warmed her bones and lightened her chest; it was a sense of companionship, comfort that she wasn't alone in this place. On impulse she squeezed his hand, laughed when he pulled a bemused face, and turned her attention to pouring them a drink.

'Aye, Easter Monday, it were. Eeh, what a dark one it was, an' all.'

'What's this?' Livvy asked over her shoulder as her grandfather took a dramatic pause to share a grim nod with his cousin, which Ned returned.

'Passchendaele,' Madge informed her wearily. Livvy flashed her a grin with a roll of her eyes. Clearly, the beers Morris had downed in quick succession were taking effect.

'About three in the morn, our platoon sergeant comes along and orders all the men awake. We dragged ourselves up quick smart – well, you had to, aye. Take your sweet time following an order and you'd find a boot up your arse for your troubles and not sit down forra week. Well, frozen to the marrow and dead on our feet, we scurried about in the pitch-black wind and rain, gathering up our equipment and filling our bottles at the water cart, you know? Oh, bad, it were—'

'Mayhem, aye,' Ned countered, then at Morris's glare nodded for the storyteller to continue.

'Anyroad, we has our breakfast of hot tea and boiled bacon by candlelight, which helped gear us all up a bit. Ay, we needed that, aye. We knew what were afoot—'

'Very true. You could have cut the tension with a knife, couldn't you?'

'Ned, who's telling this tale, me or thee?' Morris barked.

'You, lad.'

'Well then, just so we're clear. Right, where was I . . .' Muttering to himself, he scrunched up his eyes.

'Boiled bacon,' Madge proffered, her words coming from behind the back of the hand she'd held to her mouth to stifle a yawn.

'Ah – that's it. Aye, we knew what were afoot, all right. A lull afore the terrible storm: that storm being the opening barrage. Eeh, even the birds knew – must have sensed it, you know – that all hell was about to break wide. The horses, too; silent like the grave they was. Norra peep from them, nay.

'Dawn broke but did nowt for the mood – scudded with rain clouds, the sky were. At four hundred hours, our battalion was on the move. Across the Arras road we trooped and on down the slope into the valley, and all the while norra word was spoken; the all-consuming dread, it makes a mute of you. About three hundred yards from the first line, we halts. We waited. Soon, a cry went up: "Three minutes to zero, men!" By, my heart were thumping so bleedin' fast I thought it might break.'

'I nearly messed my pants,' Ned blurted, then clamped shut his mouth again quickly.

'At 4.50 a.m. to the second, the whistle screamed and we were off – we gave them bastard Huns the full might of the British army. High-explosive shells and guns . . . artillery fire like you'd not imagine. Flame and smoke and mud, and golden rain. Aye, golden rain. By, war's a bugger.'

The room remained shrouded in silence for a long moment. Livvy hazarded a glance to Clifford. His stiff face was white. She touched his shoulder and he nodded then closed his eyes.

'Go on, Morris, tell the rest,' Ned urged, breaking through the quiet. He took a long draught of his ale. 'I'm enjoying this.'

'Well, I'm not,' Madge cut in. Her gaze was directed at Celia's nephew and her granddaughter. She understood. She pointed a finger at her husband. 'No more, you hear? All this morbid bloody talk; don't you think we hear enough of it day in, day out, with this fresh lot raging? Now let's just talk about summat else.'

Morris, squinting at the ceiling, searched about inside his head for a minute, then snapped his fingers. 'I met Gandhi once,' he announced.

'Oh, God help us, not this owd yarn,' Madge murmured on a groan.

'The Indian leader, aye. Came here to Bolton town, he did – did you know that, you young folks?' he queried, smiling, his gaze flicking from the sisters and Clifford in turn.

'Gracie Fields came to Bolton to make a film,' Joan piped up. 'Mind you, she didn't have as far to travel, what with her hailing from down the road in Rochdale—'

'Oi, missy. If I've told you once, I've told you a million times: I'll not have her name mentioned beneath this roof!'

'But you like her music, you do, especially "Wish Me Luck".'

'Correction: I did.'

'Oh, Grandad!'

'Nay.' Morris was insistent. 'Wedding herself to an Italian – humph. I don't know what this world's coming to; ruddy traitor, she's nowt else. Anyroad, as I were saying – aye, nice he were, Mahatma . . .'

'Huh! Listen to him – on first-name terms, are youse, you and your good pal Gandhi?'

He ignored Madge and, giving a sniff, continued, '. . . and taller than I'd expected.'

This proved too much for his wife – she exploded with laughter. 'By gum, you don't half spout some rot! Taller – how the devil would you know that? You only glimpsed him from the platform forra few

45

seconds at Trinity Street Station – and he never even stepped foot off the train!'

'Aye, a secret mission to Lancashire, he was on,' her husband continued, unperturbed. 'India wanted her independence, didn't she, and was threatening to boycott our cloth, meaning the closure of our mills. He came to sweet-talk the cotton workers.'

'When was this, Mr Tattersall?' Clifford asked. A little of the colour had returned to his cheeks now and he appeared once again relaxed.

Livvy dug him in the ribs, much to his amusement: 'Don't encourage him!'

'Oh, you'd likely not remember, lad, would've been but a nipper: 25 September 1931,' he proclaimed on a proud rush, making the party giggle. 'Never forget that date, I'll not. Saw him, I did, from t' train window, as clear as I'm looking at you now, in his little iron-rimmed spectacles.'

'And did it work?' Clifford pressed, dodging Livvy's second attack with a grin. 'The sweet-talk, I mean?'

Morris hesitated. 'Oh, erm . . .' Finally, he threw his arms up. 'I'm buggered if I know.'

'Eeh, I don't know, you mad dog,' Madge told her husband. She had tears of mirth running down her podgy cheeks. 'You're getting worse, you are, I'm sure.'

'Put the wireless on, lass, see if there's owt on,'

Livvy said to Joan. 'Quick, now, before he thinks up summat else,' she added, and poked her tongue out when the old man shook his fist at her.

'Oh ay, aye – I like this one!' Morris wheezed, hauling himself up. He held out a gnarled hand to his wife. 'Come on, wench, take a turn with me and let's show this wet-behind-the-ears lot how it's done.'

'What? We could out-waltz you any day of the week – watch this!' Joan said, dragging nearby Clifford to his feet.

Daft as a bucket-load of wasps, Livvy thought to herself later with a contented sigh at her lips and love in her heart as she looked around at the cheery, dancing party. By, but she wouldn't bc without thcm, not for a gold clock.

'You look nice.'

It was evening and the house was quiet. Madge had returned to number nineteen with Celia and Clifford, Ned had gone home, and Morris had taken himself up to his bed 'for forty winks'. The sisters had cleared up and washed the dishes, and now it was time for Livvy to head out to work.

Meeting the girl's gaze through the mirror, she smiled. 'Ta, lass.'

'I can't wait until I can go out to pubs and dance halls – this town'll not know what's hit it when me and Doris are old enough. Paint it red, we will.'

Livvy snorted. 'I can well believe it. Anyroad, you shouldn't wish your life away. Enjoy your youth, my lass, whilst it's here – it's all downhill, you know, once you hit adulthood.'

Joan cocked her head. 'Nah, I'll bet it's reet good fun. 'Ere, I'll be able to come and visit you at work. That'll be gradely, eh?'

Banking down a grimace, she turned on her heel and reached for her coat, which was draped over the back of the chair. 'Right, well, I'm off. You'll be all right?'

'Aye.'

'Ta-ra, then, for now.'

The comment remained with Livvy throughout the journey to the tram stop. One day in the not too distant future, Joan *would* be free to come and go as she pleased, wouldn't she? What then? *Lord help them all.*

Her mind was still a jumble of niggling worries when she reached the Fleece Hotel and pushed open the door distractedly. Therefore, when the man approached and greeted her all smiles, she at first struggled to place him. 'Sorry, I . . . Do I know you?'

'Sure you do, honey! We met last night?'

Oh God, it was him. The Yank. 'Oh. Aye. Now I remember.' Livvy scanned the bar area in search of her friend.

'Vera's over there, at my table.' He nodded across.

Sure enough, following his direction, Livvy saw the woman beckoning her – half-heartedly, she returned her wave. 'You sit yourself down, honey, I'll get you a drink.'

'All right, Livvy?'

'I was,' she muttered, dropping into a chair next to Vera. 'What's he doing here?'

'Aw, don't be mean. He's really rather nice when you get to know him.'

She eyed Vera with an understanding nod. Clearly, her friend's invitation for the man to join her last night had extended much further, if her words were anything to go by. 'Got *well* acquainted with each other after I left, did youse?' she asked drily.

'You know me, girl. I ain't one to pass up an opportunity of making a bit of extra brass. Very generous with it he is, too. I ain't bought a single round yet.'

Overpaid, oversexed and over here. The well-used British saying with regards to their Atlantic cousins was true to form in this instance, all right. 'He's full of himself.'

'So what? Ain't most Yanks? Most fellas, actually, come to that.'

Livvy gave her a crooked smile. 'Suppose so.'

'Here you go, ladies.' Having appeared with a tray of drinks, the American placed it carefully on the table, wiped a bronzed hand down his trouser leg, then held it out to Livvy. 'I never got the chance to

49

properly introduce myself last night. Private Carl Rivera, ma'am, at your service.'

Looking into large brown eyes bright now with friendliness, all trace of arrogance and annoyance at her snub during their previous encounter nowhere to be seen, Livvy relented.

She slid her hand into his. 'Olive Bryant – Livvy to my pals.'

'I hope I might have the honour of that title, now?' And at her shrug: 'Gee, swell! Nice to meet you, *Livvy.*'

As she sipped her beverage, she took him in discreetly over the rim of her glass.

The US army base of Burtonwood had been set up last year in Warrington. Men stationed there would flood the pubs and dance halls of nearby towns and cities at the weekend – and Bolton was no exception. The Fleece, with its relaxed and, some might say, bawdy reputation ensured a lively time and was a particular draw – so much so it had been dubbed the American Embassy. You could barely move on Bradshawgate on a Saturday night for US servicemen.

GIs, so named after the 'General Issue' stamp on their equipment, had begun making their arrival on British shores in the spring of last year in preparation for the Allied offensives against Germany, following the attack on the US fleet at Pearl Harbor, which had forced America into the conflict, expanding the war into Asia and the Pacific. For a war-torn, weary Britain, which had already endured three years of death, destruction and grinding austerity, these exotic-seeming foreigners brought glamour and glitz, and a much-needed injection of fun.

And there was no shortage of men-starved, war-tired women for them to have their way with.

Hungry for a good time after so long living in loneliness, doom and shortages, plenty were drawn to the confident and devilishly good-looking Yanks in their smart uniforms like moths to a flame. In turn the men, who earned almost three pounds a week more than the Tommies – a staggering amount – had, unlike their British fighting counterparts, money to burn and would shower females who caught their eye with all manner of lavish gifts. And luxuries they were deemed when for so long they had been nigh on impossible to come by here, such as nylons and chocolate. The cheeky query from girls, 'Got any gum, chum?' was a common one.

The pull was insatiable. Unsurprisingly, the GIs received short shrift from local men, who resented these god-like beings enticing their womenfolk away from under their noses.

The lion's share of Livvy and Vera's clientele now comprised of GIs, and yet the former was under no illusion that they were any better than their own home-grown men, as some women appeared to think. To her at least they were customers, a means to enjoy herself and earn to feed her family – their flirty manner and silken tongues did nothing in turning her head whatsoever.

'Smoke?' Carl proffered a cigarette to the women. Livvy brought her mind back to the here and now. Following Vera's lead and nodding thanks, she extracted a Lucky Strike from the packet. 'So, Livvy,' he asked after lighting theirs, then his own, 'tell me about yourself.'

'Why should I?' she retorted.

'Because I'm interested.'

Crossing her legs, she arched an eyebrow. 'What d'you want to know? I'm sure you've learned by now that like Vera here I'm a doxy.'

'Doxy . . .'

'A pick-up. Good-time girl. A common tart.'

'Oh, I . . .' He nodded, smiled. 'Sure, that doesn't bother me.'

'I couldn't give a rat's arse if it did.'

Carl bit his lip for a moment, then released a half-laugh. 'You sure don't hold back, do you, honey? That's what I like about you English folk. What is it you lot say here . . . Ah yes: call a spade a spade.'

He'd delivered the last part in perfect imitation of their blunt Lancashire accent, had the flat vowels down to a T – Livvy and Vera looked to one another in shared surprise.

'Eeh, how've you learned to talk like that?' Vera squeaked, face wreathed in a grin. 'That were reet good!'

'Aye,' Livvy was forced to admit, returning his smile. 'Pass for a ruddy native, you would.'

Carl threw back his head and laughed. 'I've been here long enough, hey? Besides, I have a good ear for accents.'

Despite herself, Livvy's interest was piqued. She drew on her cigarette and blew the smoke towards the ceiling. 'So where are you from?'

'Illinois. You've heard of it?' he asked at her nod.

'I've met one or two Yanks from there, aye.'

'Do you . . . do business with many Americans?'

Another puff on her cigarette. 'That's right. Mind, nationality means nowt to me. So long as they've the brass to pay and I like the look of them, I'm game.'

'Livvy,' Vera whispered.

'What?'

'Do you have to?'

She gazed at her friend in astonishment – was Vera actually blushing? Good God, she was embarrassed. But why . . . Oh. Livvy sighed to herself and shook her head. The daft mare had fallen for him. She had, must have done, and what . . . she was reluctant to have him know the gory details of their trade lest he thought less of her, was that it? Well, more fool her.

Livvy was certainly not ashamed, and hear it he would:

'Me and my friend here, we've had every type of man there is bar an eskimo! Ain't that right, Vera?' she said, giving her a cheerful nudge. 'Aye: English, Irish, Welsh, Scottish, American—'

'Even the Negroes?' Carl almost demanded.

The US army that came to Britain was segregated, a fact that not only baffled Livvy and almost everyone else she knew, but disgusted her, too. Their black servicemen were even discouraged from spending their furlough, or leave, in 'white' dance halls and pubs. Anyone would think they were the enemy, not the allies, going by some people's behaviour.

Staring him dead in the eye, she brought her chin up. 'That's right,' she confirmed resolutely, 'and why not, eh? We're all people. Skin colour, it don't mean nowt so far as I'm concerned. Nor should it to you, pal. They're your fellow countrymen, after all. What's more, they're fighting every bit as hard as the non-coloured man to bring this war to an end. For that alone, they deserve as much respect as the next fella. Wouldn't you say?'

He breathed out slowly. Vera glanced from one to the other, wide-eyed. Livvy took another drag on her Lucky Strike. The seconds ticked on.

'Hey, ladies.' Throwing up his hands, Carl laughed again. 'Come on, let's not fight.' All smiles now, he pushed back his chair and got to his feet. 'Let me buy you dolls another drink, hey, as way of apology? Come on, what d'you say? Truce?'

Vera smiled and bobbed her head readily. Livvy remained mute, and he took her lack of response as agreement – another flash of his gleaming teeth and he disappeared to the counter.

'What was all that about?' Livvy wanted to know the moment they were alone.

'Don't know what you mean . . .'

'Aye, you do. Fawning all over the bugger – by gum, girl, wake up. All his sort are after is a good time. He'll not offer you owt more—'

'And how do you know that, eh?' Vera's emerald eyes flashed steel. 'You know nowt about him!'

'Oh, and I suppose you do after one quick tumble in t' hay? Love, listen,' she added, softer now, to defuse the situation – she'd never argued with the woman before and she didn't like it – 'I'm just thinking of you, that's all. I don't want to see you get hurt. Tread careful, eh?'

Though her scowl remained, Vera eventually gave a reluctant nod. 'Aye, all right. I do like him, though, Livvy. I don't know what it is about him . . . I just do.'

Spotting Carl weaving his way back to the table through the crowd, she let the matter drop to save Vera's pride and patted her hand. Nonetheless, her gaze, as she watched the man approach, remained wary.

For reasons Livvy was yet unable to identify, she had the strongest feeling that a storm of trouble was brewing – and that Carl Rivera would be slap bang in the centre of it.

Chapter Three

'COME ON, CAN'T I tempt you with just one more drink?'

'No, really, we have to go, now.' Cupping Vera's elbow as a signal they must leave, she pulled the somewhat reluctant woman to her feet. 'Ta all the same, mind.'

'Perhaps I could join you both—'

'Absolutely not.' Livvy's tone brooked no argument on that. 'We have work to do and your presence wouldn't do us much good, would it? You'll put blokes off.'

Vera moved to whisper something into Carl's ear, making him smile, then rejoined Livvy and led the way to the door. Outside, Livvy drew her to a halt.

'What did you say to him?'

'When?'

'Just then as we left?'

'Oh.' The woman tossed her head. 'I promised as

how we'd meet him back at the Fleece later on, that's all.'

Livvy was far from pleased with this: 'Well, you shouldn't have done.'

'And why not?'

'Because I don't appreciate you making plans on my behalf. What's more, it ain't right to encourage him. Besides, I'm straight off home once we've finished with business at the Palais.'

'Then I'll enjoy a last drink or two with him on my own!'

'You do that, aye. Oh, come on, let's get a move on,' she finished, frowning, hurrying Vera along. 'We've already missed out on the best part of the night as it is sat supping with him.'

The dance hall was packed out when they arrived. Following the routine of old, they deposited their coats, ordered themselves a lemonade and secured a table in a good position. Some ten minutes later, the music and atmosphere having worked their magic, the women were swaying their shoulders and drumming their fingers on the tabletop in time to the beat, all thoughts of their recent spat forgotten.

'By, they're a bit of all right,' Livvy breathed, flicking her brows towards two extremely good-looking men in the distance. 'Shall we?'

'Aye, go on.'

'Evening, lads.' Sidling up to the one she'd had her eye on, Livvy stretched her lips in a dazzling smile. 'Here alone?'

Sizing her up, his gaze widened in appreciation. 'That's right. Yourself?'

'Aye. Fancy that, eh?'

'Fancy,' he echoed, shooting his friend a wink.

They were deep in conversation when, glancing over her shoulder, the potential customer stopped talking suddenly to frown, then asked, 'Are you here with your bullyboy?'

'Bully . . .' Realisation dawned – he meant a pimp. She opened her mouth to inform him she didn't have one, that no man owned her or took from her a farthing of her hard-earned wages, when common sense got the better of her. For all she knew, he might take the fact as opportunity to get funny or refuse payment later if he knew she had no muscle to back her up. Granted he looked the decent type, but well, you never could tell in this game. 'He's not in here,' she said instead.

'No? Then who's that bloke over there what ain't stopped gawping at us?'

Her own brow furrowing, she turned and scanned the open space. She did a double take – then gasped in surprised anger. 'I don't believe this . . .'

'What's up?' asked Vera, breaking chatter with her partner, noticing Livvy's expression.

'You just have a look-see over there and you'll find out.'

'Is that . . .'

'Aye, it bloomin' well is.'

Smiling, Carl made his way across the floor towards them. 'Ladies, hi!'

'What the devil are you doing here?' Livvy demanded. 'Are you following us?'

'Why of course not. Sure, I wasn't to know where you were headed. This is a nice coincidence, though, isn't it?'

'No, it bleedin' well ain't.' She turned to stare pointedly at Vera; catching the hint, the woman drew Carl aside and spoke to him. Moments later, he half bowed with a hand to his breast and sauntered away.

'Sorry about that, lad,' Livvy told the man whom Carl had interrupted her speaking to. Then in the next breath: ''Ere, you're not leaving?'

'I think it best . . .'

'No wait – look, that fella's gone now,' she wheedled. 'He'll not disturb us again.'

He dithered for a handful of moments before relenting. 'All right then. You've got somewhere we can go?'

'Aye. Come on, boys, let's get out of here.'

The two couples headed off, holding hands, in the direction of Vera's accommodation. When they arrived at the door, the women were giggling at something one of the men had said and didn't notice anything was amiss; it was Livvy's partner who spotted it. He put out an arm, halting their entrance.

'What's wrong, why—'

'Look,' he answered Vera, pointing ahead.

'What the . . .' The door leading up to her rooms was ajar.

'You didn't leave it open when you went out?'

'No way.' She was adamant. 'I always double-check that it's locked.'

'Well, then someone's forced entry.'

'Oh God – the ruddy swines!'

The men shot each other a grim look. One said, 'You girls wait here whilst we check what's what and secure the place. They might still be inside.'

Livvy and Vera didn't need telling twice – nodding, they huddled together chewing their nails.

Stretching themselves to their full heights, the men pushed the door wide and marched inside.

Seconds felt like hours as the women waited with bated breath. Then the men were back. They stepped out into the street shaking their heads. Livvy rushed over:

'What, what's the matter, what did you find?'

'*Who*, more like.'

'Eh?'

'Oh, go on and see for yourselfs. Anyroad, we ain't got time for all this caper, we're off.'

'But . . .' Dumb with confusion, Livvy watched them walk away. When they had gone, she turned her questioning gaze on Vera; however, her friend was as nonplussed as she. 'Someone's in there, girl.'

'Well, who?'

'I don't know, do I? We'll have to go and see.'

Clutching arms, they made their hesitant way inside.

'Hey, you two. Say, I hope you don't mind—'

'*You.*' Livvy took in the scene incredulously. It was the GI. Sitting sprawled in the easy chair by the fire, he looked for all the world like he belonged there. 'What on earth . . .'

Vera was frowning. 'How did you get in here, Carl?'

'I wanted to surprise you, baby.'

'How?' she repeated quietly.

'That sweet old lady who runs the diner—'

'The café? You mean my landlady?'

'That's right – she let me in. I might have told her just the smallest white lie,' he went on, winking. 'I said you knew I was coming and that you'd told me to ask for the spare key . . . Say, Vera.' His face falling at her expression, he stepped forward. 'You're not mad at me, are you? Sure, I really didn't think you'd mind.'

'It's all right, I'm not mad,' she murmured. 'It's just, you gave us such a shock.'

Closing her eyes, Livvy held up her hands. 'Sorry,

just let me see if I've got this right. Some stranger breaks into your home and you say it don't matter? Have you turned bloody barmy, or what?'

'He's norra stranger, is he? He's Carl, Carl Rivera.'

'Oh, Vera, come on!'

'Nor did he break in, he used a key.'

She stared at her friend in stunned silence. She was actually defending this toerag's behaviour? Good God, was she really being this stupid?

'This is my home, remember, Livvy,' Vera was saying now; twin spots of angry colour stained her cheekbones. 'I get to decide who comes and goes here, not you.'

'Right, and what's that meant to mean, like? You want me to leave, aye?'

'Well, that's up to you.'

'Ladies, ladies, please.' Carl moved between them both. 'Don't let's fight! Look, I'll go—'

'No, you'll not,' Vera interjected. 'Don't. I want you to stay.'

Swallowing down the stab of hurt at the woman's disloyalty – never before had either of them allowed a man to come between them – Livvy forced herself to ask, 'And me?'

'I want you to stay, an' all. Eeh, course I do.'

'Aye?'

'Aye.' Vera punched her arm playfully. 'Let's get

63

out of here, eh, and go and get sozzled, what d'you reckon?'

'What about work?'

'Oh, sod it for one night. Say you will, go on.'

'Sounds like a swell plan – and the drinks are on me,' Carl added. 'Come on, Livvy, what'd' you say? Can we put this behind us, start afresh?'

'For my sake?' Vera coaxed.

Livvy glanced from one to the other, her mind in a quandary. Her love-struck mate might believe everything this man said, but she didn't buy it for a minute and didn't trust him as far as she could throw him. He was a queer sort, all right. And yet she didn't want to lose her friend, either. What's more, was it wise to leave Vera alone with him? Surely if she went with them, she could keep an eye to her, make sure she was all right. But having to spend the entire evening in his company – free ale on tap or no . . . the prospect made her want to groan.

At last, she submitted; heaving a sigh, she nodded.

She only hoped she wouldn't come to regret it.

As the elderly man sitting at the old joanna started up yet another song, Carl gasped. Jumping to his feet, he clapped his hands together with gusto:

'Now this is more like it – I know this one,' he shouted to Livvy and Vera over the medley of music, singing and feet stomping. 'Come on, dolls, come and join me!'

Grinning, they accepted the hands he held out to them and took to the floor; Carl spun them at speed in turn, making them shriek with laughter.

To Livvy's surprise, the night had turned into one of the best she'd had in a long time. Her misgivings regarding a certain member of the party had initially kept her guarded, however as time moved on and Carl, true to his word, looked indeed to want to start over and behaved with the epitome of gentlemanliness, she'd slowly begun to relax. Of course, the copious amount of alcohol – he ensured that their glasses never had a chance to run dry – had also helped in that. She wouldn't have believed it possible only a few short hours since, and even now she hated to admit it, but she actually was really enjoying herself.

'That's me done – I'm fagged!' she gasped finally, flopping back into her seat. Equally out of puff, but with smiles matching her own, Vera and Carl rejoined her.

'What's say we call in at one of your delicious fish and chip shops later?' he asked after taking a long swig of his drink, and at their nods: 'Good, 'cause that song sure does make me hungry.'

The women hooted with laughter, asking in unison: 'How in God's name can a song make you hungry?'

'Ah well, you see, it's the memories it evokes. My dad would always play it on the piano at family gatherings when I was young. And at these gatherings, there sure was plenty to eat. My mom, she's one swell cook.'

Seeing the lines that had appeared at the corners of his mouth as his lips drooped and the cloud of longing that had entered his eyes, Livvy felt a pang of pity for him. Her tone was soft. 'You must miss them.'

'I do. But . . .' He spread out his hands and let his shoulders rise and fall. 'I took up the call of Uncle Sam and must see it through to the bitter end. We're all making sacrifices, huh? Until the enemy is beaten, we have a job to do, it's that simple.'

'Had you travelled much before the war?'

He shook his head. 'No, ma'am.'

'And here you find yourself now, dumped in a strange country a million miles from all you know and love. You must get homesick.'

'Well, it's not quite so many miles as all that . . . but sure. I do miss it.'

'Tell me about it, this place of your people,' she said, leaning back in her seat and crossing her ankles. 'I'm interested.'

'My people.' He grinned. 'You make me sound like a being from another planet.'

'No, you know what I mean. There must be some differences to our lot over here?'

'Oh, honey – *every*thing here is different! This for one thing.' He took another draught from his glass. 'Warm weak ale sure is an acquired taste! Boy, what I wouldn't give right now for a highball.'

'High what?'

'A bourbon and soda, honey.'

'It's a Chicago gangster you think you are, I reckon, like what we see in the films!'

He smiled. From his breast pocket, he extracted a document and held it up. 'Courtesy of the United States War Department – you see, I have been trying.'

'What's that?' Livvy scanned the bright front cover depicting an image of a soldier, his arm and legs extended to form the shape of the United Kingdom, and 'Welcome!' emblazoned across the bottom.

'"A Short Guide to Britain". The powers that be deemed it wise to publish instructions on the rules of your country. This was issued to all American troops to help us adjust here. What is it, what's funny?' he asked when the women shared a grin.

'We got them, an' all, to aid us in dealing with the Yanks,' offered Livvy.

'Gee!'

'Well, them folk what work with you lot did, anyroad; NAAFI staff and the like.'

Vera nodded, adding, 'A pamphlet, aye. My sister was employed for a time in a canteen and she were given one. She showed it to me and Livvy. It too had instructions on understanding Americans and their – your – ways,' she amended with a laugh. 'What to do and what *not* to do when meeting the Yanks. Said we should be nice to you, it did, or else we'd be helping Hitler, who wants to separate us.'

'Very true.'

'And it had drawings in it showing different insignias of rank for the men and that . . . oh, and a table of some of your sayings and what they mean in English.'

'English! And wha'd' I speak, baby, double Dutch?'

'Well, no, but by, you do spout some queer things.'

His shoulders shaking with mirth, Carl shook his head. 'Right, because this place really makes sense – I don't think!'

'How's that then?' Livvy wanted to know. 'We're not *so* different, surely?'

'You think? Take your coinage, for instance: how, in the name of all that's holy, do you cope with this crazy system? Give me dollars, cents, dimes and nickels any day! I still struggle with it, you know. Wait, let me see if I've got this right . . .' Closing one eye, he squinted at the ceiling and counted on his fingers: 'Twenty-one shillings to a guinea, twenty shillings to a pound, and . . . twelve pennies to a shilling? That's right, isn't it? Boy!'

'I've noticed as well that your lot don't say the time

proper,' Vera said, wiping tears of amusement from her eyes when the laughter had died down. 'A quarter after eight, you say, not quarter past, and twenty of ten instead of twenty *to* ten. Now that's daft!'

Carl folded his arms. 'Well, we're far ahead of you in terms of infrastructure. You take our skyscrapers, baby. Magnificent examples of advanced minds – far superior to anything you have to boast.'

'Listen, chum, you can keep your ruddy cloud ticklers!' Livvy retorted good-naturedly; she was thoroughly enjoying the repartee. 'Where's your thousand-year-old buildings, eh? Nah, can't swank about them, can you, for you've not bloody got none. We've got history, love, right on our doorsteps, every which way we turn; you ain't.'

Pulling a face then chuckling, he bowed down in defeat. 'All right, you beat me there.'

'Ha! Gotcha.' Licking her finger then striking the air, she gave a sharp nod. 'So put that in your pipe and smoke it!'

'To be fair to you, London stands not on rock as in my country but clay. So you see, you couldn't build as we do; your ground just isn't sustainable.'

Livvy and Vera shared a raised eyebrow.

'Knows a lot, this fella, don't he?'

'Aye, Vera, he does – a reet brainbox,' Livvy agreed.

Carl pretended modesty, half hiding his face with his hand: 'Oh, you're just fooling, stop it.'

'We ain't!'

'Sure you are . . . Okay then, don't stop; go on. I rather like hearing you sing my praises.'

'Nah, we're bored now,' Livvy announced dismissively, turning her attention to her nails. However, she couldn't hold back the giggles for long – simultaneously, the three of them burst out laughing.

'Well, I think our leaders would be mighty proud of us if they could see us now,' Carl stated. 'Anglo-American relations are alive and well.' He held out his drink. 'Cheers.'

'Cheers!' the women echoed, clinking glasses.

The conversation flowed freely for the next few hours, and Livvy was shocked when the bell calling time rang out. Glancing across and seeing barmaid Gwen placing towels over the pump handles, she gasped: 'Bloomin' 'eck, is it that late? I'll miss the last bus!'

'Ne'er mind,' said Vera, 'you can always stop over at mine tonight. Your Joan shan't fret none; you've done it before, after all.'

'I suppose so . . .'

'Oh, go on. Your family will survive without you for one night, I'm sure.'

Livvy relented. 'Aye, all right. So, are we calling for chips or what?'

'Oh, we are! I'm that hungry I could eat a scabby dog.'

The moment the fresh air hit them, Livvy's world began to spin; fumbling for her friend's arm, she groaned. 'I'm squiffy, me, didn't realise how much I were supping.'

'You'll be reet, just keep a hold of me – and 'ere, watch your step, friggin' blackout,' was Vera's advice.

The trio made their measured way through the pitch-dark street, apologising and giggling every few steps as they bumped into and trod on the feet of other revellers homeward bound. At last, they reached the chippy. Minutes later, cuddling her hot, steaming bundle of mouth-watering food against her chest, Livvy led the way out. Pausing by the roadside, intending to say goodnight to Carl, she was dismayed when Vera linked her arm through his and tugged him along in the direction of her rooms.

For all they had had a sound night and shared together a laugh, that was in the safety of a public place; for some reason, she felt a stir of discomfort at the notion of them being alone together in the seclusion of the flat. Yet what choice had she – Vera's home, Vera's rules, she reminded herself. Suppressing a sigh, she dragged her feet forward and followed on.

Having drawn the curtains and got the fire going, Vera crossed to the kettle to make tea. Livvy took the opportunity to ask the American: 'Why did you return here with us? Surely you have to be back at camp?'

Liberty trucks from Burtonwood, at least four of them, would fetch the GIs to Bolton for the evening during their free time. She'd seen them plenty enough times herself, parked up in the small side street near St Mary's Church. The Americans would spill out to swarm the town, and drivers would take them all back again when the dancing was over at the night's end.

'Sure, a few minutes won't do any harm. Tonight's driver is a chum of mine – he always waits a little while longer for latecomers.'

'And if he don't?' she persisted. Right now, all she desired was to have her supper and get her head down. She was dog-tired, and the onset of a headache was looming. She'd never catch a wink of sleep if he hung around. 'If this pal of yours *does* scarper without picking up stragglers, you'll finish up with the snowdrops on your back and a bashing from their nightsticks.'

'Snowdrops?'

'Aye, what us Brits call your American Military Police. Owing to the white gloves, gaiters and helmets they wear?' she explained.

'Oh, I see! Oh no, honey.' Carl dismissed her claims with a flap of his hand. 'He'll hang around. And if for some reason he doesn't – well. It's not the end of the world. I'll return at first light, say I had too much to drink and stayed with a friend. Granted, they won't be pleased, but I'll survive.' He shrugged. 'I'll see how I feel.'

Vera was approaching with the teapot and cups – Livvy forced to her lips a tight smile and let the matter lie.

They ate their food and chatted for a short while until, chuckling, Vera nodded at Livvy.

'By gum, girl, you can't keep your eyes open.'

She was relieved her friend had noticed. The sofa was where she slept whenever she stayed here, and there was no chance of relaxing until Vera decided to call it a night. 'I'm fagged, it's true.'

'We'll have to let her get some shut-eye, love,' Vera said to Carl. She'd suddenly come over all coy; looking up at him from beneath her lashes, she asked, 'What are your plans . . .'

'I'll stay, baby, if that's okay with you?'

'Aye. Course it is!'

'Swell. Well, goodnight, Livvy.' He stooped and, before she knew what was happening, planted a kiss on the side of her cheek, his bottom lip making contact with the corner of her mouth in the process – she shrank back a little.

'Aye,' she said as lightly as she could manage, didn't want to cause a fuss by calling him out on his overfamiliarity. 'Yes. Goodnight.'

'Goodnight, God bless, girl,' chirped Vera over her shoulder en route to her bedroom, almost dragging the American out in her haste to be alone with him.

Livvy repeated the woman's parting words to the already closed door. Then shaking her head and shrugging, she made for the small chest in the alcove.

From the middle drawer, she extracted two khaki army regulation blankets – Lord alone knew how Vera had got her hands on them – and carried them to the sofa. After folding one into the general shape of a pillow and turning down neatly the other with which to cover herself, she perched on the cushion edge and began to undress.

A milky low moon winked through the gap in the curtains – none of them had noticed they were not fully closed. It was a wonder the air-raid warden hadn't come banging on the door demanding they 'Put that bleedin' light out!' Clad now in just her undergarments, she moved to draw them properly – it was an automatic response; the nation was well trained about such matters after so long – then turned back on herself with a click of her tongue. She'd be extinguishing the gas lamp in a moment anyway, so what did it matter?

The coverings were itchy but didn't detract from the blessed sensation of resting her weary body and aching head. Within minutes, she was slumbering soundly.

A hand on her bare thigh brought a wisp of consciousness back; frowning, she pulled with effort the half of her exhausted brain still suspended in sleep to reality. 'Wha—'

'Sshhh. Quiet.'

'Eh? Who . . . Oh—!'

Carl moved swiftly to clamp a hand over her mouth before she could yell out. His hold, as he pressed the back of her head down into the makeshift pillow, was like iron – Livvy was immobilised.

'Baby, baby . . . Lord, I've been dreaming of this— No,' he added in the next breath, imprisoning her wrists in his free hand as she made to strike him and straddling her before she could kick out. 'Just re*lax*.'

His full weight was on her legs and her arms were twisted at an awkward angle above her head; she was trapped – trapped! Panic cascaded through her veins in a torrent. Despite her line of work and minor dealings with the occasional tricky customer, she'd never encountered anything like this before, not from any man. She'd never been forced . . . *Dear God, help me.*

'Don't worry, baby, I'll pay you.' Carl's words came out muffled against her lips as he kissed her hungrily. 'I'll pay you whatever you want . . .'

Please. No. Please.

'Stop,' she managed to rasp out past his probing tongue. 'Stop.'

'Sshh, baby,' was his response.

In a lightning move that left her senses stunned, he positioned himself in place and forced himself inside her. Pain, as he yanked aside her brassiere and clamped his teeth around her nipple, sent white sparks popping behind her eyes, paralysing her – her inner scream was deafening.

When it was over, he remained for a moment, his face and bare shoulders glistening with perspiration, looking down on her and smiling. He kissed her tenderly and rose from the sofa.

Not a word was spoken as they moved in unison: Livvy to burrow herself in the corner of the cushion, arms wrapped around her knees, which she'd brought up beneath her chin, he to straighten his clothing and collect a Lucky Strike from the packet atop the mantelpiece.

'You want one, baby?' he proffered, holding one out.

Sending her tousled hair swinging, she shook her head.

He lit his cigarette and lowered himself into the chair by the fire, hands resting loosely on the wooden arms, his legs splayed, completely at ease. Throwing him a glance, Livvy thought she might vomit.

'That was sure worth the wait,' he murmured after a time. There was a definite note of victory in the tone.

'I, I . . . said . . .'

'What's that, baby?'

'I said . . . I said stop. I wanted you to *stop*.'

Carl blinked at her through the lunar gloom. 'You did not.'

'Yes. I. Did!'

'Well.' He puffed out slowly. 'What's done is done, huh? Besides,' he finished, as cool as a spring breeze, 'who would believe you?'

Livvy's livid reply hadn't a chance to bear life – before she could utter a stream of hateful expletives, the door leading from the bedroom swung wide and slammed against the wall.

Snapping their heads around in tandem, Livvy and Carl saw Vera standing on the threshold of the living room.

Arms folded tightly, her face a mask of stone, the woman had eyes only for the American. 'I would.'

'Vera, I—'

'I would,' she repeated, moving slowly across the space towards him. 'I'd believe her, every word. And d'you know why?' She threw the words at him like knives. 'Because I've been standing the other side of that door for the last minute and heard every sordid damned detail of what's just been said.'

'Honey.' Rising, his smile fixing itself in place, he made to take her in his arms, but she shoved him aggressively in the chest, making him stagger; he gazed at her, evidently shocked that his charm wasn't having the desired effect over her this time. 'Baby, come on, you've got this all wrong—'

'Like hell I have.'

'Sure you do. I visited the rest room and must have stumbled in here by mistake. It was dark – I thought I was with you. What happened . . . it's not like Livvy says, she seduced me—'

'Get out.'

'*Baby*—'

'I'm not your friggin' baby and never were. Go! Go on, you rotten bastard, get gone!'

'Vera . . .'

'Eeh, love!' Taking Livvy into her arms when Carl had stormed from the room, slamming the door behind him, Vera held her close. 'I'm sorry. I'm so very sorry!'

'No, love, no.' Choking back miserable whimpers, Livvy shook her head. ''Tain't no fault of yours – how could it be? If any bugger's to blame it's me. I should have tried harder to stop him, should have done *summat*. I were just so shocked, and he were just so strong—'

'You did no wrong. Look at me,' Vera insisted, lifting her friend's chin with her finger to glare deep into her eyes. Tears splashed unchecked down her face. 'You did no wrong, Livvy. None, love.'

On a soft, shared sob, they threw their arms around each other and hugged tightly.

Chapter Four

'YOU HAVE TO try and eat something, Livvy.'

It was the following morning and the women, pale-faced and bleary-eyed through lack of sleep, having sat up for most of the night, were attempting break-fast. Despite Vera's advice, even she had forced inside herself but a few nibbles of toast.

'The thought makes my guts lurch – honest, love, I can't manage it. The tea's enough.'

'I meant what I said last night, you know: I am sorry,' the other woman murmured after a long silence. 'I should never have fetched him back here. I should have woken sooner, come to your rescue—'

'Vera, Vera.' Livvy's voice was weary. 'Look, as I keep saying, there's no point in raking over old ground. What's done is done. I just want to forget about it.'

'But you can't!' Aghast, she took Livvy's hand and squeezed. 'You mean you'll not even consider report-ing the swine?'

Livvy almost laughed: 'To who, pray tell? Oh, you mean the authorities? Do me a favour! I'm a prostitute, Vera – who the hell is going to want to listen to me? The police won't bat an eyelid. They'll deem me deserving of the crime, that given the way I choose to live my life I was asking for it. An occupational hazard, aye.'

'But he weren't a punter, was he?'

'That'll make no odds and you know it.'

'I thought he was a friend. I thought he liked me, you know. I feel so bloody foolish. Hoodwinked me good and proper, he did. You knew, mind, didn't you?' her friend went on, visibly cringing. 'You saw through him, sensed he were a bad lot; never did take to him, you never. You tried to warn me and I shut my bleedin' ears to it. Well, I'll tell you summat for nowt: never will a fella do me over like that again. None are getting anywhere near from now on, and that's the God's honest truth. Bastards, they are, the lot!'

A half an hour later, Livvy was standing in the street saying her goodbyes at the door. Tears were threatening once more but she swiped them away with her sleeve in desperate determination. She wouldn't crumble, give in to her emotions, couldn't. She'd go under and drown in them, else.

'Just you remember, you know where I am,' Vera said, stroking her arm. 'You need to chat, cry, rant and rave, whatever, you come to me. All right?'

'Aye.'

'Eeh, Livvy . . .'

'Don't,' she warned as the woman's face creased and her eyes turned bright, 'please don't, for you'll set me off again.' Swallowing thickly, she nodded. 'Right, I'm off.'

'Ta-ra, love.'

'Ta-ra, Vera.'

Lost in a world of her own tumbling thoughts, she recalled nothing of the journey to Top o'th' Brow. The next thing she became aware of was standing in the hallway of her house.

She removed her coat and hung it up. One deep breath – two, three. Then, plastering in place a smile, she opened the door leading to the living room and stuck her head around the frame: 'Morning!'

'Morning,' Joan and Morris, seated together, the younger darning a pair of socks and the elder busy filling his pipe, answered.

Normal, everything as it always was . . . Livvy felt the weight on her chest ease a fraction at the familiarity.

'Did you stop over at Vera's, Livvy?' her sister asked after breaking off the length of cotton with her teeth.

'She better had done, or else!' their grandfather butted in. However, there was no real accusation in his eyes – it was a running joke, a harmless mock warning should he discover she'd spent the night in the company of a male instead, and one she always played along to. *If only they knew the truth.*

81

'Course I stopped with Vera, dafty,' she told him, ruffling his thinning hair and dodging with a smile when he took a swipe at her.

'I wish you'd not do that, you aggravating bugger,' he grumbled, smoothing his palm across his head. 'I've only got a handful of strands left, you know, and half of them are due for kicking the bucket. Make yourself useful, anyroad, and put the kettle on.'

'Sorry, I can't, I'm nipping up forra bath,' she said, and before he could argue the matter she'd hurried from the room and was taking the stairs two at a time.

Her facade slipped away the moment she reached the solitude of the bathroom. Leaning with her back against the door, she closed her eyes.

Snatches of memory – Carl's face twisted at the point of climax, the burn of his touch on her skin which remained still even now – stabbed like pitch-forks at her benumbed brain. She thrust herself forward and turned on the bath taps.

'Sod the government, sod the ration, and sod this bloody war,' she growled to the gushing water, paying no heed to the five-inch restriction this day. She needed to immerse herself fully, *must* remove, if not from her mind then from her body, all trace of him.

After a thorough soak and all-over scrub, she felt little better but not altogether as bad as she had. She supposed it would have to do. Nothing, after all, could make this go away fully, nothing. Gulping back the hurt before it had a chance to consume her – she'd shed not another tear for him, this she'd vowed already – she stepped from the tub and let the water and all the terribleness it had stripped away go down the drain.

Morris was dozing in his chair when she re-entered the living room. Joan, her chore now completed and her wicker sewing basket returned to the sideboard, rose at her entrance and moved to where sat the teapot on its trivet in the centre of the table.

'Ta, lass,' Livvy said, taking from her gratefully the steaming cup she'd filled and holding it between her two hands.

'It's Lord Woolton's for dinner.'

'Lovely,' Livvy lied. She had not a shred of appetite still, doubted she'd ever eat again.

'Grandad's gorra look of Doctor Carrot, ain't he?' Joan observed, her lips piquing. 'And Grandma's the spitting image of Potato Pete.'

'Joan!'

'Well, it's true.'

'You shouldn't say such things,' Livvy chided softly. Then her own mouth stretched wide, despite her inner sufferings, and she chortled. 'Mind you, you're not ruddy wrong.'

The Ministry of Food had come up with the humanised versions of the staples during the Dig for Victory campaign when urging more people to grow and eat vegetables. The bald and bespectacled sketches of Doctor Carrot, dubbed the children's best friend, who helped you see in the dark – great for the blackout! – and his rotund and rosy-cheeked companion Potato Pete, known for his protective properties, were renowned and much-loved characters.

The vegetarian pastry dish Lord Woolton's pie meanwhile, named after the Minister of Food who popularised the recipe, had quickly become, rather surprisingly for a nation that favoured meat, a legendary wartime favourite. Consisting of root vegetables – including of course Doctor Carrot and Potato Pete – oats and spring onions, it was finished off with a potato crust. Not only was it cheap, tasty and filling but the ingredients were relatively easy to obtain. A winning combination for any struggling housewife. And Livvy, all too aware how hard her sister worked to keep the home ticking over and that wasting good grub was sacrilege during these trying times, knew she'd simply have to force it down regardless.

'Clifford called in earlier,' Joan was saying now. Livvy's heart did a hop, skip and jump at the mention of his name.

Keeping her eyes on her tea, she murmured, 'Oh?'

'He wanted to see you, but I told him you weren't back yet from t' night before.'

She suppressed a sigh at how grubby the statement, however innocently given, sounded. Which to all intents and purposes, it was. There was only ever one reason she stayed out all night at Vera's and that was due to her getting drunk after a hard evening's whoring, God help her. 'What did he want me for, did he say?'

Joan shook her head. 'He just said he'd catch you later.'

Livvy nodded, smiled and let the subject lie. Whatever he'd wanted, it would have to wait. She couldn't see him, not yet, not after . . . No, she couldn't see him.

'You are all right, ain't you, Livvy?'

Dragged from her reverie, she nodded quickly. 'Aye, course I am. Why?'

'I don't know,' the girl said, eyeing her thoughtfully. 'There's . . . a sadness, almost, about you. Nowt's occurred?'

The effort it took for her not to break down in tears was immense. A large lump had lodged itself in her windpipe; her tone was little above a whisper. 'Don't you be worrying yourself over me, lass. I'm fine, honest. 'Ere, come over here and fetch the brush.' She patted the space on the sofa beside her.

'But I've chores to see to . . .'

'Ne'er mind about them awhile. They'll still be there later.'

Smiling, Joan did her bidding and lowered herself to the floor between her sister's feet. Closing her eyes as the first stroke of the bristles glided through her golden spiral curls, she sighed. 'I'll be for falling asleep in a minute. Always makes me dozy, this does.'

'You love it, though, always have done,' Livvy murmured, swishing the brush back and to, back and to. 'Do you remember when you were a nipper and you used to sneak into my bed of a night and beg me to play with your hair, reckoned you couldn't get to sleep else? You'd have me at it for hours, you would – my poor fingers were raw the next morning.' She laughed gently. 'By, I don't half miss them days.'

'Me too. When Mam and Dad were alive and we were all together. It were nice, weren't it, Livvy?'

'It was, love, aye. But, well, you've still got me, eh? We've got each other, for now and always. All right?'

'Aye. Nowt will come between us, will it?'

'I'll kill owt what ruddy tries it, lass, you can be sure of that.'

The dinner was over with and the dishes washed when soft tapping sounded later at the window. Assuming it was their grandmother on her daily visit, Livvy moved unconsciously to open the door – then cursed herself to see who the visitor actually was. Locking eyes with him, a deep blush immediately spread across her face. 'Oh, hello, Clifford.'

'All right, Livvy. Not a bad time, is it?'

'No, no. Come on in.'

He shadowed her into the living room and sat down. 'Where's the others?'

'Grandad's out with Ned playing dominoes, and our Joan's called round to her mate Doris's house.' Her eyes fixed squarely on the brown wool rug in front of the hearth. She waited for him to speak again, however the silence grew. At last, she was forced to glance up. Clifford was staring straight back at her. He had a slight frown at his brow, and for one dreadful moment panic seized her. Did he know, had he somehow guessed? Had he read in her face what had happened, seen her secret? *Dear God, no* . . .

'Livvy?'

'Sorry?' she asked, shaking the nightmare fog from her head. She hadn't realised he'd spoken. 'What did you say?'

'I said I called in this morning but you weren't here.'

'Aye.' Again, she sent her gaze back towards the fire. 'What was it you wanted?'

'I thought it might be nice if I took our Celia out to the cinema one evening and wondered if you fancied tagging along with your grandma. It's ages since she went out anywhere, and she works hard in that house waiting on me hand and foot – she deserves it. What d'you reckon?'

That this was an excuse to get her to go out with

him, in whatever capacity he could manage, was painfully apparent. Not that he wasn't fond of his aunt and he took good care of her, but Livvy had never known him to make pains to take the woman out before now. Her face softened and her shoulders lost a little of their tautness. She took a seat facing him and crossed her legs. 'I'm not sure, lad . . . When were you thinking of?'

'Tomorrow? Unless you've got work?'

'No.' Thoughts of that right now made her queasy. She couldn't return to all that just yet. 'No, I ain't got work.'

'So . . .'

A nagging voice at the back of her mind was telling her, warning her, not to accept, that in doing so it would give him the wrong impression and false hope. *Nothing could happen between them.* However another section yearned for it, she realised. Clifford was safe, familiar. He liked her for her alone, as a person, not her body – a rarity to be sure in her life. She needed, nay was desperate for, a release from these terrible thoughts before she went stark, staring mad. She wanted escape and here was he offering to provide that, for a few hours at least. Why the hell not?

'Look, it's fine, really. If you'd rather not—'

'I'd like to,' she blurted.

'Aye?'

'Aye. I'd like to a lot.'

Clifford's face spread slowly in a warm, wide smile. He breathed out deeply and nodded. 'Right, then. Gradely. We'll call across for you about seven?'

'I'll be waiting.'

When he'd gone, she busied herself cleaning the kitchen, scrubbing the sink out and wiping down the stove. Still, there was no running from her own mind, and throughout her thoughts remained with her.

Why did that man have to go and do that to her? Why? Letting the cloth slip from her fingers, she slid to her knees on the cold floor.

He heard her say no, he did. He *knew* she hadn't wanted him, wanted that. He'd taken it from her anyway without a single thought for her. He'd humiliated her, hurt her, and afterwards behaved as though it hadn't meant a thing. Just what make of man could do that? A beastly one, that's what. Why didn't these types of males ever think what such an act might do to their victim, not once but over and over and over, for it didn't let up in the brain for a second – would it ever? She just wanted it to be over, damn it. Why wouldn't it leave her be and go away?

With great strength, she mustered herself up and put the kettle on. A cup of tea later and she felt if not better then more readily able to face her family again, who would shortly be back and expecting her to greet them in her usual easy way. And this she would do – she wouldn't disappoint them.

The twilight hours in bed later were worse, she very soon came to realise, than the daytime ones. At least then she had means to occupy to an extent her ruminations – here, lying tossing and turning in the still darkness without a hope of release in sleep was torturous. She'd almost given up and was about to leave to go back downstairs when, suddenly, another face swam forth behind her eyes to replace the repugnant one of the American: Clifford.

She allowed herself a smile. Tiny and fleeting, but a smile all the same.

Wrapping the bedclothes around herself more tightly, she let her lids close once more.

'Livvy!'

'Hello, Vera. Can I come in?'

'Eeh, course you can. I've been that worried about you, yer know. You've not been far from my mind once since you left yesterday.'

'I just had to get out from them four walls forra bit.'

The women, once they had a hot drink each clasped in their hands, sat staring at one another across the small pine table – Livvy refused to step foot near the sofa.

'So how're you fettling?' Vera asked quietly.

Rubbing her cheek, she answered with mirthless laughter.

'Sorry, that were a daft question. I meant, how have you been . . . Oh, I can't summon the right *words*—'

'It's all right, really,' Livvy cut in softly, putting her friend out of her misery. 'I've . . . Well, I'm coping, you know?'

'No, love, I don't. I can't begin to imagine what you're going through, I . . .' Vera cleared her throat. 'Have you told anyone: your grandma, grandad?'

'Good God, no. I couldn't. They'd not understand.'

Silence descended for a time, thcn: 'Will you come back to work, do you think?'

Livvy took a long while to answer. 'I don't know,' she admitted. 'The thought of it now . . .'

'Aye. I understand.'

'You do?'

Vera nodded. 'What will you do for brass otherwise, d'you reckon?'

'Happen I could try my hand at bar work. For real and proper this time,' she added with a crooked smile. 'The family believe already that's what I do, anyroad. It shan't be so bad, eh?'

'The money ain't as good, mind.'

'No, but that don't seem to matter now.' And Livvy spoke truth. It really didn't.

'We'll still be mates, love, won't we?'

'Eeh, Vera.' Placing her cup on the tabletop, Livvy stretched her arms across and took her friend's waiting hands in hers. '*Course* we will. Us toiling at different professions, it won't make a scrap of difference to owt. As if you even need to ask.'

'Everything's changed, ain't it?' Vera surmised after a while. 'And all because of that rotten—'

'Don't, love. Don't say his name.'

The woman breathed out heavily through flared nostrils, then nodded. 'Aye. Sorry. I'm just spitting bloody mad, I am! He wants stringing up! Are you sure you'll not consider reporting him, Livvy? To his commanding officer, if not the law – surely there's summat his superiors could do? I'll march all the way to Burtonwood for you and alert them myself, I will. You've only to say the word and—'

'No. I mean it, no. But ta all the same; I know you mean well.'

'Livvy?' Vera whispered several minutes later.

'What?'

'I didn't know whether I ought . . . don't know if I should mention it, but . . .'

'What?' she repeated, quieter now. Dread like thrashing eels had taken possession of her guts – something bad was coming if her mate's expression was anything to go by.

'He's been back here.'

She swallowed hard. 'When? Why?'

'Yesterday evening. He wanted to see you, he said.'

'See me? What the hell for?'

'I don't know, love. I didn't give him the chance to go on, told him instead just exactly what I thought of him and slammed the door in his phizzog.'

'How did he look?' Not that it mattered, but she wanted to know anyway. 'Did he seem . . . sorry?'

'He didn't, no, I'm afraid to say. The swagger was there, and he carried about him still that air of arrogance, you know the one. What's more, he appeared norra bit mithered at my rant. I don't believe we've heard the last from him, Livvy,' she finished grimly.

Her heart was thumping. She licked her dry lips. 'You reckon he'll be back?'

'I do, aye. In fact, I'd stake good money on it. He's a queer 'un, that one, and no mistake.'

Vera's words plagued Livvy the whole way home. What if he did return? What if he got angry, violent, took his warped frustrations out on her friend? It wasn't exactly an impossibility, was it? From what he'd shown of himself thus far, she reckoned he was capable of anything when push came to shove. Would Vera suffer his dark side next? Was she in danger? As for herself: why on earth had he come seeking her out after everything? Would his urge to see her burn out or only strengthen? Should she be the one looking over her shoulder also? – for how long? Just when would all this know an end?

Upon reaching the estate, Livvy, instead of turning for Glaister Lane, carried on straight towards New Lane and the small parade of shops. She needed breathing space, time to calm down; home and the false pretence at normality she must adopt there was the last thing she had the nerve for right now.

Leaning against the strip of wall between two stores, she heaved a long breath. How she wished it was Sunday still; the grocer's, butcher's and confectioner's were closed then and all was quiet. No such luck this Monday morning – the place was bustling. Her neighbours and fellow residents, judgemental people with their narrow-minded views, bar a select few . . . she closed her eyes and ears to each one who passed. Oh, what she wouldn't give in this moment for a friendly face, a listening ear to spill her guts to and—

'Livvy?'

Half turning as the voice rang out, she let out a sigh. *Christ, that's all she needed.*

'Eeh, these friggin' eyes of mine are not what they were . . . That you, lass?' the caller persisted, louder now, squinting across the stretch of road in front.

With reluctance, she raised a hand: 'Aye, it's me, Grandma.'

Madge, her head wrapped severely in a floral scarf,

94

trundled over. She'd clearly just come the short distance from Celia's house – nonetheless, her cheeks were glowing from the excursion. 'What you doing, hanging about here on your lonesome? Shops are for buying from, you know.'

'Aye, I'm not daft.'

'Well then?'

She glanced off into the distance. 'Oh, you know, just thinking.'

'And you can't do that at home?'

She shook her head.

'Summat's afoot with thee, in't it?'

The effect of the simple observation surprised Livvy; the words acted like a pin popping a balloon – her face crumpled and she began to weep silently.

Madge, not known for her oversentimentality, didn't panic or cry out. Nor did she move to throw her arms about her granddaughter. Instead, she put one hand on an ample hip and sighed understandingly. 'I thought so. Well, that's life for you; a swine it is at times, lass.'

'Aye.'

'You'd have come to me if you wanted to get whatever it is off your chest. But you've not, so you don't.'

'No.'

'And that's your God-given right,' she stated simply, but with benevolence. 'I'll not force your hand, nay. Just know my ears are open day or night if you change your mind. All right?'

'Aye. Thanks, Grandma.'

'Well, I'd best get on with the shopping. Celia's shoulder-deep in suds doing the weekly wash, so I must bring home the bacon, so to speak – ha!' She laughed at her own joke and flapped the ration books she carried in the direction of the butcher's. 'Gordon Wallace shall be all sold out of meat if I don't get my skates on. You still on for the pictures later?' she added.

The cinema outing with Clifford and entourage – of course, she'd almost forgotten. She answered in the positive.

'Good. Right, well, I'll see you later then.'

'Ta-ra for now, Grandma.'

Madge rubbed Livvy's cheek in a brusque caress, nodded and waddled on her way.

Alone again, Livvy sniffed decisively and wiped her eyes. Shape up, she told herself. Tears won't bring you nowt but a snotty nose and ugly blotched eyes, so just you give over. Gaining some strength from the self-affirmative talk, she pushed herself off and made with renewed purpose for home.

'Eeh, he were a handsome bugger, that fella in the film,' Madge stated. Having made the small party wait when they exited the cinema, needing to catch her puff before tackling the six steps leading to the street, she was regaling them with her opinion on the screening. 'That lass, mind, what played along-side him, all skin and bone, she were – aye, a reet good meal she's short of. By, but I do love the Odeon, don't you?'

Celia had a ready nod. 'I were here the very first day, in 1937.'

'And me, love! Eeh, fancy that, and we never knew each other then.' The friends had met a short time afterwards upon becoming neighbours on the com-pletion of their housing estate being built. Smiling, Madge stared ahead in happy remembrance. 'I came with my daughter and son-in-law – Livvy's parents. It was shortly before . . . God rest their souls.'

Clifford shot Livvy a look of sympathy, but she gave him a smile that said it was fine – Madge found com-fort in talking about them, and she liked to listen. It made her feel closer to them, helped keep their memory alive, and for this she was thankful.

'Aye, special, it were, the opening night here. When the First Battalion of the Royal Scots struck up the music it sent shivers down my spine. Gaumont British Sound News, a cartoon and the feature film.'

'*Dark Journey* starring Vivien Leigh.'

'Aye and Conrad Veidt.' Madge threw Celia a wink. 'He were handsome, an' all, weren't he?'

'Oh ay, aye. He died, you know, a few months back.'

'He never did! How d'you know that?'

'I read it in t' paper – heart attack, playing golf.'

'Bloody hell fire. Eeh, what a shame.'

'Aye, he were bonny—'

'Right, you two, when you've finished your drooling,' Clifford cut in, chuckling. 'Shall we make a move?'

Innocent the statement might have been, but Livvy felt her jaw tighten in apprehension all the same. Her old stomping ground was far too close for comfort for her liking.

She'd attempted suggesting they visit another picture house further away, however her grandmother wouldn't hear of it: the Odeon it had to be. The massive building on its corner site, with its stepped ceiling and fluted walls, did boast a lovely setting; still, Livvy would have much preferred another venue. All she could do now was pray that the women, who were partial to a tipple, didn't demand they round off the evening with a trip to the pub.

Suppose they opted for somewhere Livvy was well known, such as the Fleece Hotel? The notion didn't bear thinking about. Mind you, she consoled herself, it was unlikely. It was a good five minutes' walk from where they stood on Ashburner Street – surely that was enough to put Madge off. And Clifford would, she was certain, prove an ally if needed – he was a staunch teetotaller.

'Eeh, place don't feel the same, though, you know, with this blackout,' Madge went on, regardless of Clifford's prompting, and made no attempt to move. 'How nice was it at night, lit up all bright, Celia?'

'Aye.' The woman trained her gaze along the cream exterior and the black and green tiles – up, up, to the Odeon lettering, which before the war dazzled in neon light. 'A shame.'

'Remember when them bombs fell, beginning of '41?' Madge paused for dramatic effect, then whispered: 'I were here.'

'No!' Her friend was well aware of it, but nonetheless she leaned in intently and awaited the telling to come, as was expected of her.

'I was, Celia, no word of a lie. Weren't I, Livvy?' Madge demanded, and at her granddaughter's nod, 'Me and Morris, aye.'

'Eeh, Madge, love . . .' Celia was agog.

'Ruddy frightening, it were. Livvy here had offered to sit in with our Joan, so we thought sod it, let's have an evening out. Aye, and some evening it turned out to be!'

'What occurred, love?'

'Well, bombs fell.'

'No, I mean what was it like? Were any of youse hurt?'

99

'Oh. No, glory be. We were sat there, sound as you like, minding our own, and a message flashed on t' screen to say an air raid was occurring and where to find the nearest shelter. Well, you know how it was back then: not many let it bother them, did they, and would stay on to watch the film? And that's what we did. A few left, but we never. We've paid, we thought, and we're going nowhere, we'll get our money's worth! Anyroad, next news, the manager appeared on t' platform to tell us all they'd had a yellow warning.'

'Oh 'eck.'

'Then it turned into a red warning.'

'Oh dear!'

'Aye. We were told to stay where we were, and we all just stood there in silence, looking up – we could hear them, you see, the bombs coming. Stood there like one of Lewis's dummies, aye, frozen in fear. And next thing you know, there came these almighty great bangs. In all honesty, we felt them walls move then shift back again – the vibrations, you know? Our heads and shoulders were covered in fallen plaster.'

'What did you do, Madge, scarper?'

'Huh! Not us. We stopped on and enjoyed the rest of the film.'

'Eeh!'

'The bombs, they landed either side of the cinema. Either side – how lucky was that? The bonded warehouse behind went up – whoosh! Mind, I think there was alcohol stored in there, spirits and the like – it caused a dreadful fire.'

'What a waste of good ale.'

'Aye. And life, Celia, don't forget: one poor fella perished in that attack. I'll tell you summat, though, just imagine how much worse it could have been. There was a full house here that night: nearly two thousand souls. A couple of yards the wrong way and it would have come right through this roof. The lot of us could have been wiped out in the blink of an eye.'

'Weren't your time to go, love. The Lord's gorra plan for you yet.'

'That's right, that's what I said. Morris though, he reckoned we were just bloody jammy.'

'Aye well, you're all right now, eh, Madge?' Clifford got in before she and his aunt had a chance to go off on another tangent. Smiling, he edged towards the steps. 'Shall we go?'

They were halfway down the road when Madge suddenly halted. Assuming she was breathless again, Livvy didn't give it a second thought, however she was wrong.

'I fancy a sup.'

'Wet the whistle, aye,' Celia agreed, licking her lips.

The women glanced about, and Clifford gave a

roll of his eyes. For her part, Livvy had gone cold with dread. Think. *Think.*

'The Founders Arms on St George's Street – you know, opposite the old town hall?' Celia announced. 'Eeh, I've fond memories of that pub, used to love going in there—'

'No!' Livvy blurted. That would take them right through the heart of Bradshawgate and her patch – they couldn't. *What if, by some chance, they ran into Carl Rivera?* She covered her urgency with a laugh. 'What I mean is, I've not got the energy for trekking over there – oh!' *Thank you,* she said inwardly as an idea sprang to mind. 'You know we've drink left over from Grandad's birthday! How's about we head back to Breightmet and enjoy a tipple in comfort at home? I'll get the chip pan on?' she coaxed when it looked as though Madge wasn't to be persuaded.

To her relief, her last suggestion did the trick – her grandmother nodded. 'Sounds good to me, lass. Come on, Celia.'

Livvy was clearing away the plates and glasses and inwardly congratulating herself still on her quick thinking when Clifford rose to help her. She gave him a smile and, leaving the older women nattering with Morris and Joan, led the way into the kitchen.

'Just put them on the draining board, please, lad; I'll wash them up later. It's been a good day, ain't it?'

102

she continued after depositing her own load. Leaning her hip against the stove, she folded her arms. 'Ta for inviting me along. I enjoyed it.'

'Aye?'

'Aye.'

'Me too, Livvy.'

He was looking at her intently, as though he desperately wanted to say more but hadn't the nerve to – she recognised the demeanour only too well. Nodding back towards the living room, she made to join the others before he had a chance to switch the conversation to something more intimate. However, he stopped her:

'Wait, please. There's summat I wanted to say.'

Her response was guarded. 'Go on.'

'I've been wanting an opportunity to speak to you alone all night.'

'Oh?'

'That's why I were trying my best to hurry the owd girls along earlier after the film. By, your grandma can't half gab when she gets going.'

Livvy couldn't help but grin. 'You're not wrong!'

'I thought when we got back and the two of them had gone on home, I could speak to you privately, like. Only you invited everyone back here, and . . .' He stopped to stare at the ground. 'Did you sense it, Livvy, what I had in mind and that's why you asked them? Only I can't help suspecting you're never really happy being on your own with me.'

A rush of sadness tinged with guilt swept through her at his hound-dog expression – she touched his arm. 'No, Clifford, you're wrong. I had no clue. I didn't want to go to a pub because I really didn't feel like it. Really,' she went on when he brought his eyes back to hers. 'And I do like spending time with you, course I do, only . . . I don't know. I just don't like to give you false hope,' she finished softly but honestly. 'You like me and—'

'And you don't like me?'

She did. *I do. But lad, it can never be . . .* 'I can't be who you want me to be,' she said at length. It seemed the most truthful way in which to reply.

'But I wouldn't want you any other way. I want you for you.'

'Eeh, lad . . .'

He stepped closer and ever so tenderly took her hand. 'I'm very fond of you, lass.'

'And I of you,' she admitted, closing her eyes and sending the tears that had welled up within them bowling down her cheeks. 'But you deserve better, Clifford. I, I just can't . . .'

'Livvy, please—'

However, she'd already skirted past him and escaped into the next room.

He left very soon afterwards on the excuse that he

had a headache and needed an early night; Livvy sat on for the next half an hour with the rest of the company, her throat tight with suppressed emotions and her heart in ribbons.

When at last she deemed it acceptable to make her own exit, she had to force herself not to dash from the room.

Upstairs, she closed the bedroom door behind her and lay fully clothed on top of the bed. A voice in her head told her she was a fool. Clifford was fine and decent; never would he harm her, hurt her, as others would – and had done. He was a good man – and therein, she knew, lay the problem: he was *too* good. Too good for the likes of her.

She'd already given herself heart, body and soul once . . . it felt like a lifetime ago now. And look where that had got her. Alone, half mad with grief and shattered forever beyond repair.

Lord, please don't let me dream of Red Lane. Don't let me dream of him . . .

No. She and Clifford could never be.

She wouldn't allow such a mistake again.

Chapter Five

THE SUN WAS basking high above the rooftops. The sky sparkled azure, and birds sang their hearts out and hopped in high jinks in their gladness to be alive about the chimney pots. Watching absently from the chair she'd carried out to the garden and placed beneath the front window, Livvy bit her lip in indecision. It was Saturday, and for the past hour she'd been contemplating whether to go and visit Vera later.

Not having been one for sitting in at home, now, for as long as she could recall, the inactivity was slowly beginning to get her down and was driving her to distraction.

A lone wasp hovered close to her face and she swatted at it irritably. Why the hell shouldn't she go to see her friend, anyway? She should become a recluse, was that it? Never put her foot over the step ever again, and all because of the American and his disgusting actions? He'd dictate from afar her every waking moment, choose when and if she could come and go? She'd allow him power over her for evermore, call all her decisions, have her leading a near-non-existent life?

She must have employment besides anything else. She'd been squirrelling away money for a while and had a fair few pounds put by, but that wouldn't last. She needed to earn a regular wage; her family depended on it.

Again, the wasp made a nosedive in her direction and she rose with a growl and snatched up the chair. After placing it back beneath the table indoors with the others, she stood for a moment in the centre of the floor, eyes thoughtful. Then straightening her shoulders, her mind made up, she strode from the room and up the stairs.

Her clothes, hanging neatly in the wardrobe, spurred her decision on further – running her fingers along the familiar garments, she gave a wistful smile. Most women would kill for even one of the items here in these times of austerity, she knew, when the maxim 'Make Do and Mend' had become the grinding norm, and plenty, struggling by on their meagre coupons, couldn't remember the last time they had owned anything patch and darn free, new.

When clothing rationing came into force in Britain at the beginning of June 1941, civilian wear had had to take a back seat so that textile manufacturers could focus their attention on military equipment and uniforms. This led to inflation and shortages, and the rationing of clothing was a means of distributing limited supplies fairly. By the end of the year, the Board of Trade, in an effort to resolve the shortfall, introduced the CC41 Utility Clothing Scheme. It would shortly afterwards be adopted on other staples, such as bedding and furniture.

Restrictions meant that more than ever before, clothing had to be durable. CC41 mass-produced items – CC stood for civilian clothing or controlled commodity, although it was commonly referred to as the two cheeses, due to its quirky logo – were of much simpler design and offered good quality and affordability.

The bulk of Livvy's collection was indeed of the utility variety, however this didn't matter; they were, it was true, of sound standard. Besides, it was the quantity which mattered. Vera's black-market contacts really could get their hands on anything – so long as the price was right, of course.

Her half a dozen pairs of shoes standing on the wardrobe floor beneath, and the pretty handbags in an assortment of shades to match her outfits, produced another smile. The suede block heels, which she'd almost ruined fighting off the gravy-loving dog, had a wry laugh bubbling up in her throat. By no means amusing at the time, but she could see the funny side now, the scoundrel.

She opted for one of her favourite dresses: a crêpe de Chine number that reached just below the knee in a rich, swirling pallet of deep mauve, fuchsia and turquoise, and pulled it out. A pair of white, strappy heeled sandals came next, followed by a bouquet brooch to finish off the look, and Livvy carried everything to the bed.

She was dressed to perfection and her hair and make-up immaculate when she entered the living room again some half an hour later. Joan, reading a magazine with Doris by the fire, nudged her friend at her sister's entrance; they smiled in appreciation.

'Will I do?' Livvy asked.

'Eeh, our Livvy, you look smashing.'

'Like a film star,' Doris adjoined.

'Huh. If you ask me, she's inviting trouble, parading about looking like that,' Morris added from the sofa.

Livvy ignored him. Funnily enough, his quips, harmlessly intended as they were, didn't quite hit the same now. 'Ah, ta very much, girls.' A last look at the clock and pat of her curls and she was ready. 'You'll be all right, lass, aye?'

Joan nodded. 'See you later.'

'Ta-ra for now.'

Despite her farewell, Livvy found she couldn't leave right away. Her heart had suddenly begun to pound and her legs felt oddly wobbly; she halted in the seclusion of the hall to take calming breaths. Truth was, in spite of her front, she was nervous as hell.

Just what would she do if she encountered the Yank? More to the point, what would *he* do?

That he'd returned to Vera's wanting to 'see her' had really shaken her up. She wanted him nowhere near her ever again; Lord, she didn't even want to hear his name mentioned, never mind clap eyes on him. Was she really doing the right thing here . . .?

'You're going.' She mouthed the words to herself with a trembling urgency that quickly grew into firm resolve. 'Move yourself. Go – go!'

Nose up, chin out, she reached for the latch and opened the door. Seconds later, she was passing with purpose through the square.

Vera's surprised delight was tangible when she answered Livvy's knock. A low whistle escaped her; she clapped her hands slowly several times: 'Look at *you*. Come in.'

'I'm not going back to it,' Livvy was quick to make clear when they reached the woman's rooms. 'As I said, I'm done with that now. No, it's bar work I'm aiming for. I intend putting some feelers out this evening, asking about.'

'As you like. I'm just glad to see you.'

Livvy nodded, smiled, then when it became evident Vera wasn't going to bring the subject up herself, she asked, 'Has he . . .?'

'I've seen nowt of him, no,' her friend revealed, much to Livvy's relief.

'Thank God for that. Happen he's grown bored, now, and will leave me alone?'

The look Vera gave her in answer to this provided Livvy with little reassurance.

'Anyroad, let him try his damned worst. He's not dictating my life for evermore, no ruddy way. I'm hiding away at home no longer. It's time to begin living again.'

'That's the spirit – good on you, girl!'

'Ta, Vera.'

'But Livvy?'

'Aye?'

'Just you be careful, eh?'

The drumming in her breast started up once more. She swallowed. 'Will you come with me, love, to look for work? Please?' she pressed when the woman hesitated. 'I know it's selfish of me to ask when you've your own brass to be making, but . . . just forra few hours?'

'I do wish you'd shop that bugger in. Your problems would be solved; there'd be no looking over your shoulder, then, would there? Course I'll come with you,' she went on when Livvy dropped her gaze. 'But love, we ain't joined at the hip; I can't be with you all the time. What if you do get taken on someplace? I can't be your chaperone at work, can I?'

111

'I know. Don't worry, I'll . . .' She shrugged, hadn't the solution right now. 'I'll cross that bridge when I come to it,' she said at last. 'One thing at a time.'

They headed, once Vera was finished getting ready, not in their usual direction but towards the opposite side of town, where they were less known. This, Livvy felt, was a fresh start. Best to begin the quest on an even footing. However, they yielded little result. At each pub they tried, either they were not in need of new staff or the proprietors were brusque and gave the women short shrift; their reputation preceded them, Livvy suspected, and landlords wanted no whore – former or not – on their workforce.

'What about Gwen?' Vera almost pleaded with her friend eventually, leaning against the wall of Woolworths and easing off a shoe to rub her aching foot. 'I've a ruddy blister forming here . . . Well, Livvy? She knows you and is a gradely sort – happen you'll have more luck.'

'But the Fleece, though, Vera?' Livvy was far from enthusiastic at the prospect. 'It's bursting at the seams with GIs at the weekends. What if . . . *you* know.'

'So what if Carl Rivera does stop in and sees you toiling there – sod the swine!' her friend snapped. She rammed her shoe back on and folded her arms. 'You can't run from this forever. If you'll not consider reporting him and getting him locked away, then you'll likely have to face him sometime. This war ain't going away anytime soon, Livvy, and that means neither are the Americans. So, are we going or what? It's either ask Gwen or go skint, so far as I can see, for folk ain't exactly falling over theirselfs to employ you, are they? Or . . .'

'Or what?'

'*Or* you could always come along to the Palais with me. Stick to what you know, what you're good at? Choice is yours, but for Christ's sake will you make your mind up about it quick. I'm half crippled here, with all the walking – my hooves ain't half sore.'

Livvy didn't take long to decide. What was there to dither on, after all? She couldn't go back to prostitution, which left only one option open to her: 'Lead the way to Bradshawgate,' she said on a sigh.

The Fleece's regular patrons greeted them with their usual enthusiasm and Livvy warmed somewhat at the sight of the friendly faces. However, there was one in particular she kept her eyes peeled for and wished to God she wouldn't see – the Yank's. To her great relief, she realised, having scoured the area several times, there seemed to be no sign of him. Letting her shoulders relax, she went to join Vera at the counter.

'All right?'

Sweeping the space a final time, just to be absolutely certain, and spotting nothing of the man, Livvy finally nodded to Vera.

'Good. Now then, where's she . . . Ah, there she is,' she added, motioning to the far end of the bar. 'Gwen, love?' she bawled over the hubbub. 'My mate here would like a word when you've a minute.'

Watching the barmaid's approach, Livvy had butterflies – though she couldn't rightly define exactly what she was most nervous about: not securing a position and being out of regular employ for the foreseeable, or getting taken on and inevitably having to face her attacker. She was stuck between a rock and a hard place, she realised. Both prospects were far from pleasant ones.

'What can I do you for, love?' Gwen asked, having reached them, her mouth as ever holding a ready smile.

Livvy explained that she'd decided on a change of career and queried whether there might be any shifts for her here. Crossing her fingers behind her back, she held her breath.

'I reckon there might be a few hours' work going begging at the weekends,' Gwen said, scratching her chin. 'As you can see, we get awfully busy then. As for full-time, though, Livvy . . .' She shook her head. 'No, love, sorry.'

'It's all right, Gwen.' Two days of wages out of the week just weren't sufficient to survive. 'Ta all the same.'

'How d'you feel about chip fat?' Gwen asked suddenly.

Sharing a look with Vera, Livvy frowned. 'I don't understand . . .'

'What I mean is, are you fussy about stinking of the stuff?'

'Well, I wouldn't choose to, obviously – who would!'

The barmaid grinned. 'Someone in need of a job.'

'Oh. You know of one going, then?'

'My sister,' she explained, 'she runs that little chippy across the way. Her daughter, our Jean, she's ready for dropping her second kiddy and shall have to give up working any day now. Our Bertha will be short-staffed – you could always ask there. There's no harm in trying?'

Gwen was referring to the chip shop she and Vera had visited the previous week with . . . him. And later, what had followed . . . that was the night . . .

'Love?'

Livvy shook herself back to the present. 'Sorry, Gwen. No, I ain't too proud of ponging of oil, am I 'eck. Ta ever so much. I'll ask your Bertha, aye.'

'Well then, that were a bit of luck, weren't it?' Vera said when the barmaid moved off to return to her duties. ''Ere, you'd best slip me a free fish in with my order when I come in!'

'By gum, love, I ain't got the friggin' job yet!'

Laughing, they downed their drinks and ordered another.

It was Livvy's round and as she was sorting through the coins in her purse she noticed Vera tense beside her. And she knew, she just knew . . .

Her hand froze. Turning her head a few inches, she followed the direction of her friend's gaze.

Carl spotted Livvy in the same instant and juddered to a halt in the doorway. Standing stock still, he gazed at her for what felt like an age, and locked in shock she could do nothing but stare back. Then he was on the move. Thrusting his hands in his pockets, his lips peaking in smile, he headed with his easy rolling gait, as though he hadn't a care in the world, in their direction.

'I won't . . . I *can't* . . .' Livvy's words came in short, sharp gasps. 'Make him go away, Vera, please – make him go away!'

'You've got some bleedin' brass neck—'

He cut Vera off with a click of his fingers. 'Look, honey, I don't want any trouble. I just want to talk to Livvy here.'

'Not on your friggin' nelly!' Vera's eyes bulged. 'By, I've a good mind to—'

'Tsk, tsk.' Having caught her wrist as she made to strike out at him, he shook his head. 'Calm down, little firecracker.' Without looking at Livvy, he added, 'Baby, can we talk?'

'She's not your baby! She's nowt to you, d'you hear me?' Vera was yelling now, and one or two customers

116

were glancing across. 'Get the hell from this pub or I swear to you, I'll leap right up on to this counter and tell every last person here just what you did. What you are. Beast,' she hissed into his face. '*Beast!*'

Carl was silent for a moment. He released Vera's arm. Then he swivelled his head and, finally, looked at Livvy. There was nothing behind the eyes, she saw. Not desperation to be heard, and certainly no guilt. Not even anger. Nothing, not a thing. It was like standing before a statue. His gaze was blank, dead, and it chilled her to the marrow. She took a step back.

'Can we talk, Livvy?' he murmured.

She shook her head.

'Can we talk?' he repeated.

'No,' she whispered. Then, gathering every ounce of her strength: 'I want you to leave me alone. Please.'

His eyes bore into her for several moments more. Then without another word he brushed past them and sauntered away.

'Bastard!' Vera was raging. 'Are you all right, love?'

'A drink,' Livvy stuttered, sagging. Her palms were clammy; she thought her legs might give way at any second. 'I need a drink.'

Ten minutes later, after a thorough scour of the vicinity and satisfied that the American had left, Vera returned to Livvy's side and escorted her outside.

'Let's get you home.'

'You don't have to wait with me,' Livvy told her when they reached the bus stop, though praying secretly she would. 'You go on, enjoy the rest of your night.'

'And take the risk of that mad sod accosting you? He could be lurking around the next corner, for all we know—'

'Eeh, don't say that! You don't reckon he is, do you?' she asked, flicking her fearful gaze around.

'I ain't taking the chance. No ruddy way!'

'What am I going to do, Vera?' Tears were building; she blinked them back furiously. 'Why can't he leave me be?'

'I don't know, love. 'Cause he's not made right in the head.'

'I can't go on like this. Summat has to be done.'

'Aye? What, like, when you'll not get the law involved?'

'Oh, for the love of . . . they won't care, Vera! How many times do I have to say it?'

'What then? What else is there?'

Sucking in a ragged breath, Livvy closed her eyes. 'I'll speak with him.'

'Who?'

'*Him.*'

'What!'

'I'll speak with him,' she repeated, though it made her physically ill to utter it. 'I'll do as he wants. Then, hopefully, he'll go away and let me alone.'

118

'And if he don't? What then?'

Livvy let her shoulders rise and fall in a helpless motion. He *had* to.

'You'll be for getting the shove from that job of yourn, you will, if you're not careful.'

It was the following day and Livvy was serving the breakfast. Her grandmother was here to join them in the meal, as she was wont to some mornings, and the foursome were seated together around the table.

'Arrived home last evening, she did, after being gone only a handful of hours,' Morris went on to Madge.

'Oh aye?'

'I told you, Grandad, I weren't feeling too clever, had a dicky stomach, and they let me home,' Livvy said patiently.

'You'd only just had a week off. A full ruddy week – and at the employer's insistence! I've never heard the like in all my born days.'

To explain away her absence from work following the attack, Livvy had told her family that her boss said she worked too hard and deserved a break. Though their reactions had varied in levels of incredulousness, they hadn't been in the least suspicious; had believed her without question, bless them. 'Aye, well, they're a kindly sort.'

'Kindly? Bloody saintly if you ask me! By, I could

have been at death's door when I toiled as a labourer and my gaffer would still have expected me in. "What's that, Tattersall, you've come down with the bubonic and can't stand? No fear, we'll prop you up!"' he mimicked, making them laugh.

'I might have a new position lined up, anyroad,' Livvy revealed with some caution. The last thing she wanted to do was slip up somewhere in the telling. 'The pub game, it don't much appeal to me as it once did,' she told them as she poured out the tea. 'The noise and rowdy customers . . . it gets tiresome after a while, you know? And so I thought I'd try my hand at summat else. I've heard there'll be a place going soon at a chippy and thought I might give it a try.' Murmurs of interest rippled around the table – taking advantage of their enthusiasm, she went on, 'Eeh, you never know, I might be allowed to fetch home the unsold grub at the end of the night.'

'Well, I for one hope you're successful, lass!' Madge announced. Her eyes had lit up at the mention of free chips on tap. 'When will you find out?'

'I thought I'd go and see Bertha – she's the one what runs the place – this afternoon. Strike whilst the iron's hot, eh? I don't want to give her the chance of finding someone else.'

True to her word, a few hours later Livvy was making her way into town.

At least this time there was no question of bumping into the Yank, who would be well away from Bolton and back at base in Warrington, the weekend over with, glory be. Then, just as quickly as thoughts of him entered her head she banished them again. He would take up no room in her mind; she wouldn't allow it. Today was about securing herself a job and nothing more.

It being Sunday, the chippy was closed for trading, but she took a punt on the owner living on the premises and made her way to the door at the back of the building. Upon reaching it, she paused to straighten her sensible brown skirt and cardigan and make sure her brogues weren't soiled. First impressions were everything, after all, and she didn't want to appear slovenly. Then, satisfied, she took a deep breath, nodded and knocked.

'Hello? Who's there?' came a voice through the wood.

'Er, hello . . . Am I talking to Bertha?'

'That you are. And who might you be?'

'My name's Livvy – Olive, Olive Bryant – and I wondered if I might speak to you. Gwen sent me,' she added.

As she'd hoped it would, this last impartation went in her favour – the opening of the door sounded almost immediately.

'Afternoon,' Livvy said, smiling, when a woman in

her middle years appeared. 'By, you're the bloody double of your sister! Sorry,' she went on quickly, hadn't meant to blurt the observation out and swear in the process; it had merely taken her aback. 'I hope you don't mind me saying so . . .'

'Course not.' Bertha chuckled. 'Don't worry, we get it all the time, and I'd have been surprised if you hadn't mentioned it. I should think we do look alike: Gwen and me are twins.'

'Oh right! Well, the resemblance is uncanny.'

'So what can I do you for, lass?'

Livvy explained her situation and the information given to her by Gwen, continuing with, 'I hope you don't think me brazen turning up here like this and disturbing your Sunday, only I really need a job, missis, and didn't want to let the opportunity slip through my fingers. I'm a hard worker,' she finished. 'And I'm not proud, neither; really, I'll do owt.'

Bertha eyed her keenly. 'Are you married, kiddies?'

The unexpected questioning caught her off guard. A clear-cut vision of Red Lane, of a little house with a blue door, smashed into her mind – sucking in air, she stumbled a little.

'Are you all right, lass?'

'Aye. Sorry, I . . .' Tears were forming. She shook herself and swallowed hard. 'No,' she said at last. 'No, I'm not married.' Another gulp: 'No children.'

'I only ask so I know what your availability is, you understand . . . Are you sure you're all right?' Bertha pressed, stepping forward to touch Livvy's shoulder. 'Your colour's gone as grey as the grave.'

'Could I possibly sit . . . sit down, I . . .'

''Ere, come on, lass, come inside.'

Bertha shepherded her up a short flight of stairs to her private living room and guided her to a chair. The world hazy and her vision swimming, Livvy took in next to nothing of her surroundings and allowed herself to be led, as docile as a toddler.

After several minutes of sitting hunched with her head between her knees, the nausea began to subside. She accepted a cup of tea from the woman gratefully and with trembling hands took tiny sips.

'I'm so sorry, Mrs . . .'

'Call me Bertha, lass. And there's no need for apologies. How you fettling?'

'I'm all right, now, ta.' Oh, but she was embarrassed. 'I don't know what came over me.' A lie if ever there was one – she knew exactly what had caused her to become overcome as she had. 'I, I think I'd better just leave, forget all about the job, and—'

'Hang about, hang about. There's no need for all that.' Bertha eased her back into the seat. 'Now then. What's this really all in aid of? Come on, lass, you can tell me.'

123

Livvy's voice was barely above a whisper. 'Red Lane, that house we spent such a short time in, him . . . They haunt me, Bertha. I *was* married,' she added on a broken cry.

'You're a widow.'

She nodded. 'Me and Clive, we met during Whit Week, on the walks. We'd not known each other long when he proposed, but we knew it was love, you know? I didn't even have to think about the answer. It could only ever have been yes.'

'He perished in the war, did he, lass?'

'He was along with the first to be called up at the declaration: he'd been a regular soldier in the territorials for years, you see. He was killed right at the very start of things. Not that I'd believe it at first. I was convinced he'd return and spent every minute glued to the wireless or reading the papers, desperate forra miracle and a mention of him. Then, when that never bore fruit, I took to visiting the cinemas, would scour the news reels before the main feature, hoping to pick out his face amongst the many soldiers on the screen. Course, I never did.' Lifting her gaze swimming with tears, she smiled sorrowfully. 'We'd only been wed a fortnight. Just fourteen short days, Bertha, and Clive was snatched from me. How can that be right? Why's this world so friggin' *cruel*.'

'Eeh, lass.'

The words tumbled on as though her tongue had

taken on a life of its own. 'He'd tell me over and over, when I were worried, like, about him being injured or worse, that nothing could happen to him. Completely convinced of it, he were. You see, his parents hailed from a small village in Lancaster called Nether Kellet, and not a single soldier from this village was killed during the Great War. Well, Clive was convinced that this second war would prove likewise. He reckoned that Nether Kellet men were blessed somehow and that God would protect the next generation too – his generation – as He had done the last one.

'I pointed out to him once that he might be wrong, that he'd been born not there but here in Bolton, but he just laughed. He said he carried in his blood Nether Kellet luck passed on to him from his mam and dad, that nothing could touch him.' She laughed softly. 'Bloody fool. He were proved wrong on that, all right.'

Shaking her head, Bertha reached across to refill Livvy's cup. 'What a rotten shame.'

'Aye well, it's life, in't it? Bad things occur and we have to accept it. Mind, I weren't so logical about the situation to begin with. I couldn't function after getting that telegram, just totally fell to pieces.' Pulling back the cuffs of her sleeves to reveal the faded white scars scoring her wrists, she nodded to the woman. 'Aye – went clean off my rocker, I did.

'I reckon I must get that from my owd fella. He

went doolally as well, when Mam went. The cancer took her, and the drink took him not long after. He'd turned to it, the ale, to block out his pain. Unlike him, though, I weren't successful in my attempt at escaping this life. I couldn't believe it when I came to in that hospital bed, I was so angry . . . It was in there that the nurses discovered I were expecting.'

'Oh. Ay, you poor young thing. But, you said you had no children . . .'

'That's right, I don't. I lost it. Ruptured summat inside, as well, in the process, and can't ever have no more. At least I didn't have to worry about getting into trouble in my last job, eh? Aye, being barren is a big advantage for a whore.'

'Liv—'

'That's right, Bertha, I was a prostitute until a week back. It's just summat I sort of . . . slipped into, you know? Oh, it weren't about the money; no, not at first. I were lonely, just so lonely. I met a bloke in a pub – out drowning my sorrows, I was. Well, I finished up back at his house and one thing led to the next. It felt good, aye, being held again, caressed, feeling a fella's skin against my own. Next morning as I were leaving, he took my hand. I thought he was going to kiss it, ask to see me again, but no: he pressed five bob into it instead and sent me on my way. And I did, I just went and took the brass with me, didn't say owt. It was the shock I think, I don't know.'

'Livvy—'

'Anyroad, not long after, I met Vera, a lass in t' same trade. And well, I just carried on. Teamed up together, we did. I enjoy it, Bertha, the sex, I do. I think women are meant to feel ashamed to say that, I don't know why, but I ain't. I like it. How it feels, the closeness . . . And aye, the money did help. Then this GI, Carl Rivera his name is, he forced himself on me, and now it's all been changed. I'm done with it, can't go back to it, no. Don't fret none, I'll not expect you to want to take me on now, knowing this – why would you?'

'Lass, give your gob a rest forra second, eh, and let me speak?'

The woman had spoken not unkindly; Livvy blinked then nodded.

'I don't care a fig what's gone before, what you've done or ain't, all right?' she said, and proving she had so much more in common with Gwen than mere appearance. 'All's I'm interested in knowing is whether you're handy with a knife.'

'Knife?'

'That's right – you're capable of peeling and chipping potatoes, aye?'

'I . . . Aye. *Aye*. Eeh, Bertha. You mean . . .'

'Position's yours, lass, if you want it.'

'Even after all I've just told you? Everything you now know, what I revealed?'

127

'Like I said, I ain't mithered about your past. That's private to you alone and no one else. So. Can you start tomorrow?'

Livvy came away from the chippy soon afterwards in a daze.

What, in the name of God, had possessed her to behave as she had? Her cheeks burned in remembrance of it.

Spilling her guts like that to a complete stranger? She wouldn't have been surprised if Bertha had got her certified – thrown her out on her ear at the very least. But no, that golden-hearted woman had done neither. She'd instead offered her the job! Still Livvy could scarcely comprehend it.

Revealing her innermost darkest and deeply intimate secrets was something she hadn't anticipated she'd ever be able to do. Even Vera, her best friend, wasn't aware of any of it. Naturally, her family knew, but none ever brought the subject up, not these days. Best lay what had passed to bed, and leave it to rest there, was how they saw it.

She'd been filled to capacity, she realised. On the cusp of overflowing with grief and heartache for so long, it had at last tipped over the edges and encapsulated her whole. She'd desperately needed the release as it was – Carl's actions were the catalyst. The unburdening, she was slowly coming to understand, had probably saved her. She'd have surely suffocated at some point soon, otherwise, beneath the weight of her feelings. Maybe, just maybe, she'd garnered more from this afternoon than just gainful employment.

A lightness she scarcely recognised, it had been so long in the knowing, settled inside her chest, and Livvy smiled. Picking up the pace, she walked on for home.

Chapter Six

THOUGH RATIONING WASN'T implemented at eateries such as restaurants, cafés and chip shops, some foodstuffs could find themselves in short supply, much to customers' disgruntlement. Bertha was a master at smoothing troubled waters on occasions when fresh fish was running low and she was forced to limit customers to one per order, to help make things stretch. She'd explain calmly but firmly the situation and her soothing personality would soon do the trick. Not once did Livvy see a customer of Bertha's leave her shop without a smile.

As for Livvy herself, she absolutely loved her new position. True, it wasn't glamorous by any means. The uniform of a long white coat had replaced her beautiful dresses, a hairnet and snowy cap her carefully styled dos, and the money was nowhere near what she was earning before. Nonetheless, she got from this job a sense of quiet pride and achievement the like of which she hadn't with the last one. She felt . . . normal. Aye, that was the word. What's more, it felt good, *right*. There was no question about it that she'd made the correct decision.

Over a cup of tea and a custard cream on their midday breaks, Bertha had regaled Livvy with tales of the business and more colourful characters over the years, and would oftentimes have her in stitches. The woman told how, during the earlier years of the war when air-raid warnings over the town were far more frequent, she and her customers would troop down to the cellar beneath the shop when the sirens sounded. Bertha would take along with her all of the cooked food and they would all have a feast whilst they waited for the all-clear. It helped to lighten the mood and alleviate fear.

Bertha also revealed how, if a customer was short of money, she let them exchange whatever ration coupons they could spare for a fish supper, and advised Livvy to do likewise. Times were hard and fretting about how to feed the family was an extra burden her friends, as Bertha referred to the customers, could well do without. Not that the selfless Bertha benefited from those she acquired through these means; she instead passed them on to her daughter, Jean – the sweet coupons in particular were most welcomed by her young grandson.

Livvy thought her new employer a thoroughly wonderful person. How fortunate she'd been to bag herself not only a great little job that she enjoyed but a kind and generous boss into the bargain. She truly had struck gold.

As the weekend rolled around, and with it the prospect of the GIs swarming into the town, Livvy found that she wasn't nearly half as nervous as she'd feared she would be.

Carl might very well come back to the chippy, it was true. It was also correct that if she wasn't busy out back preparing potatoes and was instead on the shop floor serving, he'd spot her immediately and know where she worked, where to find her whenever he chose to. He'd no doubt pester her to speak with him again; this, she was certain, was a definite. And yet she really wasn't in dread of it now. The real fear had gone, leaving only a focused readiness.

She'd face him, and she'd do so with her head held high. No cowering and pleading with him to leave her alone, no panic. She was in control of her life again, of this, and she would decide how to resolve it. Since baring her heart to Bertha, Livvy had never felt so clear of mind. It seemed she'd returned to herself, was back to who she'd once been at long last. Not for anything would she become lost, forget who she really was, ever again.

'Two penn'orth of fish and one of chips, please, lass.'

The door had just moments before been unlocked

– Bertha's was a popular destination. Smiling at the first Saturday customer of the evening, Livvy crossed to the fryer to fulfil the request.

'And the same for me, love,' another voice rang out.

'Be with you in a sec,' Livvy called over the shoulder. 'Oh!' she added in the next breath, and a wide smile stretched her mouth. 'Hello, Vera!'

Grinning, the woman crossed to the counter and leaned her elbows on the top. 'You got the job, then?'

'I did. Eeh, love, it's gradely. Sorry, hang on.' She hurried to finish off the customer's order, sent her on her way with a cheery wave, and returned to face Vera. 'Aye, it's a reet nice place this. And Bertha's an angel.'

'That warms my heart summat lovely to hear, girl. By, but you do seem different,' the woman added after some moments, studying Livvy in mild wonder. 'I can't explain it . . . you've a light about you. You're brighter.'

Livvy's smile widened. 'And I feel it, too. D'you know, I've not been this happy in many a long year.'

'Good, love. That's good.'

'Vera?' A sudden cloud had passed over her friend's countenance. 'What is it?'

'Livvy . . .'

'Carl.' She nodded. 'I'm right, ain't I? You've seen him.'

'Eeh, he's a bastard and nowt else! He's so hard-faced he could knock nails in with it!'

'Tell me.'

Vera thrust out an arm. Jabbing her forefinger at the window, she pointed northward. 'Collared me, he did, not five minutes past. Just appeared out of nowhere like a bleedin' phantom. It took me all of my time to get shot of him; he only let me be because I flagged down two passing soldiers and told them he were bothering me. They hawked the swine off.'

'He wanted to know where I was. To talk. Is that it?'

'Aye.'

'Then tell him.'

'But—'

'Honest, it's fine.' Livvy's tone was measured, resolved. 'The next time you happen across him, tell him where to find me. Direct him here.'

'Love, you're sure . . .'

'I am.'

'But what will you do?'

'Exactly as he wants: speak with him. Happen then it'll all be finished with and he'll leave the pair of us in peace.'

Her friend left shortly afterwards with her brow knitted in concern at Livvy's request and looking far from convinced that it would have the desired result. Livvy straightened her cap, nodded and got back to work.

It was approaching eighty thirty when he arrived.

Bertha was serving at the till, and she shouted through to Livvy, who was busy chipping spuds in the back room: 'Someone's asking to see you, lass!'

She took her time wiping the starch from her hands on her coarse apron. Then she took a deep breath and made her way to the front of the shop.

Locking gazes with him, Livvy ignored his smile and stared back calmly. 'Can I take my break now, Bertha?' she asked, her eyes never leaving Carl's face.

'Aye, go on. Try not to be too long, though, if you don't mind; it's growing busier by the minute.'

'This won't take long,' Livvy murmured. However, that's as far as she went; she gave away no further details. Fear of the woman's wrath should she deem that Livvy had brought trouble to her door made her refrain from revealing the identity of her unwelcome visitor. The last thing she wanted to risk was possible dismissal. She flicked her head at the American, indicating that he follow, and led the way outside.

'So.' Clasping her hands together in front of her, she asked, 'What have you got to say?'

'Well, I . . .'

'Spit it out, I ain't got all day.'

Evidently thrown by her cool indifference this time around, he floundered momentarily. Then regaining his wits, he laughed. 'Hey, baby, I've missed you.'

'That's it, is it? That's what you've been wanting to say to me? Right. Fine. I'll be on my way, now—'

'Hold up! *Jeez.*' He ran a hand through his slicked-back hair. 'How are you?'

'How am I?' Her eyebrows rose to meet her hairline. 'How *am* I? I'm bloody marvellous, lad. Grand, aye. Top of the world—'

'I'm getting the distinct feeling that you're mad with me?' he interjected to say, eyes creasing in confusion.

Was this man for real? She gazed back incredulously.

'Baby, what exactly have I done to upset you? You provided a service and I . . . Oh!' He slapped a hand to his forehead. 'Christ, Livvy, I'm sorry. It completely went out of my mind.'

Frowning, she watched as he dug his hand into his trouser pocket. When he extracted it again, clutching a fistful of coins, her stomach turned over – she smacked his arm away with a growl.

'You think that's what the issue is here? That you failed to *pay* me? You raped me, you bastard.'

'Hey, I did not.'

'You did! You did!'

'You did nothing to stop me, honey, so don't try that ol' number on me.'

'I couldn't, I—'

'Look, I liked you, Livvy. Sure, I *still* like you, a

136

helluva lot. You knew it too, didn't you, but you wouldn't let me near, didn't want me as you do all the others. Christ, you even prefer the coloureds to me! Why, huh?' he demanded, leaning in close. 'What's so wrong with Carl Rivera?'

'That's it, ain't it.' In an instant, everything slotted into place. She swung her head slowly from side to side. 'You took me with force because you couldn't get at me any other way. Because I choose – I *chose* – to bed fellas I liked the look of, that I fancied – and you weren't one of them. You wanted what you couldn't have.'

'*I* wanted *you*. From the first moment I set eyes on you I was struck; I think I love you, Livvy—'

'You don't love me!' A harsh bark of laughter leaked from her. 'You don't know the meaning of the damn word! It's the thrill of the chase you're driven by, and when you realised you wouldn't snare me with your oily charm you set a trap, ambushed me like prey instead. It's all just sport to you.'

'It is not—'

'Aye, it is. Carl wants it, so Carl must have it. By, you're nowt but a spoilt bloody boy.'

'I love you. I can't get you out of my mind—'

'Tough.' Her chin coming up, she pushed her face into his. She spoke quietly, concisely. 'I care nought for you. Do you understand that? You're nothing,

nothing, to me. Now do us both a favour. Turn around, walk away, and stay the hell out of my life.'

He blinked, lips parted, eyes wide with shock. Then: 'No.'

'What d'you mean, no – I'm warning you!'

'I can't do it, baby. I need you. What's more, I know for a fact that if you'd only get to know me better, you'll soon love me too. I *will* have you, Livvy.'

'You're barmy,' she whispered. 'Stark, staring mad . . .'

'Mad for you, you're right. Come on, honey, just give me a chance, hm?' His smile had made an appearance now; he winked. 'Let me take you out, show you a good time. I can guarantee,' he went on with heavy patronisation, tapping the tip of her nose with his finger as one would a truculent child refusing to obey, 'that by the end of the night you'll have changed your mind about me. You'll soon come to see it, baby: I'm one helluva catch.'

'I'm going back inside, now.' She spoke unpanicked, though inside she was feeling anything but. The man wasn't a full shilling. Deluded to the point of disturbed, he presented a whole other level of threat to her. She didn't know where on earth she stood now. 'Please just leave me alone.'

'I don't think you quite understand.'

Glancing down at the hand he'd clamped around

her wrist to halt her escape, she did her utmost to remain calm. 'Leave go of me.'

'Haven't you been listening? Christ, I've just poured my heart out to you and what, you just walk away? You unfeeling bitch.'

'Leave go of me,' she repeated, a slight quaver behind the words now, which she couldn't repress. 'Now, Carl.'

He released her, thrusting her away from him with a grunt. 'There. Happy now?'

'Aye. Goodbye.'

'For now, perhaps.' Walking away backwards, he nodded with sheer conviction. 'I'll see you again real soon, baby. *Real* soon.'

Bertha did a double take when Livvy half stumbled back inside the chippy. 'Eeh, what? Are you all right, lass? Has summat occurred?'

'No. Nowt. I'm all right.'

'You're sure? Only you look —'

'I'm fine, Bertha, honest. I'd best get back to work.'

Alone in the back room, Livvy let the act fall away; trembling from head to toe, she leaned against the wall for support and pressed her hot cheek against the cool plaster. Good God. *Good God.*

She'd been so naïve, so stupid, to think she'd get a handle on this. It wasn't going to go away.

This was bad. Really bad.

Just what the hell had she found herself mixed up with? More to the point, where would it end?

'May the Lord strike me down dead, it's no word of a lie. He wore a suit of bees, aye. A *suit* of *bees*!'

Having entered her house, and catching from the living room beyond sound of the conversation mid-flow and her grandfather's excitable voice, Livvy hovered in the hallway, reluctant to enter. Joan was staying over at Doris's house tonight, so they had company, it seemed – this was the last thing she had strength for. After this evening's antics, she desired only to shut herself away in her bedroom and try to somehow make sense of everything Carl had said. And, if possible, try to figure out a solution. *Please, God.*

'Aye, a little lad of six, I were, and on a visit to London with my grandparents. They ran their own boot menders, you know, were quite well-to-do . . . Anyroad, we were strolling along Oxford Circus, as you do, minding our own, when this fella walks past us, calm as you like as though in a daze – frozen in fear, he were. And for good reason. For his back was covered, from collar to waist, in bees. And another ruddy great cloud of the things buzzed over his head.

'As you can imagine, a big crowd had started to follow him to see what would happen, and though I tried to join them my granny was having none of it;

140

slapped my legs for me, she did, and told me I weren't going nowhere near, no bloody how. Well, I watched that bloke the length of the street until he disappeared from sight, bees an' all. Turns out, or so we heard later, that he'd been asked to carry a basket of the things to the railway station and, somehow, the lid came loose. Never did find out what happened to him. For all we know, the poor cock might still be wandering the capital to this day with his merry band of stingers. Who's to say, eh?

'Eeh aye, they're a queer lot them Londoners. Not like us northern folk, eh? Got all our marbles intact, we have! Oh aye, and this other time—'

'I'm home!' Livvy called out at last, more for Morris's listener's sake than anything else. Her grandfather couldn't half gab when he wanted, could talk the hind legs off a donkey. 'All right— Oh. You're here.' She gave Clifford, who had half risen from his seat, his face lighting up, a shy smile. 'Keeping you entertained, is he, Grandad?'

Clifford flashed a crooked smile, nodded. 'You're keeping well, Livvy?'

'Can't complain, ta,' she lied. She could complain, all right, with the terrible mess she was in. Oh, she could. 'And yourself?'

'Fair to middling, you know?'

'Aye, aye.'

Thick silence took hold – she let her gaze stray to

the far wall; anything was better than staring at one another in awkward silence.

'Sit thee down, lass, I'm just in t' middle of telling a story.' Morris's statement was more demand than invitation. If there was one thing he loved above all else it was an audience. 'Well go on, then, shape yourself, afore I lose track of where I'm at!'

Though certain she would have heard the tale at least a half dozen times already, she hid a sigh and did as she was told. Best to let him have his way or she'd never hear the end of it.

'Picture this,' Morris continued, getting back into his stride and crossing his slippered feet. 'Young buck of eighteen, I were, as free and gay as a bird. I'd not yet met my Madge, you see, so hadn't a care in t' world.' He paused to give a gravelly laugh at his own quip. 'Anyroad – it were the second most extraordinary sight my two eyes ever did see. There I was on a nice summer afternoon, strolling through Stainton village on a visit to family, as you do – 'ere, did I ever tell you I hailed from North Yorkshire, lad? Nay? Well, it's true. Get about, I do. Oh aye, been places, I have – and aye, minding my own, when this horse careers past, gone clean out of its mind with the madness. Go on, you have a guess as to why.'

'I don't know . . .'

'Bees, lad! Bleedin' bees again! Three whole waggonloads of hives this time. Can you fathom that?

142

Imagine it! Oh carnage, *carn*age. The first waggon had given a lurch, you see, and overtipped one of the hives. Well! All these bees made a beeline – haw, see what I did there! – for the beast and his driver. Getting stung to buggery, the horse starts rearing and whinnying like a thing possessed and sets off at a gallop, thinking he can outrun them. As if it stood a chance, poor divil. And well, what should occur? The whole ruddy waggon went over, didn't it! Made the situation twelve times worse, the daft animal did, for now a dozen hives were broken and thousands upon thousands more bees were let free.

'Well, I thinks to myself, watching on from a distance, this shan't end well. And guess what, lad. Go on, guess.'

Shaking his head, Clifford shrugged.

'It didn't. End well, that is. By 'ell, no it did not. Driver and his boy what were on-board managed to roll off and get away, but the horse . . .' Morris tut-tutted gravely. 'Kicked and smashed itself free from shafts and waggon it might have done, but them bees weren't done with it yet. Covered the full body of the thing, they did. Stinging, stinging, stinging . . .! In t' end, the horse gave up and dropped down dead. Ay, a crying shame, it were. Oh, and listen to this: this other time—!'

'Brew?' Livvy interrupted, jumping to her feet. *By Christ, they would be here all night if she didn't put an end*

143

to this. 'Grandad? And you, Clifford, you'll have a sup?' she said, pleading to him with her eyes.

Catching her meaning, the younger man nodded. 'I could murder a cup, ta. Hang about, I'll give you a hand.'

Facing one another in the kitchen once the door was closed, Livvy and Clifford blew out air and grinned.

'What's with all the bees?' she wanted to know.

'For my sins, I just happened to mention in passing how I was nearly stung this morning whilst tending the garden.'

'Oh God.' Livvy couldn't help but laugh.

'And well, Morris . . .'

'It started him off on his own experiences with the insects?'

'That's the top and bottom of it, aye. Invited me into the house, he did, to hear them. That was over an hour ago.'

'No!'

'Aye.'

'Eeh, lad.' She dissolved into giggles once more.

Clifford's grin returned. 'I couldn't very well say no, could I?'

'Course you could. He's ruddy murder when he starts.'

'Nah. He's all right. Anyroad, I reckon he gets a bit

lonely in on his own. I don't mind keeping him company, really.'

They returned their attentions to the task: Clifford collecting the milk from the cold slab in the larder and Livvy scalding the tea leaves in the pot. After loading the tray, and before they returned to the living room, she turned once more to face him, knew she had to mention it. She still harboured guilt from their last meeting and the way the conversation had turned. Clifford had evidently been keeping a low profile and she'd seen nothing of him since that night. Nor had she attempted to seek him out – what would there have been to say? Regardless, the last thing she'd wanted was for them to fall out, and she was keen now to ensure they had returned to an even footing:

'It's nice to see you, lad, you know?'

He cleared his throat, nodded. 'And you.'

The tension was building. Glad of something to do, she reached for the tray. 'Right, well . . . We'd best get back in.'

Morris retired to bed after two cups of tea and three further retellings of his earlier exploits, much to his audience's relief – his footfalls died away on the stairs and they flopped in their seats, grinning.

'By gum!' Clifford groaned.

'I don't know where he finds the energy,' Livvy snorted in full agreement. 'I reckon he'd fetch the war to a halt, you know, if ever there was a chance to stick him in a room alone with Hitler. He'd bore the bugger to death!'

'Eeh, don't be mean,' Clifford whispered, however he'd delivered the words from behind his hand, which he'd clamped to his mouth to stem his laughter. 'Poor owd sod.'

'Mean tripe. I've a thundering headache on me after that lot.'

'Oh. Erm . . .' He shifted to the edge of the sofa. 'I'll get off home, eh, let you get some rest . . .?'

'No, you're all right! I weren't hinting for you to leave, lad.'

'Aye?'

'Course. Stop a bit, finish your brew.'

They sat in companiable silence for a few minutes. Livvy kicked off her shoes, tucked her feet in beneath her and rested her head against Clifford's shoulder. A long sigh escaped her. She smiled.

'All right?' he asked quietly.

'I am now – oh, but it's nice to relax.'

'A trying shift, was it?'

Her smile slipped. She nodded. 'Aye, you could say that.'

'Madge mentioned you'd got a new position; how's it going?'

'Good, aye. I bet I pong of chip fat, don't I?' Nonetheless, she made no attempt to move away from him and instead snuggled up a little nearer. His warm arm against her own was a comfort, soothing.

'A bit,' he admitted, smiling when she clicked her tongue, 'but I don't mind.'

'No?'

'No,' he murmured. Then: 'I'd suffer owt to be close to you.'

Her heart flipped over and tears stung. She closed her eyes. 'Clifford . . .'

'Livvy, can I ask you summat? Something very serious?'

Oh God. *Please don't make me turn you down again. It's just as painful for me as it is for you.* 'I . . . suppose.'

'And you swear you'll give me an honest answer?'

Lad, lad. 'I . . .'

'You must promise me.' His tone was thick with intensity. 'Say it.'

'I promise,' she whispered after an eternity. She held her breath.

'Are all them stories of your grandad's really true?'

'Wha—' She let out air again slowly. 'That's it, what you wanted to ask me? You swine!' she said when he threw back his head and laughed. 'I thought . . .'

'You thought it was going to be summat really deep?' It was his turn to release a long breath. He leaned his head back against the sofa cushion. 'I'm sorry.'

'For what?'

'Coming on strong.'

'It don't matter—'

'Aye, it does.' He turned suddenly to face her. 'From now on, I'll back off, all right? I promise. All I ask is this: might there ever be a chance . . .'

She licked her dry lips. The urge to scream to him yes – and the struggle not to – was like a physical pain.

'Just mebbe? One day?'

'Mebbe,' she admitted. After all, who could say what might happen? No one, of course. Could she indeed resist him for the remainder of her days; was it possible? *Oh, but how very different things could have been, in another life* . . .

'Right. Well then. Good.' He ran a hand that shook ever so slightly across his mouth. His eyes were wide and shining. 'That's good.'

'I only said maybe, Clifford . . .' she had to point out. 'Remember?'

'Aye, but that means there's hope. And that's more than I had a couple of minutes ago.'

'Eeh, lad.'

'I'll wait patiently, Livvy. I will. I'll not pester you nor try to force your hand. And who knows: if I wish for it hard enough then sometime in t' future, you might be ready, eh? You're worth it,' he finished simply.

Burrowing her head into his waiting arms, Livvy allowed a tear or two to fall.

Chapter Seven

'DID YOU HEAR the news on t' wireless, lass? About Mussolini being overthrown?'

Livvy nodded and a smile crept across her lips. There had been talk of nothing else at home since. Joan had taken great enjoyment in winding their grandfather up with talk of a new government being formed in Italy, and likelihood that it wouldn't be long until it surrendered to the Allies. If Italy did turn on the Germans and effectively joined Britain's side, that would mean they were no longer our enemy – we could all listen to Gracie Fields again! the girl had stated, throwing Morris into apoplectics. All week, the mumpsimus old man had almost been tripping over his bottom lip dragging on the floor, in a terrible sulk.

'That Lord Haw-Haw will no doubt have had summat not worth listening to, to say on t' matter,' Bertha went on with a roll of her eyes. 'As soon as that awful, plummy, nasal voice comes through the speakers, it gets my back up. Aye, gets right on my wick, he does.'

'And me. "Germany calling! Germany calling!"'

The nickname had been given to a now infamous anonymous man who, since shortly after the outbreak of war, had begun broadcasting Nazi propaganda to the United Kingdom in an affected upper-crust English accent. The goal was to discourage troops and the British population alike. Nevertheless, despite the inflammatory nature of the announcements and the fact they were often peppered with inaccuracies, many did choose to listen in to the programme for any scraps of information regarding details of what was happening behind enemy lines. Home reports of casualties were often played down so as not to damage morale, and if nothing else Haw-Haw could always be relied upon to spill the beans instead, albeit with heavy exaggeration.

Bertha grimaced at Livvy's on-the-mark imitation. 'At first, you know, I hated him whoever he might be, would swear he had a heart as black as Hitler's moustache to spout with such relish the rot that he does. Now, it don't rightly mither me as much. In fact, I almost feel sorry for the fool.'

'Aye, it's a comic act he's become these days so far as most folk are concerned,' Livvy agreed. However, her mind wasn't fully on the conversation at hand.

For today was Saturday yet again – by far her worst day of the week now – and she had a horrible feeling a certain someone would be paying her a visit before it was through, God help her.

'I still can't get over how long this thing's dragged on for, you know, lass,' Bertha continued, unaware of her employee's discombobulation. 'The war I mean. Eeh, shall it ever know a conclusion, I wonder? Every time summat big occurs, I think this is it now, *this* will bring a certain stop to it, surely, but no. At the end of February when us and America began round-the-clock bombing of Germany, I thought the finish line was in sight. Again, in May, when the Axis forces in Tunisia surrendered. Then the Dambusters Raid days later. And just a few weeks back when we invaded Sicily. Yet no! It just grinds on and on and on ... That fed up with it, I am.'

'"We shall ride out the storms of war and outlive the menace of tyranny, if necessary for years ..."' Livvy reminded her with a soft smile of one of the Prime Minister's most memorable speeches. 'It's all we can do, Bertha.'

'Aye, lass. And 'ere: we *will* defend to the death our native soil – oh yes. Eeh, lends me strength and plenty of hope, do his words. Mind you, I'll be ruddy ready when peace does come, you watch and see. Dancing in t' street is where you'll find me, aye!'

'It'll be queer listening to church bells ringing

151

again when it's all over with, eh?' Livvy mused before taking a mouthful of her tea. They had been silenced at the start of hostilities and would only be sounded again either to alert the public of an enemy invasion or to announce the end of the war.

'Queer, but lovely. I reckon I'll cry when I hear their sweet toll.'

'Let's just pray your tears are for the right reasons,' she pointed out, and both women nodded solemnly.

'Just think, no threat of bomb blasts will mean no more tape criss-crossing the windows and no sandbags ... everything back looking nice and normal again, aye. Eeh, and no blackout – by, imagine that again: lights at night! I'll be skipping round t' house like a young lass ripping the blackout curtains down, I will.'

'What will they do about the pavements?' Livvy wanted to know. 'You know, how they've coloured the edges white to aid us to see a bit better where we're walking in t' dark – what when we don't need them? Will they scrub them all clean or just let it fade away?'

'Oh, I don't know ...' Bertha frowned thoughtfully. 'Surely, though, the cows shall be a different matter. Fancy them painting white lines on the poor things. What when they're grooming theirselves – don't it poison them, make them ill? Unless it's a special sort of paint? Mind you, do cows even groom theirselves . . .'

'I don't know.' Livvy laughed. Oh, but they didn't half wander off track and chat some nonsense on their breaks. What's more, she loved it. You just never knew what Bertha would come out with next.

'The mind boggles, I don't know how the powers that be think them up. Aye, they'll have to clean them, eh, surely, the cows?'

'I suppose so.' Then in the next breath, she said, 'Ay, let's talk of summat else, eh?' War, war, war: it was all anyone ever spoke about, she'd come to realise since working here and being in close contact with the general public. She was thoroughly fed up with it.

'Well, you think of the topic and I'll follow on,' Bertha announced, getting to her feet. 'Mind you, we'll have to gab as we toil: it's nearly time for opening, and hungry folk shall be bashing down the door in a minute. Hop to it, lass, come on.'

It wasn't until a lull in work much later into the evening that Livvy realised Carl hadn't made an appearance. She'd been kept so busy that she hadn't noticed – now, her heart rose in blessed hope. Happen he wouldn't show after all? Perhaps he'd actually got the message and that was the end of it . . . was it possible? Could she really dare believe it true? *Please, Lord.* Sure enough, when her shift drew to a close and there had still been no sign of him, she began to trust it possible. She was almost giddy with the relief of it. He must have surely got bored with her and wouldn't show his face again. Oh, thank God!

'I'll be seeing you, lass,' Bertha called as Livvy made for the door, waving her on her way with a warm smile. 'You take care now in that dark, won't you?'

'I will – ta-ra, Bertha. See you Monday.'

Livvy's smile remained in place the length of the street. When she neared the bus stop and spotted a huddle of shapes illuminated against the moon – others waiting to travel, too – she felt even better. Should Carl somehow happen to appear after all, at least she wasn't alone and there were others present who would possibly come to her aid if need be. Surely even he, bold as he was, wasn't so hard-faced as to try anything with her in front of an audience. No, she'd be fine now. As the saying went, there was safety in numbers.

The dimmed headlamps of the bus appeared in the distance, their slits of light breaking through the cloying darkness, and she shuffled forward in readiness with everyone else. It came to a stop and she stepped aside to allow those there before her to climb aboard. At last, she located a seat and dropped on to it gratefully. Closing her eyes, she settled back with a sigh.

She might call into number nineteen when she arrived back, see Clifford, she mused as the bus crawled with care through the night towards her destination. He'd be pleased of a chat with her, and she would very much like to see him.

Since laying themselves bare during their talk, something had shifted in their relationship, and she was more than a little glad of it. She felt much more at ease around him now – in fact, she rather suspected he felt the same way.

There were no expectations now they had laid their cards on the table and knew for certain where they stood, no awkwardness; the tension had gone. It was nice to simply be around one another, enjoy the other's company, the special friendship, without fear of upsetting – or being upset by – the other. Now, instead of the quiet dread and gnawing guilt – or more painful still, the desperate yearning – whenever he was around she found her heart leaping and her face widening in gladsomeness when they did meet.

Clifford too seemed happier, most likely because she was, and much more relaxed when they were together than she'd known him to be previously. She could only hope things continued the way they were going, for both their sakes.

The streets were eerily quiet and completely deserted when she reached Top o'th' Brow. Few folk these days strayed outdoors unless they really needed to once the evening drew in; Livvy didn't blame them. Everything seemed different at night. Shapes materialised where through the daytime there were none, and sounds appeared magnified tenfold. Glancing up at the branches of a tree in the garden she was passing, silhouetted black like long witches' talons against the star-pricked, silver-blue of the sky, she shivered. Pulling her coat closer around her chin, she hurried her pace.

She'd reached Bridson Lane and was about to turn the bend into Glaister Lane when a noise sounding distinctly like a sharp intake of breath reached her ears – she whipped around instinctively.

By now, her eyes had become accustomed to the lack of light; nonetheless, it was impossible to make out anything further than a few feet away. However, bar herself there didn't look to be another soul alive around so far as she could see.

Then the sound came again, this time seemingly from right beside her.

The fine hairs on her arms sprang to attention; standing stock still, her eyes creased in concentration, she scoured the short stretch of road once more. But again, there was nothing.

Remembering the small torch in her handbag, but that she'd forgotten to change the dead batteries inside it, she cursed inwardly. She took a last look

156

around. Then, turning on her heel, she picked up her feet and set off at a sprint for number nineteen.

Clifford, dressed in just his shirt and braced trousers, no shoes on his socked feet, no jacket or tie and his sleeves rolled to the elbows, appeared as though he'd just woken from a nap. Stifling a yawn, he smoothed a hand across his tousled hair. 'Livvy, hello. Sorry, I must have nodded off . . .' He stretched, smiled. 'Will you come in?'

'Aye, please.'

Celia's little abode was neat and cosy; as always when she visited, Livvy felt at home right away. She removed her coat and draped it over the arm of the sofa before sitting down. 'Where's the owd birds at?' she asked.

'Gone to the pictures. They've gorra taste for it now, I think, since we all went. They've been three times this week already.'

'And no doubt a few swift drinks at the pub afterwards! Oh 'eck. I hope they'll be all right in the blackout.'

'Ho! I don't think they'll have any bother with your grandma there, do you? Put it this way: I'd not want to mess with Madge, no way no how!'

Livvy tried to return his grin, but her lips wouldn't respond; her gaze strayed towards the window. 'Even so . . .'

'Don't be fretting, lass, they'll be just fine . . . Hey,

what's up, what is it?' Clifford asked, moving to sit beside her as she bit her lip. 'Livvy?'

'It's probably nowt . . . I heard someone, just now when I were on my way here. Breathing – but I couldn't see no one, and it's made me a bit jumpy, I—'

'All right, it's all right.' He took her hand, which was trembling, and chafed it between his own.

'Eeh, sorry, lad. I feel daft now, only the dark . . .'

'Don't be sorry, I understand. It's human nature to be wary and on your guard when you can't see your ruddy hand in front of your face. Are you sure it was a "someone"? Could it not have been summat else, say a dog?'

'Aye, probably.' Nodding, she rolled her eyes. She'd stake her last sixpence on him being right – and that she knew the culprit. 'Now you come to mention it,' she told him, chuckling, 'there's a dog I've had bother with before. I bloody bet it was that. Eeh, the swine! Near gave me a heart attack, it did.'

'Well, you're safe now,' he said in amusement. 'Tea?'

'Aye, I am.' She met his gaze, and a pleasing warmness ran through her. She smiled. 'And tea would be lovely.'

They had been chatting for a handful of minutes when Clifford said on a rush, as though he'd been trying to pluck up the courage to suggest it, 'Fancy a trip to Blackpool?'

'Blackpool?' She put down her cup on the small, dark wood table in front of the sofa. 'I don't know . . . Who with?'

'Me. No funny business,' he hastened to add, holding up his hands. 'I'm in need of a change of scene and reckon it'd do you no harm, neither. We could book into a boarding house for the night – separate rooms, of course. What d'you say?'

His face was taut with expectancy, his eyes creased with hope – Livvy's spirits leapt; she clapped her hands with childlike exuberance. 'Don't look so worried – I'd love to!'

'Aye? Eeh!'

'On one condition, though.'

'Owt. Name it.'

'We visit the Tower Ballroom forra dance whilst we're there. I've always wanted to go.'

Clifford's nod came without hesitation: 'You're on! Ay, Livvy, I'm that pleased you've said aye. We'll have a gradely time, lass, you just watch and see.'

'Mind you . . .' She bit her lip, the thought only now occurring to her. 'What will we tell the others? Your aunt, and my grandma and grandad? They'll certainly have summat to say about it, you know. Me and you, the two of us alone, off to the seaside together overnight . . . They'll be thinking all sorts, lad, and no wonder.'

'Nowt untoward will be going on.'

'As if they'll believe that! Unless . . .'

'What?'

'We could . . . bend the truth? Just a bit, like. I could tell them I'm spending the night with Vera, and *you* could say you're stopping over with some friend or other? That way, they'd not have the chance to jump to any conclusions. They'd never find out, and it'd save a whole lot of bother.' A wicked smile appeared. She wiggled her brows. 'What d'you say?'

'Aye, I'm game,' he told her, grinning back. 'When shall we go, then? How about next weekend?'

'Aye, all right. I could ask Bertha to let me leave earlier on Saturday; she'll agree, I'm sure. I'll take a bag with my things to work with me on the day, and if you meet me outside the chippy, we can head straight for the train station. Does that suit you?'

Clifford confirmed that it did. 'I can't wait, now.'

'Nor me,' Livvy said with genuine excitement. 'It's been years since I went.'

They parted company at the step soon afterwards, both still wearing matching smiles.

'Remember, norra word to a soul,' she whispered theatrically, holding a finger to her lips.

'Our secret,' he agreed, crossing his chest where his heart was with an over-dramatic wink.

Reaching for one another's hand, they laughed.

'Goodnight, God bless, Livvy.'

'Goodnight, God bless, lad, sweet dreams,' she murmured, returning the pressure of his hold before reluctantly breaking away. 'Ta-ra for now.'

She covered the short distance to her own home in less than ten seconds. When she reached her door, she glanced back to see Clifford was still standing where she'd left him, making sure she got in safely. *So thoughtful, always.* Sighing with a mixture of pleasure and gratefulness, she waved to him and, when he'd returned it, let herself into the house.

'All right, Grandad?' she greeted the old man cheerfully, and planted a loud kiss on his brow for good measure.

'You're chirpy for someone who's just done a hard day's graft. Lost a tanner and found a pound, have you?'

'Huh! I wish. Nah, I'm just happy, is all. Is our Joan in?'

'She's round at that pal's of hers. She'd best not be much longer, neither; time's getting on. Aye, knowing her, she'll likely stop out the night through – a reet little madam she's turning into and no mistake. Aye, I wonder who she takes after, eh?'

'Ooh, what's to do with you?' Livvy cooed. 'Are you *still* sulking about Gracie Fields? Eeh, I don't know! Joan'll be back soon, don't worry— Ah, see, what did I say?' she added smugly with a nod, making Morris sniff irritably at being proved wrong when the door opening sounded. 'Grumpy git, you're nowt else.'

'Mind that tongue of yourn, you. You're not too big forra good hiding, you know.'

Livvy hooted with laughter. 'If you say so – I'd like to see you ruddy try! I'd clock you one straight back, an' all.'

'What's all this?' her sister enquired, entering the living room. 'You two fighting again?'

'Oh, it's him, lass, take no notice. You know what he's like . . .' Livvy broke off, frowning, to nod at the package Joan carried. 'What's that?'

She shrugged. 'I've just found it on t' doorstep. It's addressed to you.'

'Me? Well, who's leaving stuff here and at this time?'

'Well, I don't know, do I? Look inside and find out – there might be a message.'

'Did you see anyone when you reached home? Anyone walking away or lurking about?'

'Norra soul.'

Her bemusement growing, Livvy took the brown-paper-wrapped parcel from her and carried it to the table. However, she didn't attempt to open it. Just how, in the space of a mere half a minute slot between herself and Joan arriving, had someone managed to deliver this without being seen? There had been no one in the street, had there, when she'd left Clifford

– and besides, he would have noticed, too. Who would be giving her gifts, anyway? More to the point, why leave it outside without attempting to knock? Why not hand it to her personally? It didn't make sense.

'Go on, our Livvy, have a look-see,' Joan said, coming to stand beside her. She poked at it with her finger. 'I'm intrigued, now.'

'I will later.'

'But why? Aw, go on—'

'Later,' Livvy repeated. Something didn't feel right here, and she was more than a little reluctant to discover what. Best she investigated the mysterious package and its contents when she was alone.

'Right, well, I'm going to bed.' Joan's disappointment was evident. 'It's not like there's owt to stop up for, is there . . .' A sigh, then: 'Night, each.'

'Night, God bless, lass,' Livvy said, flashing her a soft and apologetic smile. 'See you in t' morn.'

'Night,' the girl said to Morris, and when he returned it an impish glint appeared in her eye. 'What, that's it, Grandad? Ain't you going to wish me luck and wave me goodbye . . .'

'See, you see!' he exploded to Livvy, jabbing a finger at the girl, who was now helpless with guffaws. 'That one just won't let up, nay – hounding me with her antics, she is, bold bugger!'

This only made Joan laugh all the harder, and

163

Morris turned another shade of puce: 'Aggravating young—'

'All right, all right – that's enough,' Livvy called over the hullabaloo. 'By gum, it's like refereeing a couple of infants. No more about Gracie ruddy Fields, and that goes for the pair of youse. You hear?' *Lord, get me in Blackpool and away from this madhouse for a few hours!* she added to herself. It couldn't come quickly enough. 'Now, Joan, give over and go on off to bed. Why don't you take yourself up as well, Grandad? Go on, leave me in peace, eh? I'm tired and want a bit of quiet to myself.'

Still bickering, the pair did as she bid and headed from the room and upstairs. Livvy heaved a sigh and flopped down on to the sofa.

The package, though, bore a hole into the back of her head from across the room, refusing to let her rest, and at last she rose and walked hesitantly towards it.

A length of twine secured it – she plucked it off and for a few seconds more stood staring at it. Then, picking it up, she carried it back to the sofa and tore open the paper.

Her lips parting, she trawled her gaze over the items in her lap. Tinned peaches and ham. Stockings and chocolate. And lastly, sitting atop the pile, a packet of Lucky Strike cigarettes.

There was no note, however the lack of one mattered not; none was needed.

She'd had enough things from Vera and her many contacts in the past to know where these originated from. These had come from PX – the Post Exchange. The American equivalent of the NAAFI.

Only a Yank could have left them. Nor did it take much working out to know which one.

This meant but one thing. Her rapist knew where she lived.

'He followed me home, Vera, must have done.'

Looking to the ceiling, her friend shook her head.

'What the hell am I going to do?'

'What you should have done right at the beginning: shop the warped, evil swine!'

Livvy dropped her face in her hands. Unsurprisingly, she'd got not a wink of sleep and her head throbbed from exhaustion. 'I can't relax there, not now, not after this,' she whispered, bringing her bloodshot eyes up to meet the woman's. 'I spent the whole night through checking and rechecking that the doors were locked and all of the windows secure. Where will it end? What next, eh? What else has he got up his sleeve? This was a message, aye, and I got it all right, loud and clear. He wants me to see what he's capable of, what he can do. Why? Why is he doing this? I can't go on like this, Vera.'

'Then *go* to the police. Please, Livvy, do it. I'm that frickened for you.'

She nodded.

'You'll do it?'

'Aye.'

'Well, thank God for that!'

'Will you come with me, love?'

Scooching across the sofa to put an arm around Livvy's shaking shoulders, Vera said, 'Just you try and stop me.'

They arrived at the central police station a short time later but didn't enter right away; Livvy needed time to gather her bearings first, was a bundle of dread.

'You'll be just fine; I'm here and I shan't leave your side,' Vera soothed. 'Don't you forget, love, you're not the bad guy, ain't done a single thing wrong. Now come on, eh, let's get this over with.'

She trailed behind her friend, who had taken the lead, and approached the tall and stockily built police constable on duty in the enquiry office. 'Good morning, sir. I . . .' She glanced to Vera, unsure what to do – nodding, her friend nudged her aside and faced the lawman determinedly:

'My mate here wants to report a crime,' she almost yelled.

The man looked from one to the other with brow furrowed. 'Is that so? And what crime might that be?'

166

'A very serious one, lad: sexual assault.'

He reached for pencil and paper and inclined his head at Livvy to speak. 'I'll need some details. Name?'

'Bryant,' she whispered. 'Olive.'

'*Miss* Bryant, I assume?' he pressed, shooting a glance to the third finger of her left hand in search of a ring, and finding none.

'I . . .' Avoiding Vera's eye, she murmured finally, 'It's Mrs, actually, sir. I'm widowed.'

Her friend released a small gasp but didn't pass comment. Livvy was glad of it. She returned her attention to the constable's questioning.

'Now, can you explain what happened?' he said at last.

She told him what had transpired leading up to the incident and with tears in her throat went on to relay the attack itself. By the time she'd finished, her eyes were burning and her chest ached painfully from the heavy drumming of her heart. 'Carl Rivera is his name, sir, and he's a Yank based at Burtonwood army base. I just wanted to forget about the whole business, but I can't, for he'll not leave me be. He's been to see me since at my work at Bertha's chippy down yonder, and got reet threatening. And last night, he followed me home to Breightmet.

'It was dark, you understand,' she continued, 'and so I didn't see him hanging about, but he must have been. He sneaked on t' bus behind me, had to have done, and tailed me home to see where I lived. I thought I heard summat but put it down to a dog or some such; no, it was him, I'm certain of it now.'

'Those with mischief in mind can, I'm afraid to say, get away with a lot more since the blackout.'

This from him didn't make her feel any better. She shuddered. 'Fair makes my skin crawl to think on it, imagining him skulking in the shadows close by and I had no idea . . . Anyroad, I know it was him as not long after I got in, a package was left on t' doorstep. It had inside it American supplies from the PX.'

'Supplies?'

'Aye, peaches and the like, and a packet of Lucky Strikes.'

The constable nodded. 'You say he's been to your place of work?'

'That's right.' She bit her lip. 'You'll not have to speak to my employer, will you? I've not been there long, sir, you see, and I wouldn't want Bertha getting upset with me for fetching the police to her door.'

'Did you work there when the alleged incident occurred?'

'She did, aye,' Vera answered for her rapidly.

He looked from one to the other, then back again. 'Mrs Bryant?' he pressed sternly, evidently having noticed the flush to Livvy's cheeks at the deception. 'Well?'

'No, I . . .' Faltering, she looked to Vera again, but

168

the woman hadn't the answer this time and only sighed. Both knew what was coming.

'Mrs Bryant?'

'Sir, I . . .'

'Yes?'

Livvy took a deep breath: 'I was earning my money as a prostitute. But Carl Rivera wasn't a customer,' she hastened to make clear quickly at the expression that had now taken hold of the policeman's face. 'He was just a friend – at least that's what he pretended to me. No brass changed hands.'

'Perhaps,' he said, tossing aside his pencil, 'that's the real issue here? Am I right?' His attitude was swiftly altered. All interest had left his countenance, and indifference had taken its place. He sniffed. 'He failed to pay you for . . . services rendered, shall we say, and you're seeking revenge.'

'No. No, that's not true—'

'False claims such as this are not only extremely serious but leave a detrimental mark on innocent men, Mrs Bryant.' His clipped voice was deep with censure. 'I suggest you think very carefully before continuing with this charade.'

'Charade?' Vera pushed her nose close to his. 'She's speaking nowt but the truth, you sod, and I'll stand up in a court of law and say the same! Take her into the CID office right now, go on,' she demanded before the now-blustering man could get a word in.

169

'Let her speak to the Detective Constable. You'd better, for we're not moving from here until you do!'

'Let's go.'

'But Livvy—'

'It'll be us under arrest and thrown in t' cells in a minute,' she snapped, dragging Vera unceremoniously towards the door. 'It's useless – didn't I say they'd not care? Let's just leave.'

'What you just said in there, about you being a widow . . .' Vera put to Livvy when they were outside. 'Why didn't you ever tell me, love?'

'I don't know. I don't like to talk about it. Anyroad, where would have been the point? It wouldn't have changed owt, would it? It'd not have brought him back.'

They retraced their steps through the streets to Vera's rooms in silence. What was there to say, after all? As Livvy suspected, no one in authority gave a damn about an accusation made by a common whore – former or not. Take the word of a streetwalker over a brave and heroic serviceman doing his bit for their country? As if. She should have stuck to her guns and stopped away, should never have let Vera talk her into visiting the station. She'd gained nothing from the fruitless trek bar smothering humiliation and brokenheartedness. Christ, she felt worse now than she ever had.

'Will you come in?' Vera asked, seeing Livvy

hesitate when they reached her door. That she'd lost her temper, in the process escalating the already delicate situation, and felt guilt for how things had turned out back there, was plain.

'I won't, ta all the same. I just want to go home.'

'Love . . .'

'It's all right, Vera. Honest,' she assured her, squeezing her arm. 'You were only defending me, I get it. Besides, whether you'd shot your mouth off or no, it wouldn't have altered the outcome. That constable had my cards marked from the minute he found out about my past. He'd never have done nowt regardless.'

'Men.' Vera spat on the ground. 'I'm beginning to detest the whole friggin' shower of 'em!'

'There's still a few good 'uns out there, love,' Livvy said quietly, with Clifford in mind. 'Anyroad, I'll be seeing you.'

'I'll come and visit you at the chippy, shall I? Tomorrow?' the woman called after her.

'Aye, that'd be nice. Ta-ra, Vera.'

The moment she turned the corner out of view, Livvy ground to a halt and took several shuddering breaths. Tears threatened again but she shook her head furiously, refused to give way to them.

This was it, the end of any possible help from an authoritative corner. No way would she lower herself, put herself out there again, with the only other option left open to her: the commanding officer at Burtonwood. Where would be the use at all? She'd garner nothing from it, just as she'd done with the police, but further pain and embarrassment.

No. All hopes of Carl facing punishment and being made to leave her alone had been shattered to dust.

She was on her own.

Chapter Eight

A BRIGHT AFTERNOON had succeeded the somewhat dull morning. Shooting yet another glance to the cloth bag holding her few bits and items of clothing, Livvy prayed again that the weather would continue to hold out.

Bertha had indeed given her employee her blessing to leave earlier today, and without any awkward questions. Now all Livvy had to do was see the next hour through and enjoy her time away from Bolton with Clifford. She could barely breathe with the anticipation of it.

A steady stream of customers kept her busy, and she looked up with a confused frown when a light tapping came at the large window beside her. Then, seeing Clifford, looking smart in his overcoat and trilby, his smiling face staring back at her, she gasped and her mouth split into a joyous grin. 'One minute,' she mimed to him through the pane, holding up a finger. 'Let me get my bag.'

Seconds later, she was standing on the pavement in the warm evening sunshine. At his insistence, she handed her things to Clifford and drew her arm through the crook of his, linking him.

'Ready?' he asked. His face was alive with gladness at the adventure to come.

'You bet.' She pointed ahead in the direction of Trinity Street Station. 'Lead the way, good sir!'

'Hey, baby.'

The dreaded voice pierced her ears and the world seemed to tilt and sway. Livvy staggered. *Oh God, please no . . .*

'Going someplace?' Carl persisted. He'd sidestepped in front of them, forcing them to a stop, and stood with legs parted, a twisted smile playing about his lips.

'Who . . .' Clifford looked from one to the other.

'Allow me to introduce myself. I'm Carl Rivera, and—'

'He's a regular at the chippy,' Livvy blurted almost on a yell. 'We've got to know one another.' She could feel her cheeks flaming and beads of perspiration had sprung out on her top lip. Mortified wasn't the half of it. She'd done no wrong, of this she was fully aware, however the truth left her feeling none the better for it. Their grubby little secret couldn't become common knowledge; she'd die from the shame of it. Clifford, in particular, could never find out. He couldn't. *He couldn't.* 'That's right, ain't it?' she forced herself to address the American, all the while praying for a miracle.

Carl said nothing, merely smirked. Instead, he turned his attention back to the other man. 'And you are . . .'

'Clifford.' His voice was low with dislike. 'Livvy's friend.'

'Ah. Livvy's *friend.* She has lots of friends – don't you, baby?' he almost demanded, flicking his head back to face her. 'Me, though, I'm her *very* good friend, isn't that so—'

'We have to be on our way,' she cut in on a stammer, tugging at Clifford's arm. 'We'll miss our train.'

'Train? What train? Where're you going?'

'Come on, lad,' she said to Clifford, who appeared as if he wasn't going to leave; his frown was deep and dark and he was glaring at Carl as though he might hit him. 'Please, lad.'

'Honey?' Carl pressed on, seemingly oblivious to the other man's quite obvious anger. 'When will you be back? I need to know!'

'Soon. Now will you just *go.*'

He opened his mouth, then closed it again. A last long look of Clifford up and down, then he snorted arrogantly, swung around and sauntered away.

'Come on, Clifford.' Livvy was trembling, couldn't help it. Linking his arm again, she hurried him on as fast as she was able, desperate to put some distance between them and Carl.

'Who in Christ's name was that?'

Head down, she didn't respond for a long moment, then: 'I told you, he's just a customer—'

'Humph.'

'What?'

'That was one hell of a pushy fella, Livvy. Are youse . . .'

Bile rose in her throat at the assumption. She turned to look at him fully, her eyes creased with a level of hurt he would never understand. 'No,' she said firmly. 'Never. I swear it.'

'Don't feel you have to lie, Livvy. I've no claim on you, after all . . .'

'I'm not. I'm not,' she repeated, quieter now but every bit as earnestly. 'He just . . . He'll not . . .' She released a ragged breath. 'He'll get the message soon enough that I'm not interested,' she finished at last. 'Now, can we please just forget all about that man and go and enjoy ourselves as we planned?' *Please.* 'Or would you prefer we called the whole thing off and went home?' she made herself ask. 'I'll, I'll understand if you do decide—'

'No. Course not. Course we should go.'

'Aye? Really, Clifford?'

He nodded. Though his countenance had lost a little of its stiffness now, his eyes remained hooded still in a frown. He made a concerted effort to smile, failed somewhat, and cleared his throat. 'Let's forget it happened, eh? Put it from our minds and carry on with what we were about?' He tried another smile, this time with better results, much to her relief. 'Come on. There should be a train just due.'

Allowing herself to breathe properly at last, Livvy nodded. Sending a silent thank you up to the heavens, she picked up the pace to match Clifford's long stride.

'These look nice.'

'They do – decent, aye.'

Slowing to a halt, the pair swept their gazes along the length of Grosvenor Street in shared approval. The large three-storey houses with steps leading up to the freshly painted front doors, and snow-white drapes at the bay windows, made a good first impression. Making for the abode directly in front of them – 'Clark House' proclaimed a blue sign affixed to the awning – they unlatched the small wooden gate, ascended the scrubbed stones and knocked.

'We're looking for accommodation for the night,' Clifford told the apron-clad woman who answered. 'The sign in t' window says you have vacancies?'

'I do indeed.' She stepped aside to admit them. 'Come in.'

They followed her through to the entrance hall,

each discreetly marvelling further at the clean and spick-and-span surroundings.

'The daily rate is ten shillings and sixpence.' Opening up a ledger from the desk at Clifford's nod of acceptance, she asked, 'Name?'

'Mr Bamford,' he replied. Then, shooting Livvy the softest of winks, he added, 'And Mrs Bamford.'

The boarding-house keeper glanced to Livvy, who flashed a quick smile and hoped the woman wouldn't notice the blush stealing up her neck. Just what was Clifford playing at? He'd assured her, had he not, that he expected nothing from this visit, that they would have separate rooms. Why go back on his word? Did he expect that if he backed her into a corner like this that she'd cave and take him to her bed? The notion shocked her to the core. Never would she have believed it possible of him. He was decent, kind . . . wasn't he? It just didn't make sense.

'I cater to a respectable class of clientele at my establishment, you understand?' the keeper announced. She was staring meaningly at the couple's empty ring fingers.

'Of course,' Clifford was fast to respond. 'Me and Livvy here ain't married. We share a surname because we're related. We're brother and sister.'

The woman's face at once relaxed. 'Oh, I see. My apologies, Mr Bamford, only I'm sure you'll appreciate that we get all types passing through this town. You can't be too careful—'

'No apologies needed, I understand,' he interjected cheerfully. 'Naturally, we'll be requiring two rooms.'

'Naturally,' she echoed, crossing towards the staircase. 'If you'd both like to follow me?'

They held back whilst the woman moved off to unlock from a large bunch of keys attached to a chain beneath her apron two doors facing one another across the landing. She then proceeded to show them inside and reeled off a routine list of rules and regulations. 'Now, I'll leave you to unpack,' she finished. 'If you require anything, do let me know.'

Clifford assured her that they would, extracted a pound note and shilling piece from the inside pocket of his jacket, and thanked her. With a nod, the woman left them alone and they turned to one another and smiled.

'All right?'

'Aye,' Livvy murmured. She felt utterly ashamed of herself. Fancy her imagining Clifford to have improper designs, when all along . . . She shouldn't have doubted his integrity. What you saw was what you got with him. Didn't she know this by now? By, but she did possess a mucky mind at times. 'That was a good idea of yours, you know, saying we were siblings. If you'd have told the truth, that we were just two good friends stopping here together, she'd have never believed it, would have thought this some dirty weekend and that we'd be sneaking across the landing in the dead of night to each other's rooms. She had no worries when you said what you did.'

'Exactly.' Grinning, he took her hand. 'Come on, let's choose who's to have which room.'

After a freshening up at their washbasins and a change of clothes, they made their way back down the stairs and let themselves outside.

The boarding-house keeper had informed them it was a ten- to fifteen-minute walk to the promenade, and had given them directions. Now, they turned left and set off with much gaiety.

Blackpool was by far one of the nation's most popular seaside resorts, with many millions flocking each year. It wasn't difficult to see why. It boasted countless activities to please the constant flow of crowds. It provided a particularly welcome break for those from places such as Bolton. Swapping for a short time their grey and smoky industrial towns for the radically altered scenery of clear blue skies, golden sands and the sea that sparkled in the sun was a magical shock to the senses.

As well as the draw of these natural attractions, visitors were deluged with a never-ending supply of entertainments, from the zoo and the circus to the famous Pleasure Beach theme park, which, much to the delight of the masses, had remained open during the war. Once they had exhausted all of this, there was always the array of weird and wonderful stalls that lined the Golden Mile. And ice cream, sticks of rock and the town's renowned fish and chips ensured you kept your energy up whilst taking in the sights.

For obvious reasons, the illuminations had been suspended until peacetime. Nonetheless, here, everything shone in technicolour – and then some. At Blackpool, the possibilities were endless, and it was loved by young and old alike.

Of course, as with everywhere, it did have its murky side. Fortune-tellers were rife, and police came down heavily on them. Darker yet, Blackpool was said to hold the unfavourable title of prostitute centre of Britain. If true, it was hardly difficult to see how: there was a constant stream of men coming into the resort – the town was a major RAF training centre. Apparently, and to many shockingly, some theatres even had nude shows. And at least one VD clinic could be found on the promenade.

As Livvy and Clifford took a leisurely stroll along the seafront, they were soon to see that even in wonderland there was no escaping the signs of war. In fact, it was evident all across the Fylde Coast; concrete blocks had been placed in some roads to halt enemy tank storming and aircraft landings.

Meanwhile, shelters able to accommodate tens of thousands of people dotted the length of the promenade, whilst beyond it beach defences in the event of a possible invasion by sea were in full force.

Barbed wire, as well as lengths of tramlines planted vertically in the sand and resembling some strange species of giant pewter plant, were all to deter the enemy from touching down on the shore. At one point on their walk, Clifford pointed out a large, black spiky object – a British sea mine, intended to ward off any invading fleet, he'd informed Livvy – that had broken loose from its moorings. Soon afterwards, the bomb-disposal officers arrived on the scene to deal with it, and the couple continued on their way.

Even the iconic Blackpool Tower hadn't escaped the trappings, they saw, as they paused to rest on a nearby bench and eat the hot food they had purchased from a friendly vendor. Look-out observers were stationed on it, and the top section of the structure had been removed to be used as a radar station.

'D'you know,' Livvy said, as she tucked into her portion of delicious, locally caught cod, so fresh she reckoned the kiss of life might have brought it back, 'our Joan wanted to be an evacuee when she heard kiddies were being sent here.' The memory brought a rush of gentle happiness, as looking back on the past was wont to do. 'Bawled her eyes out forra week, she did, when she discovered that Bolton children wouldn't be in danger and weren't going anywhere.'

Clifford smiled. 'I can see why. I love this place and I'm a full-grown man. It must be dazzling to the younger lot. Mind, she'd not have lasted long, I bet; norra lot did.'

Those from the towns and cities that would become sitting ducks for the German Luftwaffe and vulnerable to heavy bombing had, at the very start of hostilities, been shipped off to more peaceful, rural areas of Lancashire. Blackpool had been one such place that took in and offered sanctuary to evacuees. Countless people from places such as Liverpool, Manchester and London had arrived here in their droves and billeted in both private and boarding houses. Homesickness had soon driven many of them back; however, some had remained.

'It must have been terrible, you know, for them mams what had to hand their little 'uns over to strangers,' she murmured. 'It was for their own good, mind, eh? I wonder how many who went back ended up copping for it? They should have stayed. This great upheaval for men, women and children right across the country, it's not been ideal by any stretch, but it's needed, aye – what can you do? We just have to grit our teeth and get on with it.'

'I can understand the poor mites missing home, and their mothers in turn missing them, but Blackpool would have been safer,' Clifford agreed. Like Bolton, it had thus far been spared the dreadful bombing. Most high explosives that did fall happened at Squires Gate in an attempt to destroy aircraft production. 'They've only suffered one really deadly attack, here, ain't they? A few years back, aye. An enemy plane on the way back from giving Manchester a pounding dropped a few bombs it must have had left over. I remember reading about it in t' paper.'

'Aye, I did, too. Eight people died. They reckoned the target was most likely the railway sidings.'

They lapsed into silence for a while until he said, nodding to the Tower rising majestically into the dusk-darkened sky up ahead, 'Did you know that a replica stands on the hills in North Wales?'

'What, the Tower?'

'Aye, as a decoy to confuse German pilots on reconnaissance missions and throw them off course. Clever, eh?'

'I bet it took them ages to build – it's bloomin' massive!'

Clifford chuckled, then thinking of something else it grew louder and he said, ''Ere, d'you know that barmy Lord Haw-Haw once announced that the Luftwaffe had bombed Blackpool Tower? He told folk that a picture of it had been published in the German papers, lying on the beach destroyed. Course, it was all fabrication. Bloody silly git, he is.'

Watching Clifford wipe the tears of mirth from his eyes, Livvy tried to laugh along, however she found that she couldn't. Mention of Haw-Haw had made her think of her conversation regarding him with Bertha – and with it home and Carl.

Since arriving, she'd done her utmost to push from her head the awful confrontation earlier, along with all other thoughts of him, loath to let it spoil this precious time, but it was impossible. Despite her best efforts, there he remained, skulking in the recesses of her mind, always. Lord, how she despised him and all that he'd come to represent. Yet more so, she hated herself for allowing him this power over her.

'Speaking of the Tower . . .' Clifford rose and held out a hand. 'Shall we go and sample this ballroom, then, lass?'

Though she placed her hand in his, she made no attempt to stand. 'Lad, about Carl . . .'

'Livvy, I told you. It doesn't matter—'

'It does,' she insisted. And it very obviously did if his instant stony expression at the mention of the American was anything to go by. 'I need you to know that I was telling the truth. There really ain't nowt between me and him, you know.'

'Really?' he asked after a long moment.

'*Really*. You do believe me?'

He tightened his hand around hers and lifted her from the seat. They were standing just inches apart, so close that she could smell the Brylcreem and faint aroma of tobacco on him. Her heart lurched then gave a series of heady thumps in response to it. *If only things were different and circumstances altered – for two pins, she'd have leaned in right here and now and kissed the life from him, she would . . .*

'Livvy?'

'What?' Realising he was gazing at her with a lop-sided smile, she shook herself back to the present. Then: 'Please tell me I didn't say all that out loud!' she blurted in horror, the terrible prospect occurring to her and making its escape before she could stop it.

'Say what out loud? Why, what were you thinking?'

Thank Christ for that. 'Nowt, nowt.'

'Your lips were moving, but no words came out.' His eyes deepened along with his smile. 'Come on, spill: you've got me all intrigued, now.'

'Really, lad, there's nowt to know. Come on, then,' she added, keen to bring the subject to a close and setting forth for the Tower. 'Are we going boogying or what?'

'Well, we'd be daft to pay a visit to Dancing Town, as this place is well known as, and not do, eh?'

As they had expected it would be, the popular Tower Ballroom was packed to the rafters. Stopping dead, Livvy and Clifford gazed around in awe.

Men, the majority in uniform, certainly predominated. As with most places these days, there was a shortage of females in the town, and the arrival of so many personnel had only tipped the imbalance further. Neither were the males just British; the company was made up of an array of nationalities.

The presence of Poles was unsurprising; following Dunkirk, Blackpool had become the administrative headquarters of the Polish Air Force. In fact, the influx to the town had been so great that all of the signs at the Pleasure Beach had been translated into Polish. Moreover, in recent times children and expectant mothers were not the only ones to have been billeted here: GIs, stationed at Warton, had too. As with back home, it was heaving with American servicemen.

Livvy, however, wasn't put off by this. Not all Yanks were alike, after all – in fact, she'd known a great deal who were thoroughly decent sorts. No, you couldn't tar them all with the same brush. One bad apple didn't have to spoil the barrel.

Add to the mix the thousands of civil servants sent

here from the capital, the locals, and tourists like Livvy and Clifford – and every last one desperate for fun and a break from the drudge and grind of the usual routine and work – it could be easily estimated just how bustling was the resort. It was little wonder that entertainment had boomed. The needs and wants of patrons to its many and varied establishments were catered to exuberantly – it was, after all, vital to morale – and they were treated to the best shows and musicals from the biggest stars and the most famous dance bands in the business.

'Eeh, in't it gradely, lad,' Livvy breathed, soaking in the sumptuous surroundings and atmosphere with relish.

Clifford answered with a grin and, whipping her around, making her squeal with laughter, led her on to the dance floor.

They waltzed until their feet ached, and then waltzed some more. At last, Livvy threw up her hands, begging mercy: 'I'm all in.'

'Shall we get ourselves a drink?'

'Ooh, lovely. I could murder one.'

They found a table and Livvy sat down gratefully whilst Clifford went to the bar. Alone, she watched the couples swaying along to the music, then flicked her gaze towards Clifford across the room, and a contented sigh escaped her. It had felt such a novelty, dancing. She hadn't had much experience of it, had she, in the past? The men with whom she'd previously spent time had been a commodity, there to serve a basic function, and the clock had always been ticking. To be close, in a non-sexual sense, and just revel in the mere enjoyment of one another's company with no expectations was alien to her, but very, very nice. She could have remained in his capable arms for ever.

'This has been really great, Livvy,' Clifford said minutes later as they were sipping their drinks. 'Ta for coming, lass.'

'Ta for asking me,' she breathed. 'It's been one of the best days of my life.'

'If I've not said it already, you look absolutely knockout tonight.'

She smiled shyly, which surprised her; she was no shrinking violet, not by any stretch of the imagination. She couldn't pin down what it was about this man; he brought out another side to her, made her feel as giddy and awkward as a schoolgirl when he spoke so. 'You did say, before we left the boarding house earlier. But thanks very much all the same.'

'Thank *you* for choosing to be here with me. Every bloke in the room has his eye on you, you know. I felt like a king just now, holding you on the floor.'

'Eeh, lad.' The touching sentiment, spoken with such open honesty, brought a lump to her throat. 'And I felt like your queen.'

They danced some more, rested and repleted themselves with further drinks, and repeated several more times throughout the night. At last, securing another table and sitting down, they settled back to chat.

'Growing up, it was just me and Mam. She was a gradely woman, Livvy – you would have got on like a house on fire. Toiled her fingers to the knuckles, she did, to keep us; had a series of daily jobs. She even worked as a knocker-upper for years, waking up folk for their work of a morning with her peashooter at the bedroom windows, earning sixpence a day.' He nodded when Livvy smiled. 'Well, it all totted up, the pennies. Aye, a woman of many trades was my mam.'

'She sounds lovely.'

'Aye. When she died, I were adrift. It was all I'd ever known, just me and her. I'll always be thankful to our Celia for taking me in. She helped me climb out from the pit of grief. I'm very fond of my aunt, aye. It's why I'll not fight, you know,' he said suddenly in the next breath – Livvy's eyes widened. He normally never brought up the subject of his conscientious objectiveness.

'My mam, she begged me, made me vow to her on her deathbed that I'd not go. Said I must do whatever it took but I must not join up. She said that if she passed over to the other side and I were to meet her there shortly after, she'd tan my backside for me and never speak to me again, heaven or not.' He flashed a half-smile. 'She was plagued with thoughts of me mangled or blown to bits on a battlefield in truth, that's the top and bottom of it. My father had perished the same way in the first lot; she couldn't bear the same thing happening with me. Thoughts of it almost sent her mad.'

Livvy swallowed hard at this and nodded. She could understand that, all right. Her nightmares about Clive suffering the same fate haunted her still.

'I don't really remember him, Dad; I was young, you see. Mind you, I do have one cloudy memory of him having me march to the kitchen when I wanted a jam butty . . .' Clifford smiled again. 'He was full of fun, aye, by all accounts, and a good man. Anyroad, when Mam had gone, I talked with Celia about what she'd had me do. I were tortured, you see. Watching fellas at every turn taking up the call to arms without a second thought, and there was me, sitting back happy to do nowt . . . well, I weren't happy. I were miserable, sick to my stomach with myself and wracked with shame. Celia was horrified. She insisted I upheld Mam's wishes, said it was unforgivable to go back on a dying promise. So I did. I did, and every day since I've hated myself for it.'

Livvy remained silent as he let his gaze travel around the room at the servicemen with an almost hungry expression, understanding that he needed to speak this, must have the release, in his own time and way. She wouldn't prompt him.

'None of the blokes at work speak to me, you know,' he continued after an age. 'They reckon I'm subnormal – mebbe I am. A freak, a coward. Less than, a half-man—'

'Don't,' she intervened quietly at last, wouldn't hear him badmouthing himself. 'You're none of them things.'

'No? Try telling folk that. My reasoning to them just don't make sense, and I can't say as I blame them for it. Others, other conchies, they have real convictions, you know? Although like me they're torn between duty to their land and to themselves, hounded by self-doubt, that's where the similarities end. For whether it be on religious grounds or moral ones, a feeling that war is unacceptable and murder a mortal sin, it's true beliefs they carry, aye. Even them what won't fight because they're scared witless – and what's wrong with that, eh? We're only human at the day's end, can't all be heroes – they too have good reason not to join the ranks.

'Me, on t' other hand? I stop behind because my mother said I must. Christ, how pathetic does that sound . . . I had to bend the truth on that at the tribunal; couldn't admit the real reason, or they'd have never passed me. Nah, unlike the others, I've no thoughts on the matter either way, no anti-war sentiment or otherwise, no strong opinions – not even weak ones. Nor am I frightened. Nowt. I'm just disloyal to my country.'

'You are not, Clifford Bamford.' Taking his hand, she lifted it to her lips and kissed it tenderly. 'Not to me.'

He closed his eyes and turned his head. 'As much as I love you even more for saying it, lass, it shan't change what's in here.' He tapped his breast. 'I hide away whilst there's universal bloodshed and suffering going on at every which turn, every second of the day. It's a hell I'm in, just like those in the army, only a private one of my own what no one sees. No, this inner conflict shan't leave me. It's summat I shall have to live with on my conscience for the rest of my life.'

'You'll not renounce your status one day, will you? Join the military?' The merest notion of it brought Livvy out in a cold sweat. 'I can see it in your eyes; it's like a fire smouldering there . . . Please say you'll not.'

'Livvy, don't ask that of me—'

'Please, lad, you mustn't. I'll not let them have you, too. They'll not have another man that I—' She paused to lick her lips, her breathing heavy. 'I'm . . . sorry, I . . .'

'Another man that you what, Livvy?'

'Love,' she whispered. 'I love you.'

He did nothing for a full minute. Then, taking a deep breath, he blew out air slowly. 'Clive,' he murmured.

'Wha—' Her shock was absolute. 'You know, that I was wed before?'

'Madge,' he explained. 'She told me a bit ago.'

'But . . . Grandma don't speak of it; nobody does!'

'I think she felt she had to,' he said, lowering his gaze. 'It was after that night in your kitchen: you remember, after the cinema? I'd told you how fond I was of you, and you said summat like you couldn't be who I wanted you to be? Well, I put it to Madge when her and Celia got home. I poured out my heart to her, told her how much I . . . Well, you know.'

How much he loved her. Livvy did.

'She told me a bit about what happened.'

'Clive. The house we shared on Red Lane.'

'Aye.'

'The baby?'

He nodded. 'I know there can't be any more children – and lass, I don't care a fig. So, if that's it, what's kept you from being with me, then don't let's be parted any more. By, if you could only see into my heart, what I hold there for you—'

'And I you. But, lad, it's not just that. There's things, other things that I've . . . Who I was. What has happened. You deserve so much better than me. Eeh, you do.'

194

'Tell me. I guarantee you, there's not a thing you could say that could change how I feel about you.'

She agonised over whether she should for all of half a second before shaking her head. As surprisingly cathartic as their heart to heart had been, for them both she sensed, she wasn't ready and was unsure whether she ever would be to talk about the prostitution – even less so Carl Rivera. She didn't doubt that Clifford loved her, but warts and all? Would he really be able to see past it all? *There's not a thing you could say that could change how I feel* . . . Words were all well and good, however reality had a way of turning out rather differently. The prospect of him viewing her in another light, his outrage, disgust, would break her. She couldn't – wouldn't – risk it.

'Not yet,' she told him at last. 'Not yet.'

Their walk back to the boarding house shortly afterwards was fraught. Emotive tension crackled in the air between them. When they reached the landing, they stood facing one another closely in the dim light.

'Goodnight, Clifford.'

'Goodnight, Livvy.'

She stood on tiptoe and pressed her lips against his waiting ones in a long, slow kiss. Then she turned and made her lone way to her room.

The strength it took to keep moving forward and not run back to him almost killed her.

Chapter Nine

'JOAN, LASS? WHAT the ruddy hell are you doing?'

The girl whipped around, onion and knife in hand, and taking in her appearance fully from the front, Livvy fell about chortling.

'Laugh all you like, but I think it's a good idea.' Joan's muffled response from behind the gas mask she wore was barely intelligible. 'Strong, these onions are. I couldn't see a thing trying to peel them – my eyes were streaming.'

Still chuckling, Livvy shook her head. 'By, you're a tonic, you. You're right, mind, it is good thinking, that. Them things have come in useful after all. I know a woman what were telling me that she dons hers whenever she has to change the baby's dirty napkin.'

Dragging off the rubber contraption, Joan sucked in fresh air gratefully. 'This don't smell much better. Pooh, the pong!'

'I can imagine!'

'So did you have a nice time at Vera's?'

Livvy crossed to the kettle, saying vaguely over her shoulder, 'Aye, it was all right.'

'Grandma should be here soon. She's coming round for dinner, asked me to set out another place.'

This had her smiling. She enjoyed their family Sunday meals. 'Where's Grandad?'

'Spending a penny. I think his piles are playing him up again; he's been up there ages.'

'Oh, how lovely, and just when we're about to eat,' Livvy muttered. *Oh, to be back home!* 'D'you need any help, lass?'

'No, you're all right. I'm nearly done, just have to shove the dish in t' oven.'

She smiled again, stroked Joan's hair, and made back for the living room. Morris appeared just as she was settling down in the chair by the hearth. He flicked his finger at her, indicating that she must move, and she rose with a roll of her eyes and relinquished the seat to him, crossing instead to the sofa.

'All right, lass?'

'I am. You?'

'No, I bloody well ain't. My you-know-whats are giving me gyp. Terrible, it is; I'd not even wish this on Hitler hisself—'

'All right, all right. There's no need to go on. Anyroad, shurrup, you'll be putting us all off our grub.'

He harrumphed and reached for his pipe and

newspaper. 'Well, pardon me for bleedin' breathing, I'm sure.'

Though Livvy clicked her tongue, her eyes were filled with affection. 'And don't you be harping on about it when Grandma arrives – you know what she's like. I fancy a bit of peace today.'

'Blimey, you can't do nowt beneath this roof without getting a rollicking for it! I must have been one bad bugger in a former life to deserve this. Aye, a *reet* bad bugger.'

'Now you remember what I said,' she told him, getting to her feet as a knock sounded at the front door. 'Just keep your mucky ailments to yourself.'

'Mucky? Mucky? There's nowt mucky about me, you bold swine. Had a stand-up, all-over wash at the sink just this morn, I did!'

Grinning and shaking her head, Livvy went to admit her grandmother.

'What's he blathering on about this time? I could hear that gob of his from the end of the path.'

'Come in.' Livvy chuckled, pressing herself flat against the hallway wall to allow Madge's frame room enough to fit past. 'The kettle's just on.'

Their dinner was over with and the dishes washed when Madge said to Livvy, after making sure first that the attentions of the others were on the wireless, 'So, has whatever that was making you melancholy passed, now?'

She thought about her answer for a moment. She'd cried to Madge on the shops over her troubles concerning Carl, and nothing had improved nor been resolved on that score. Nonetheless, she wasn't in so dark a frame of mind as she had been. 'Not really, Grandma, but I am feeling brighter than I was.'

'Good. I don't like seeing thee – seeing either of my lasses – blue. It don't do you no favours, you know, getting down in the dumps. You must fight them urges – they'll swamp you, else.'

If only it were that simple. 'Sometimes you can't help it, though, can you?'

'No, for as I've said afore, life's a swine at times,' was Madge's dry reply. 'Mind, it's how we choose to handle them situations that sorts the wheat from the chaff. You're made from sturdy stock, Livvy. Just remember that.'

She hadn't been lying just now; despite everything, she was feeling all right. She and Clifford had left one another on good terms this morning upon their return to Bolton. They had decided not to walk the full length home together and had parted company at Blair Lane. It was true that their presence together this morning, after them both spending the night away from the estate, may possibly have raised some suspicion, however it hadn't really been worry of censure that had led their decision. In fact, they found it rather amusing – and ultimately a little thrilling, playing out the cloak-and-dagger act.

Last night's outpourings hadn't been mentioned, and Livvy had been happy to follow suit and let the incident lie. She'd said all that she was prepared to, at least for the time being – best it remained in the past now. Their declarations for one another, however, had been acknowledged if not in words then by looks and hand squeezes, particularly on the train journey home.

Where was this all leading, Livvy had asked of herself over and over, and knew that Clifford surely wondered the same. So much stood in the way of them being together, it was impossible to imagine a point when things might be different. She supposed that the main thing was that he now knew without question what was in her heart, as she did with him. It wasn't enough, of course not, if they couldn't progress with this knowledge further, but there was no getting around the issue just yet. For the time being, security in the surety of their feelings for one another would have to do.

'I've been thinking,' Joan announced, pulling her sister from her reverie.

'Bet that was painful,' mumbled Morris, then grinned when the girl poked her tongue out at him.

'I want to get a job.'

'Aye?' Livvy asked. 'What's brought this on, lass?'

'Doris has got herself a new job at Whitaker's in town, and she said they're looking to take on more staff. It'd be gradely, us two working together, and I would like to earn my own money. I could help out, tip up brass towards the housekeeping.'

Livvy nodded slowly. Since working at the chippy, her income had seriously depleted. A few extra bob coming in might well solve the problem. Besides, it really was time to let Joan spread her wings. Being cooped up at home with only a cantankerous old man for company and her days filled with washing, cleaning and cooking wasn't healthy. The poor girl should be out there in the world, meeting people, experiencing new things, gaining new skills – and more importantly having some fun. She'd end up an old maid before her time if they weren't careful. All in all, it was a splendid idea.

'Well, I for one think you should go for it, lass.'

'Honest, Livvy? You really do?'

'Aye. And 'ere, they'd be lucky to have you.'

'Can I go round and see Doris now, tell her the news?' Joan was hopping from foot to foot. 'Eeh, she'll be pleased as punch. Can I?'

'Course you can, go on. Don't be too late back, mind, in the blackout.'

When she'd gone, the adults shared looks with one another and smiled.

'The child's all grown up,' Madge stated softly.

Morris and Livvy, the definite trace of a tear in the latter's eye, nodded concurrence.

'Hello, stranger.'

Returning the greeting, Vera leaned her elbows on the counter. 'How you fettling, Livvy?'

'Oh, you know.'

'You've seen the blighter again, ain't you?'

Putting a finger to her lips and inclining her head to the back room, where Bertha was busy, she said through the side of her mouth, 'Have I! He only collared me on Saturday last, in front of Clifford.' She'd told Vera months ago of the man's budding feelings for her and that she felt the same. 'D'you know he actually stopped us in the street outside and demanded to know where we were headed? The brass-necked cheek of him. Honestly, I didn't know where to look.'

'Oo-er. Did you tell Clifford the truth, what the sod did to you?'

'Did I bloomin' 'eck.'

'Then how did you explain Carl away? Surely Clifford wanted to know who he were?'

'I brazened it out, had to, said he was just a customer who'd taken a shine to me. I thought forra minute they might come to fisticuffs.'

'Happen they should have! You should tell him, you know, Clifford. Let him give that Yank the damn

202

good hiding he deserves. That's what he's short of, you know. *That* would halt his canter, all right!'

'I can't, Vera. Clifford can never know.'

'Why not? I've told you before, you've done nowt wrong—'

'Just drop it, eh?' Livvy's tone was harsher than intended. She sighed. 'Sorry, love. I just ... I just can't tell him.'

'Where was the two of you going, anyroad?' Vera asked after a minute when Livvy had finished serving a new customer.

'Actually, we ... well, Clifford invited me to Blackpool.'

'Did you stop over?'

'We did.'

'Just the two of you?'

The smile that crept along Livvy's face evoked laughter as dirty as a drain from her friend – she pointed a warning finger, grinning. 'Nowt happened, Vera, not like that, so you can get them mucky thoughts from your mind. I did finally tell him, mind, how I really feel.'

'Eeh, love. At last.' Vera's smile was filled with genuine happiness for her. 'So what happens now?'

'How d'you mean?'

'Well, surely youse'll move things forward, now you both know where you stand?'

'That's just it.' Livvy let her shoulder rise and fall in a helpless motion. 'We don't.'

'Livvy, love, you're not making sense.'

She went on to explain about her predicaments preventing her from taking matters further. 'Now do you see? I can't tell him about Carl because the truth about the prostitution might come out. Then where would I be? Who in God's name is ever going to want a whore for a wife, Vera?'

The woman made a strange sound in the back of her throat and lowered her head.

'Oh. Love. I'm sorry. I didn't mean . . .'

'No, it's fine. It is, really. I know I'm destined to be a crusty owd spinster, don't worry about it—'

'Don't be angry. It came out all wrong, that's all. Anyroad, it were me I was on about, not you. You'll find someone, aye.'

Vera didn't respond to this, simply trained her gaze on the street outside.

'Look, love, why don't we have a night out, eh? Just me and you, have a reet good laugh, like we used to. What d'you say?'

The woman glanced back at her, her interest piqued. 'Where at?'

'We could go to the Palais. To actually dance, this time,' she added meaningfully, with an arched eyebrow. 'Come on, let's let our hair down and live a little, shall we? Have ourselfs some fun?'

'Go on then, you've twisted my arm.' Vera's smile was firmly back in place. 'It'll be nice, aye. I have missed you, yer know.'

'And me you, love,' Livvy said, pressing her hand. 'Meet me here later at finishing. We'll nip to yours and I can borrow one of your frocks. We should just make the interval if we're quick about it.'

Getting ready later at Vera's rooms was lovely and felt just like old times. They were in good spirits when they left and headed off the short distance to the Palais.

'Shall we pay our sixpences and go up to the balcony for a coffee, listen to the band?' Livvy suggested shortly after they arrived. 'I like it there.'

'Aye, if you like.'

'Come on, let's get our tickets.'

Swaying in time to the music, they were chatting until Vera broke off mid-conversation. Something – or someone – had clearly caught her eye. Watching her friend's squint widen and her lips part in obvious surprise, Livvy almost didn't dare look. *Please Lord, no.* Surely, it couldn't be . . . On a Monday? But the GIs were away and busy at their base during the week – weren't they? How . . .?

'Love? You need to see this.'

'Vera, is it . . . Is he . . .'

'Find out for yourself – there, on the floor! Blind as a bat I might well be, but I'd know that lovely mop of curls anywhere.'

Livvy swivelled her eyes downwards.

At first, she didn't believe what she was seeing. She did a double take, then another. Then her mouth fell wide and she gasped aloud. 'What the . . . Why, the young minx!'

Joan, her head thrown back, and laughing without a care in the world, was dancing in the centre of the floor with a soldier. Beside her, her friend Doris was equally enthralled in the music with a dashing man in uniform. Livvy was dumbstruck.

'She's grown up since last I saw her,' Vera remarked in amusement. 'How old is she now?'

'Fif-bloody-teen. Well, sixteen in a few weeks, but . . .'

'Ah, well then. Ay, cut the lass some slack. I were going out to dance halls way before that – just turned fourteen, I think I was, when I started.'

This did nothing to ease Livvy's concerns – quite the opposite, coming from who it had. She could only be grateful that tonight had been about enjoying themselves and nothing more – and thank God she'd given all that stuff up altogether. To think what would have happened had she still been picking up men here and the girl had witnessed it . . . The prospect didn't bear thinking about.

'She shouldn't be here, she's far too young. And look, look at that!' she blustered, pointing. 'The bold devil's wearing one of my best frocks. We'll see about

206

this – watch her face in a minute when she cops sight of me!'

When she reached the floor, Livvy stood watching for a moment, hands on hips. Then, dodging dancers and striding forward, she tapped Joan on the shoulder. 'Enjoying yourself, are you?'

'Oh. Livvy! Hello . . .' The girl's expression was indeed one to behold.

'Fancy seeing you here.'

'We were just . . . I were just . . .'

'I know exactly what "you were just".' Flicking her chin to her sister's dance partner, she added, 'You, sonny, hop it.'

'You can't do that!' Joan's stance now matched her own – planting her hands on her hips, she stared Livvy out, her sapphire eyes flashing. 'You're *embarrassing* me. Anyroad, I ain't doing no harm!'

'Grandma and Grandad would have kittens if they knew where you were—'

'Well, they're not going to, are they?' Joan countered. 'Not unless you telltale on me.'

This attitude was unfamiliar; Livvy was thrown. Joan had her moments, like any teenager, of course she did, but this boldness and outright defiance was quite new to her – she was momentarily at a loss how best to approach it. 'Lass, listen—'

'Why should I? You never listen to me!'

'What?'

'Don't you even want to know why we're here, me and Doris? You ain't even asked. Well, I'll tell you: I got the position at Whitaker's. Aye, had the interview this afternoon, I did, and they've taken me on. We were celebrating.'

'Eeh . . . Well, that is good news, but—'

'Why must there always be a "but"? I'm sick of you always trying to tell me what to do. You ain't my mam, Livvy, however much you might like to think yourself as such. Nor am I a babby no more. Just leave me alone, eh?'

The vitriol left her shaken to the core. Stunned, she could but stare back in silence. The lambasting had stung. She hardly recognised the girl.

'I'll look after her, honest.' Doris, appearing now decidedly uncomfortable and evidently keen to defuse matters, patted Livvy's arm awkwardly. 'My mam and dad know where I am and don't mind – they met here, you see, at one of the weekly mill dances. Well, it was my mam who worked in t' mill, Dad didn't. But you could still attend the dances even if you weren't employed there – someone from the company, who had hired the hall here, would sell tickets on the door to normal members of the public, and—'

'I know how mill dances work,' Livvy snapped, slicing through her babble. Then, seeing the girl flinch, she said on a sigh, 'I'm sorry, Doris, didn't mean to shout at you. It's just . . .' Bringing her gaze back to rest on her sister, she let her shoulders rise and fall. 'I worry about you because I love you.'

'But there's no need: the Palais is safe!'

Oh Joan. It's not you I don't trust, don't you see that? A master in all things relating to the male of the species, Livvy knew exactly the workings of a man's mind and just what some were capable of. The thought of some lech attempting to take advantage of the innocent, precious being before her was like a rotting in the pit of her guts.

'We'll be reet, really we will,' her sister went on. Her tone was cajoling now. She smiled. 'Go on, our Livvy, let me stay. Please?'

'You've got to let go sometime, love. Now's as good a time as any. Give her a chance to prove herself, eh?' Vera said quietly in her ear. 'What do you have to lose?'

That was exactly what Livvy was afraid of.

'She'd better be back when I get home.'

'Course she will. Stop fretting.'

Livvy, after much persuading from her friend, had agreed not to cramp the girls' style by staying and had left them to enjoy themselves at the Palais. She and Vera had taken themselves off to the Fleece, where the latter had insisted that Livvy would feel better when she had a few drinks inside her. The assumption couldn't have been further from the truth. Several beers in and Livvy, rather than being relaxed, had turned maudlin.

'We were only saying yesterday, me and the others, how Joan's growing up. Well, I don't like it. It's hard, you know, letting go.'

'Ruddy hell, love.' Vera rolled her eyes. 'You sound like a mother hen mourning its empty coop!'

Losing herself at the bottom of her glass, Livvy agreed inwardly. After everything, Joan did feel like a product of her making, it was true. Hadn't she had to step up and be a parent to her after theirs had passed away? However, it wasn't only that, was it, she admitted to herself, and her mood dipped further still. Unable to have another child of her own, she'd turned all of her love and attentions on to the girl even more, had poured her soul into caring for her, raising her, keeping her safe. Now Joan was a woman, didn't need her any more. Livvy's job was done. What's more, she hadn't a clue what to do. Just what was her role now; what on earth would she do with herself?

'You ought to be proud rather than sad that Joan has turned into such a headstrong and independent lass,' Vera pressed on. 'You've done a gradely job.'

'I suppose.'

'Eeh, come on. Let's get another drink.'

A half an hour later and Livvy, with no small help

from her friend, was feeling marginally better. Vera had coaxed a regular into pounding out a few tunes on the piano and soon, the whole pub was singing along.

''Ere, Vera, guess what I found myself doing earlier?' she said with a wink and a smile over the jovial medley.

Grinning, the woman leaned in, eager for some juicy gossip. 'Ooh, I don't know – what? Was it summat mucky?'

'You, girl, have a one-track mind! No, it weren't mucky, you daft beggar. I did my bit for the war effort – summat decent this time!' she was swift to add when Vera cackled. It had been a running joke when they worked together, their servicing of the army's men, as they saw it, and doing their bit by sending them off happy. 'You know them members of the Red Cross, what stand at their selling centre on Oxford Street flogging emblems?'

'Aye?'

'Well, I bought one from them whilst passing, on my way back from getting a butter pie for my dinner from Ye Olde Pastie Shoppe. As I were leaving, I overheard one of the women saying they needed more volunteers. I offered my services. I'm to help out forra few hours once a week.'

'You?' Vera bent double with mirth.

'Aye, what's wrong with that?'

'Oh, I can just see you now, dressed in that get-up!'

Picturing in her mind's eye the long white apron with bold scarlet cross emblazoned on the bib, and bandana-style white hat bearing the same stigmata, Livvy chuckled. Her friend did have a point.

'There you'll be,' Vera went on, 'with your collection tin and cardboard tray hanging from your neck holding all the little emblems for sale, shouting: "Keep this flag flying! Give all you can!"'

'Give over, you,' Livvy laughed, swatting at the guffawing woman. 'It just felt right to. Anyroad, it ain't much different to what I wear at the chippy, really, is it?'

'I don't suppose it is. You know, there ain't half been some change in you these past weeks. I'm not saying it's a bad thing,' she went on when Livvy frowned. 'No, it's nice, really. You're different. Normal.'

'What about you, Vera?' Livvy's tone was soft. 'Don't you ever think about giving it all up, getting yourself a regular job?'

'Sometimes,' she admitted. 'Truth is, I don't much look at it in t' same light any more. Not since you went your separate way and I'm back to doing it alone. To be honest, it's becoming a bit tiresome.'

'Look for summat new, then. Eeh, you'd not regret

it, you know. It's the best thing I ever did. You could happen give war work a try again, aye.'

When in the spring of 1941 women between the ages of eighteen and sixty had been required to register for essential war work, and later in the year those aged between twenty and thirty conscripted, Livvy, despite falling into this category, hadn't met the criteria and wasn't required to comply. Joan had been under fourteen, and Livvy's domestic duties had been heavy – both Madge and Morris had been suffering from poor health at the time. Livvy's delicate mental state following her tragic losses was an additional factor.

Left half blind due to illness during childhood, the same applied to Vera. It had been her dream, she'd revealed, to be a barrage balloon operator, but her medical exam had let her down.

'I know your eyesight's not too clever,' added Livvy, 'but I'm sure you'd find something.'

'Mebbe,' was the woman's thoughtful reply.

The friends enjoyed a few more drinks before parting ways on the corner of Bradshawgate – Vera to make for the local pubs to try to pick up one or two punters before calling it a night, and Livvy to head to the bus stop and Top o'th' Brow.

'Call into the Palais if you can, will you, love, make sure our Joan's not still hanging about?' she called to

213

the woman's retreating back. 'If you do spot her, you send the beggar home!'

'Will do,' Vera assured her with a chuckle, lifting an arm in farewell.

Throughout the journey, she kept her fingers crossed that her sister hadn't let her down and that, as Vera suspected, she'd be there waiting for her upon her return. Sure enough, when she entered the living room, Joan was seated with their grandfather on the sofa, listening to a late show on the wireless. Smiling, Livvy inwardly sighed in relief.

'All right?'

Joan nodded, then: 'Another parcel came for you.'

The smile slid at once from her face.

'Don't worry, I'll not ask to see what's inside – I know you'll only say no like last time.'

Ignoring the girl's caustic remark, Livvy crossed to the table, where, sitting atop, was indeed a package, smaller this time, but wrapped once more in the same brown paper. How had he even managed to get this here tonight?

'Who're they from, anyroad?'

'I told you, lass, I don't know,' she lied. 'Left on the doorstep again, was it?'

'That's right. Will you just bin it without looking what it is, as you did the other one?'

She'd had to spin the story to avoid awkward questions. 'Aye, probably.'

'Well, I think you're barmy. I reckon you've gone and got yourself an admirer. Aye, there could be all sorts of goodies in it.'

'I don't care, I don't want them. Now,' she continued, desperate to change the subject, 'who fancies a sup of tea?'

That night, long after the others had retired to their beds, Livvy found herself once more standing over the table chewing her nail.

'Damn you,' she whispered to the empty room. '*Damn* you – why can't you just leave me be?'

Knowing it had to be done, she removed the twine and tore at the paper – and let out a strangled cry.

A butchered pig's heart was staring back at her.

There was a note included this time. With shaking hands, she lifted the blood-smeared page and unfolded it:

If I could tear out my own and give it to you, I would.

Instead, this will have to do.

Love you, baby.

Groping for a chair and dropping into it, Livvy buried her head in her arms.

Chapter Ten

THE THIRD DAY of September marked four years since the outbreak of war and had left many this bright blue morning with a sense of despondency. Who would have thought, given all the false talk in the beginning of the conflict being over by Christmas, that they would be stuck in the same position after so long, the world a battlefield still. Livvy certainly wouldn't have.

Joan's birthday had been and gone, and the girl was thoroughly enjoying her new job. More so, however, she seemed intent on enjoying the new-found freedoms it gave her. With regular money in her pocket and fewer demands from indoor obligations, it was clear she now viewed the world as her oyster. Barely a night went by when she wasn't out with Doris, painting the town red, just as she'd vowed that they would.

News that the Allies had invaded Italy was the talk of the shops when Livvy had been for provisions just now. Not that she paid much attention; she had far more pressing matters on her mind. Namely a certain American serviceman whose reign of harassment over her showed no signs of diminishing.

Not only were his visits to the chip shop when he knew her to be on shift still occurring, but the disturbing parcels to her door had become ever more frequent. What's more, he'd discovered her by chance one day carrying out her new voluntary duties with the Red Cross. His presence even there, lounging on the corner of Oxford Street watching her every move intently, was a regular one. There really was no escaping him any which way she turned.

She'd exhausted every option. She'd warned, threatened and, when that failed, resorted to pleading with him to leave her alone, yet all to no avail. He was determined to make her love him, he insisted, and nothing she said or did would alter his mission. His delusionality knew no bounds, it seemed, which only frightened her all the more.

At her tether's end, she'd taken to once again staying at home as much as was possible. Besides work and nipping across the way to see Clifford, she hardly set foot outside the door.

Joan was chatting at number nineteen's gate with Madge and Celia when Livvy arrived back at Glaister Lane. Crossing the small stretch of road, she made her way across to the group.

'Have you seen him, lass, the rag and bone man, on his rounds today?' her grandmother asked.

'I've not. I've been busy inside cleaning the house since I opened my eyes – why?'

'I need a new donkey stone, don't I.' Lifting a bundle of rags with which to exchange with him for the scouring block, Madge shook it irritably. 'Filthy that doorstep is of Celia's, and there's nowt I can do about it 'til the totter's been.'

Livvy smiled fondly. Dressed in her usual blue and white silk frock, as old as Joan was, voluminous pinny, heavy clogs and steel curlers peeking out from the turban covering her head, Madge looked as if she was ready to throw herself on the ragman's cart. By, but she loved the bones of her, she did. 'I'll keep an eye out for him through the window and flag him down if he shows.'

'Aye. 'Ere,' Madge announced in the next breath, jerking a thumb in her younger granddaughter's direction, 'did you know this one's gorra chap?'

'No, I didn't.' Watching as Joan lowered her eyes, a soft blush appearing and the ghost of a smile at her lips – proof if ever it was needed that the statement was indeed true – Livvy did her best to mask her hurt. The girl was so secretive and closed off from her lately; she felt she barely knew her these days. There was a time when she would come to her with anything. 'Why don't I know about this, eh?' She attempted joviality, but it sounded flat even to her own ears. 'So, who is he, then?'

'Just some lad.' Joan shrugged. 'I met him at the Palais.'

'Aye, well, you just mind yourself, d'you hear?' Madge sniffed. 'Best to keep your legs crossed now than your fingers crossed later.'

'God's sake, Grandma!'

'I speak only the truth, Joan. You've yet to learn it, my lass, but you will.'

Livvy shot her sister a 'take no notice' look and nodded down at the shopping in her hands. 'You busy?' she asked her on impulse.

Joan shook her head. 'I'm not in work on Fridays, as you know; the day's my own. Why?'

'You fancy coming on a walk?'

Again, the girl let her shoulders rise and fall. 'If you like.'

'Gradely. I'll just drop these things off indoors; I shan't be a minute.'

'I thought you said you'd keep a lookout for the totter for me?' Madge demanded as Livvy turned to hurry for home. 'Eeh, I don't know. These young-sters of today, Celia; I can't fathom them, can you?'

'Not I, Madge.'

'If you want summat doing, do it yourself, eh . . .'

Rolling her eyes, Livvy ignored it and quickened her step.

'They don't half go on, don't they?' Joan said minutes later as the sisters were passing up Monks Lane. 'Give me earhole ache, they do. And aye, Grandad's not much better.'

Livvy grinned agreement. 'Mind, we'd not be without them.'

'I bloody would,' the girl muttered. 'I can't wait to get out of this place.'

Frowning, Livvy slowed to a halt, forcing Joan to do likewise. 'What d'you mean by that?'

'Nowt.'

'Lass?'

'Well, I'm not going to stop around here forever, am I?' she retorted, folding her arms tightly in annoyance.

'No? And where *will* you go, like?'

She was silent for a long moment. Then that shrug again: 'Don't know yet. Ain't decided.'

Reasoning that she was simply sounding off and that it was best to let the matter lie lest it started a row, something all too common of late, Livvy closed her mouth. The last thing she wanted was for the girl to flounce off – another regularity – and miss out on the opportunity of spending some time with her.

'Where we going, anyway?'

Livvy held up the small wicker basket she'd brought along with her. 'Does this not give you a clue?'

'Wild fruit picking?'

'Aye!'

Joan's expression relaxed somewhat at this and she unfurled her arms, letting them swing loosely by her sides. 'We've not been for ages, have we?'

'No, lass. We should, an' all, really – every little helps, makes the rations stretch out further. I enjoy it, too, do you?' And at Joan's nod: 'I'll make a pie later, eh, with whatever we manage to scavenge.'

'That'll be nice.'

By but this lass was an enigma – her ruddy moods changed more often than the English weather. Still, no matter how grown up she liked to think herself, it seemed she still wasn't too old for whimberry pie . . . Smiling to herself, Livvy led the way on to New Lane towards the open greens of Harwood.

The basket was half filled with blackberries and elderberries – a good substitute for currants – and they had been cutting deeper through the woodland for a few minutes when they spotted the clump of hawthorn bushes up ahead. They instinctively made a beeline for them. Sugar being in such short supply as it was, making jam from the haws was out of the question. They had, however, gone towards some lovely-tasting chutney last year. Dropping to their haunches, they set to collecting the ruby fruits.

'So what's this beau of yours like, then?' Livvy asked as they were busy picking, keeping her tone as nonchalant as she could. In reality, she was itching to know all about the young buck and just what designs he had on her sister.

'Handsome,' Joan said, and when Livvy raised an eyebrow, giggled. 'Eeh, he's gradely,' she opened up, her face animated, 'and he'll not let me buy a single drink when we're out, you know. Reet kind, he is, like that.'

'Nowt stronger than lemonade, I hope.'

'Course not.'

This eased Livvy's mind at least. 'So what does he do? In t' forces, is he?'

'Aye. Oh, why can't this wicked war just be over with!' she blasted out suddenly, and tears gushed from her eyes. 'I hate it, I hate it!'

'Eeh, ay, what's to do with you?' Rushing to draw the girl into her arms, Livvy shushed her, rocking her to and fro. 'What was all that in aid of?' she asked gently when Joan's emotions had subsided. 'Come on, you can tell me.'

'I can't!'

'Course you can. You can tell me owt, you know that.'

'He's asked me to marry him.'

A long breath escaped her. 'Eeh, lass . . .' She swore beneath her breath.

'I know it's quick, Livvy – we've only been stepping out forra few weeks – but it's love. Honest, it is. He said he wants me to be his wife, but not yet, not until after the war. He don't want nowt to happen and have me left a young widow. I just want it to be *over*.'

Her throat had thickened with tears. She held Joan closer.

It was like leaving her body and looking in on herself all those years ago, with Clive. She'd known, too, hadn't she, without a shred of doubt, that steadfast surety in their love, despite the short time they had been together. It would be nothing short of arrogant to dismiss this girl's feelings as the folly of youth; sheer hypocrisy when she'd gone through exactly the same thing. At least Joan was being made to wait. That was good. God forbid she did hurtle headlong into marriage and finish up as she had: a dead husband, a dead baby, and nothing to fill her life with ever since but mind-eroding grief and an emptiness in her heart that never abated. It was a fate she wouldn't have wished upon her worst enemy.

'Well, I think that's very sensible,' she murmured finally. 'This chap of yours seems like a very mature young man.'

'You mean you're not mad?' her sister sniffed, craning her neck to lock eyes pooled with tears on to her.

'No, no.'

'I thought you'd hit the roof when you found out.'

Smiling, Livvy stroked back hair that had escaped its pins and was sticking damply to Joan's brow. 'I love you, yer dafty. That means I want only the best for you. If you say you're happy with this lad, then you have my blessings, lass. Just you be careful, eh?'

'I know, I know – keep my hand on my ha'penny,' Joan reeled off their grandfather's warning. 'I wouldn't do . . . anything . . . *you* know . . . I'm not that stupid.'

'Well, I'm glad to hear it.' Livvy laughed softly. 'There is one condition, mind, to you continuing to see him?'

'What condition, Livvy?'

'I want to meet him. Deal?'

Snuggling back into her, Joan nodded. 'Deal.'

'If he gets my seal of approval . . . Well, we'll see where we go from there.'

'Can I come in? I come bearing pie . . .'

Stooping to sniff at the cloth-covered tin Livvy carried, Clifford rubbed his stomach. 'By gum, you can, that smells gradely.'

She followed him through to the living room and on to the kitchen, saying over her shoulder, 'I'll dish you some up. Is Grandma and your aunty in?'

'Nope – cinema again.' He chuckled. 'They're becoming a right pair of screen fans, them two. So how was your day?'

Covering a yawn with her hand, she laughed. 'Does that answer your question? I'm dog tired.'

After returning from Harwood and spending the next few hours baking, she'd had to change and head into town to put in a shift at the chip shop. Then it was home again, check on Morris and Joan, tidy around and make herself presentable to pay Clifford a visit. There just never seemed to be enough hours in the day.

'Sit yourself down. I'll make us a brew.'

She put up no resistance as he led her to a seat and eased her into it. 'Eeh, ta, lad. I'll not say no.'

When the tea was made and he'd joined her on the sofa, he sat eating his slice of pie without speaking, whilst Livvy sipped her drink in peace. At last, he placed his empty plate on the floor by his feet and spoke.

'Livvy?'

'Hm?'

'Can I ask you summat?'

She nodded.

'Is somebody pestering you?'

The question knocked the wind from her sails. She scrambled about for something to say, but no words would come. In the end, and much to her chagrin, she whispered, 'Aye, a bit.'

'How so a bit?'

'I . . .' She struggled to explain without revealing too much. 'There's been a few parcels, left on t' doorstep . . .'

'Addressed specifically to you?'

'Aye.'

'And you've no idea who they might be from?'

Colour was blooming up her neck, she could feel it; she dropped her head quickly. 'How do you know all this, anyroad?' she asked, dodging the question. 'Someone told you . . .? Who?'

'Your Joan mentioned it.'

'Well, she had no right to. It's my business and mine alone—'

'Is it that American fella? Is it?' he pressed when she remained silent.

'Lad . . .'

'What was his name again? Carl . . . summat?'

'Clifford, don't.'

'What?'

'Just drop it. Please.'

'I just want to know whether—'

'Well, tough, for it's nowt to do with you!' she cried, leaping to her feet. 'I have to go.'

'I'm sorry. Livvy, wait – I'm worried about you. Livvy.' He caught her arm and forced her around. His eyes were creased with deep confusion. '*Talk* to me,' he urged. 'Tell me what's wrong.'

A maelstrom of emotions crashed in waves throughout her. Dread, terror, panic. Self-disgust and regret, yearning – yes, yearning; how she wished she could confide in him, have him make this all go away . . . She choked on a sob. 'Oh, lad!'

'Have youse . . .'

She shook her head.

'Then has *he* . . .'

'Aye,' she confirmed at last on a low wail. 'Carl Rivera, he forced himself.'

The colour slowly drained from Clifford's face. She saw it, bit by bit, trickle away, leaving the skin bone white and taut like granite.

'I'm sorry,' she mouthed. 'Lad, I'm sorry—'

'Why didn't you *tell* me?'

His tortured voice tore at her soul. 'I couldn't. I were ashamed.'

'You, ashamed? You're not to blame for that animal's actions!'

'It's not that. There's . . . other things.'

'Livvy?'

'Please, please don't make me do it.' The words came out on a rasp. 'Don't make me tell you. You don't want to *know* this, lad!'

Clifford gave the slightest incline of his head that he did. He watched her, waited.

'I worked as a prostitute.'

Even as the admission was making its way past her trembling lips, she wished she could snatch each grubby syllable back. She scoured his face wildly, desperate to gauge his reaction, however his countenance had shut down – there was nothing there. It had turned empty like his eyes.

'Lad?' she endeavoured tentatively; her heart was

beating so heavily she thought it might give out on her. 'I can explain . . . Say summat.'

He didn't. He simply continued to stare at her.

'*Please.*'

Still, silence.

Livvy searched his face for another age then dipped her chin to her chest. Mouth clamped, she turned and walked from the house.

Though she didn't look round, with every step she took towards her own door she waited, ears pricked, heart screaming out to him to shout her name, call her back.

It never came.

'We're going out.'

Sidestepping in surprise as Livvy bulldozed past her, Vera closed the door and followed her into her rooms. 'Love?'

'Get ready, and be quick about it,' she ordered. Like a caged lion, she paced the floor. 'I need a drink.'

'What's happened?'

'What's not!' she shot back. She swiped at tears with a harsh bark of laughter. 'Let's just say I were wrong – me, make a new life for myself? Huh! Nah.' She held her arms wide. 'Livvy Bryant, good-time girl, is back. And by God am I going to enjoy it.'

Vera motioned to a chair. 'Come on, sit down,' she insisted when Livvy, wired on adrenaline, shook her head. 'Now, start from the beginning; what's occurred? You're not serious about returning to the job, surely?'

'I've never been more serious about owt in my life,' was her unflinching response.

'But why? You've been doing so well—'

'Aye, and look where it got me! Anyroad, why not, eh? To hell with it. It's what I'm good for.'

'And the chippy?'

'Sod the chippy! Now,' she added, tone clipped, eyes arid once more and hard as steel, 'are you coming or what?'

Her friend dithered, frowning, for a moment. Then she gave a soft sigh and made off to the bedroom to get ready.

'Shake a leg, will you, there's men to service,' Livvy snapped, striding on in front and causing Vera to take up a trot to keep up with her. 'First, though, a drink.'

Gwen smiled in pleasant surprise when they entered the Fleece. 'Hello, you two. Livvy love, we don't see much of you these days—'

'Aye, well, you will from hereon in,' she cut in abruptly, nodding to the pumps. 'Drinks all round, and quick as you like.'

The barmaid blinked, nodded. 'Are you all right?' she asked with soft concern as she filled the first glass. 'Only you seem—'

'Just fine and dandy. Least I would be if you'd only hurry up with that ale.'

The barmaid shared a glance with Vera, who shook her head, and returned her attention to her task.

'Another,' Livvy demanded, slamming her empty glass on to the counter, having downed her ale in ten seconds flat.

'Livvy, slow down, will you?' Vera hissed. 'You'll be on your arse in no time if you carry on like this.'

'No, love, it's on my back I'll be shortly, get it right – aye, and it can't come quick enough!' Shoving her friend, she let out a raucous cackle. 'Well, that's if the staff in here would get a wriggle on and fetch me my drink first,' she continued, hooking a finger at Gwen and commanding her over, eyebrow raised. 'Another,' she repeated, tone hard. '*If* it's not too much bother.'

Vera had soon given up trying to keep pace with her. Livvy didn't care. When an hour later they emerged into the street, Vera had to take her friend's arm to prevent her from stumbling headlong into the road and oncoming traffic – ignoring Vera's chiding, a laughing Livvy squinted and pointed ahead: 'Onwards – to the boys!'

'Livvy, it's pointless trying,' the woman insisted as they neared the Palais. 'There's no way the manager will allow you entrance with the state you're in.'

She pooh-poohed the statement. 'Course he will! And well, if he tries, I'll offer him a favour somewhere private in return – you can bet a pound to a pinch of snuff he'll not turn that down!'

'Why are you doing this?'

'Doing what?' she asked, dragging the woman along in a lurching gait.

'All this! And talking like that: dirty. It's not like you and neither does it suit yer.'

She gave a single shoulder shrug. 'Why not? I'm a whore after all, so may as well act like one.'

Sure enough, minutes later the management of the dance hall point blank refused Livvy admittance. 'Bleedin' sod the lot of you, then!' she screeched, banging her fist on the door she'd just been led from. 'It's a steaming pile of shite in there anyways!'

'For God's sake – come on, you.' Apologising on her behalf, Vera forced her away and down the steps, her face like thunder.

''Ere, what's your game? I ain't done with them yet!'

'Aye, you ruddy well have. Come on, I think I'd best get you home—'

'Home? *Home?* Pah! I'm going nowhere, no bloody how!'

'All right, then, aye, go on. I've had enough. You go back to the Palais and cause further merry hell.'

'I will!'

'Aye, and what if Carl's in there? You really want to bump into him, do you?'

She faltered for a split second then huffed. 'What

of it, anyroad? The bastard will find a way of seeing me, he always does, so why not make his job easier for him?'

'And Joan?'

'Joan . . .'

'Aye – what if she's in there with Doris tonight? Do you really want her seeing you like this?'

It had the desired effect; the fight left Livvy in a rapid rush. Lowering herself on to a step, she wrapped her arms tightly around her body. 'The lass is engaged to be wed, you know.'

'I didn't think it'd take long; I've seen her a few times with a young army chap on the dance floor.'

'Does he seem decent?'

'He's a nice lad, aye.'

'Vera . . . Oh, Vera!'

'Come on, girl.' Taking her under the oxters, her friend helped her gently to her feet. 'Let's get you a nice hot cup of tea, eh?'

Snuggled up under a blanket on Vera's sofa, her hair in disarray and mascara tracks scoring her cheeks, Livvy took sips of her drink through miserable hiccups.

'All right now?'

Giving Vera a sorry sniff, she shook her head. 'I don't know what came over me, love, and I apologise – both to you and to Gwen. And I want to say . . . ta.'

'You don't have to thank me—'

'Aye, I do. You stopped me from doing summat I'd have regretted. I appreciate it.'

'With some bloke, you mean?' Vera asked knowingly.

Livvy nodded.

'I knew you didn't really want to go back to it – so what's this all about, then? Summat terrible must have occurred, for sure as eggs is eggs, I've never before seen you like that.'

'Clifford knows,' Livvy choked.

'Knows what?'

'Everything. I told him last night.'

'By gum.'

'D'you know what he did, Vera?'

The woman shook her head.

'Nowt. Norra thing. He didn't move, didn't speak. Just stood there staring at me. God, why – why did I have to go and do it? What have I *done*?'

Vera moved to sit beside her. Sighing, she put her arm around her. 'Happen he just needs some time, to get his head around it, you know?'

'Aye?'

'Perhaps. Give it a bit, then face him, try and talk to him about it. You never know, eh?'

Livvy allowed herself a few more tears, then took some shuddering breaths and wiped her eyes. 'I'm all right, now.'

'Good. You hungry? I've some tongue through yonder if you could manage a butty . . .'

'No, thanks. I could murder another brew, mind.'

When their cups were refilled and they were seated side by side once more, Livvy said, 'Poor Bertha. I've let her down bad, was meant to be working this evening. She'll give me the shove for this, won't she?'

'Likely not. She seems a kindly sort.'

'She is,' Livvy agreed. 'Even so . . . Eeh, what am I like, eh? I'm a bloody disaster.'

'Probably why we get on so well.'

Meeting one another's eye, the women chuckled softly.

'Did you ever think more on what we were talking on? You know, about you finding yourself a fresh position?' Livvy queried after a while.

'I did, as it happens.'

'Oh? What, war work?'

Putting down her cup, Vera tucked her legs beneath herself and turned fully to face her. Her eyes shone. 'You know one of my sisters works for a big firm: Burton's Factory, on Halliwell Road?'

'Aye.'

'Well, they were requisitioned a few years back for military purposes. They now make uniforms for the forces. It's trousers what our Rita works on, putting the sizes in them and such like, and making pockets. It's conveyor belt work, and aye it's fast, but she reckons I'd be able to stand the pace well enough. And I'm good with a needle, can sew with my peepers shut. She's promised to put a word in for me and let me know.'

'Love, that's gradely news.' Livvy was made up for her. 'Eeh, I do hope you're taken on.'

'Funny, in't it? Not so long ago it was you getting your life all nice and sorted out, whilst I was in the gutter. Now look at us.' As though realising what she'd said, in the next second Vera was snaking a hand to her mouth. 'Eeh, Livvy, that sounded reet bitchy! Oh, I am sorry, I didn't mean—'

'It's all right,' she murmured. 'I know what you meant. It just goes to show, eh, that this life is a queer 'un at times – you never can tell when your luck might change. I did mean what *I* said, though: I am really happy for you, honest. You deserve all the luck in the world.'

'What of you, love? Will you go and face Bertha?'

'Can't say I'm looking forward to it, but I'll have to, aye.'

'And Clifford? It'll have to be aired at some point,' she added quietly when Livvy didn't answer. 'Youse live in the same street, for Christ's sake; can't avoid one another 'til kingdom come.'

Her response to this was a sigh. Time would soon tell.

Chapter Eleven

'WHAT YOU MESSING about at there?'

Chewing her thumb, Livvy shook her head. 'Nowt, Grandad.'

'Nay? Then what's keeping you glued to that window? Are the neighbours having a set-to or summat?'

'No?'

'Is the circus in town?'

'No.'

'Happen mad owd Mrs Vine from Greenroyd Avenue has finally flipped her lid and she's parading the streets in the altogether – is that it?'

'No, of course not.'

'Well, what then? Come on, you can't kid a kidder – spit it out. It must be summat, for you've not shifted from that spot all morning—'

'Oh, it's nowt, I said. Lord, you're a nosey devil! Stop going on, will yer?'

Morris waited until she'd tossed the curtain back

into place and stalked across the room to throw herself on to the sofa before saying solemnly, 'It shan't take long, you know.'

'What won't?'

'Mrs Vine.'

Oh please, just be quiet . . .

'Gets worse, she does, by all accounts.'

Giving in to the inevitable, Livvy closed her eyes.

'Your grandma were telling me, reckons she's still convinced her boy will come back. I'd not like to witness it if he did, nay not I – poor bugger's been dead three year. You know she used to dash outside in her nightclothes and nowt on her feet whenever she heard enemy aircraft passing? Oh aye, it's true. Whilst the rest of us were scurrying for the shelters, there Mrs Vine was in the street, waving at the ruddy planes. She thought it was her son come back; laughing and crying, she'd be, calling up his name.' Morris shook his head. 'Ay. Sad, in't it?'

'Aye.'

'Rotten wars: they've gorra lot to answer for.'

She rose and wandered back to the window – then thinking the better of it when her grandfather furrowed his brow, she left the room and climbed the stairs to her bedroom to keep up her vigil from there.

She'd plucked up the nerve to call at Celia's house this morning after leaving Vera's, where she'd spent the night. Whence she'd found the courage to

237

approach the door, let alone knock, she didn't know, but she somehow had. Her efforts, however, had been a waste of time. Clifford's aunt had informed her that her nephew had left the house at the crack of dawn, and she didn't know where he was. Livvy had had no option but to thank her and drag her feet homeward.

He was purposely avoiding her, that much was plain. Just what was she going to do? The prospect of losing him was monstrous to her; she didn't think she'd cope with it. Not now, with all he'd come to mean to her. He had her whole heart.

Lost in the trappings of her mind, she almost didn't register the figure when it turned into the road. With recognition, her heart thwacked against her breastbone. She jumped to her feet, wrung her hands, sat down again. Then she stood once more and made for the landing and down the stairs.

Clifford answered the door to her light tapping. Without speaking, he held it open, and shooting him wary glances she skirted past him into the house.

In the living room, he motioned to a chair, but Livvy declined. Wordlessly, they faced one another across the space.

'I'm so very sorry, lad,' she said at last.

'You should have told me, Livvy.'

'I know.'

He stared at his boots for a moment. When he

raised his head again and held out his arms, she thought she'd misunderstood. She gasped.

'Lad?'

'Come here, lass,' he murmured.

She ran to him and crushed herself against his chest with a cry. 'Eeh, Clifford!'

'Sshhh. It's all right, now. Everything's going to be all right.'

'Aye?' she wept, tilting back her head to gaze at him.

'I'll never let owt happen to you ever again, Livvy. I'll keep you safe, my darling. Always.'

Her brain was swimming in delirium; she thought she might faint. Her laughter, when it left her, was shaky, almost manic. 'I worry this might all be a dream. Lad, I love you, so much, I thought you'd done with me, that you'd not want nowt to do with me, and I didn't know what I'd have done; I couldn't, couldn't bear to live without you now, I . . .'

Clifford soothed her as her emotions finally spilled over and she poured out her heart. Encompassed in his certain hold, she knew she'd come home.

'You can put that Yank from your mind from now on, all right? He'll not be bothering you no more.'

The quiet announcement brought her head up slowly. Clifford was looking at her with firm assurance. She blinked several times. 'But, how . . .'

'You don't need to worry about that.'

'I must know. Tell me.'

He showed her instead. Gazing at the cut and bruised knuckles, she sighed. 'Eeh, lad. You mean . . .'

'Had myself a little trip to Warrington and the army base this morning, aye,' he confirmed.

'What occurred?' she asked, her hand travelling to her throat.

'I made up some tale that I were his pal and needed to see him for a minute with urgent news. They believed me. His face were a picture when he came outside.'

'And?'

'I gave the dirty bastard the hammering of his life.'

'By, lad.'

'Don't look so surprised. Did you really think I'd keep to myself what I'd learned and not do nowt about it? I might be a pacifist on paper, Livvy, but I'm no yellow belly.'

She bit her lip. 'Did he hurt you?'

'No. He acted as all women-abusing cowards do when standing toe to toe with a man: put his hands up and bleated like a child. I warned him in no uncertain terms that from this day on, if he so much as breathed in your direction, I'd tear his subnormal head from his carcass. He'll not trouble you again, lass.'

She could barely bring herself to believe it. It was over . . . It really was? 'Eeh, I do hope you're right.'

'So do I – for his sake.'

'What I told you . . . what I was. There were reasons for it. I need to explain—'

'Not now,' he murmured. 'Not now.'

Their lips met and she melted into him like liquid. Her arms interweaved themselves around his neck, her body moulded into his in a perfect fit. Placing his hands around her waist, he swept her up from the floor and she wrapped her legs around him, her breaths coming in short spurts. Their mouths never leaving each other, they dropped to the sofa.

Clifford raised her arms and lifted off her blouse in one swift manoeuvre; his shirt was fast to follow. They dragged at the rest of their clothing like ravenous beings desperate for satiation.

Their union evoked in her sensations she had thought she'd never experience again. Countless men had come after Clive, and from most she had garnered a shared pleasure, however not once since her husband had she known this, the filling of blessed warmth throughout every vein that came only with the surety of true love. She recognised it not simply as an act of copulation to satisfy an urge but a strengthening of joined bonds and of hearts. A sacredness known from now on only to them. Tears sprang to her eyes to cascade down her face and she welcomed them; it was like a new purge, wiping away forever all that had gone before, and she was reborn.

They lay afterwards, fingers entwined, glistening

limbs in a tangle. Eyes closed, Livvy sighed through a smile as Clifford dropped slow, soft kisses on to every inch of her face.

'What?' he asked, smiling, when she began to giggle.

'I've just thought of something: my grandma and Celia ain't in, are they?'

Putting back his head, he roared with laughter. 'Oh aye, they're upstairs with a glass to the floorboards.'

'You!'

'Fret not, they're out.'

'Don't tell me, the ruddy pictures.'

'Got it in one: they wanted to see the Sunday showing.' Tracing a hand along the contours of her throat and collarbone, he whispered, 'I love you, lass.'

'And I you, lad.'

'Marry me.'

She reached up to stroke his cheek. 'Just you name the date.'

''Ere, lad, I were telling our Livvy about owd Mrs Vine earlier; you know, the mad 'un from Greenroyd? Well, did you know that during the air-raid warnings, whenever aircraft went past, she'd—'

'Not now, Grandad,' Livvy intervened – she was grinning from ear to ear.

'Huh, well that's nice, in't it? All's I were going to say is that Mrs Vine, she'd—'

'You're mad, never mind her, the poor owd cocker. Now shurrup and listen, we've some news to tell you.'

Morris had been ready with a response to Livvy's remark, however at her last sentence he closed his mouth again and sat up in his chair. 'Oh aye?'

'Hang about,' she said, dashing to the foot of the stairs to shout down her sister.

'Well?' Morris exploded when Livvy had returned to her seat and sat smiling at Clifford. 'Are you spitting this news out or ain't yer? Keeping me on bloody pins, it's not on!'

'Just wait a minute for Grandma and Celia; they're on their way across.'

When the six of them were finally gathered in the living room, Livvy called for quiet – then repeated it twice more for her grandfather's sake – and took a deep breath. Then to the gasps and low whistles of the party, she reached for her beloved's hand.

'We wanted you all to be the first to know . . . We're getting wed!'

'Eeh!'

'Oo-er!'

'By bloody gum!'

'Smashing news, that, our Livvy.' Joan added her sentiment to the medley.

Returning her embrace, Livvy doubted whether

she'd ever know a happiness to match this for the rest of her life. 'Ta, sweetheart. 'Ere, how d'you fancy being a bridesmaid?'

'Really?'

'Course, daft lass.'

'Gradely! Ta, Livvy! Ta, Clifford!'

'I'm that made up for you, my lass,' Madge told Livvy with feeling, whilst either side of her a smiling Morris and Celia nodded agreement. 'Well: one down, one to go! You'll not be far behind, Joan, I'll be bound.'

'Aye, when do we get to meet this chap of yours?' Livvy asked.

'Oh, him.' Her sister tossed her head. 'We're finished.'

Livvy was shocked. The girl's outpouring to her in the woods and declaration of undying love had seemed so genuine. 'When did this occur, then?'

'Last night. He gorra cob on because I took a turn on the dance floor with another fella, so I told him to sling his hook. No bloke's telling me what I can and can't do.'

So Joan had been at the Palais last night after all . . . Livvy sent up a silent thank you for her friend and that she'd made her see sense and leave when she did.

'Well, good on you!' Madge was preening with approval. 'You start as you mean to go on, lass, and you'll not go far wrong. Ay, I wish I'd had your sense when I were first starting out, that I do!'

'Meaning?' her husband wanted to know. 'That a jibe at me, wench, aye? You regret ever clapping eyes on me, is it, now?'

'Well, if the cap fits, Morris!'

Livvy clapped her hands to regain order. 'For God's sake. This house shall be the death of me, I'm sure. Can't you two ever be in the same room for longer than five minutes without it turning into a slanging match?'

'Less of your sauce, you,' parried Morris. 'It's how we're made, is all.'

'That's right,' Madge added, and she and her husband shared a firm nod.

'You're barmy, the pair of you.' Livvy threw up her arms. 'I tell you what, Clifford, you ought to think long and hard, my lad, before legally binding yourself to this mob.'

'I'd wed you, Livvy Bryant, even if Jack the Ripper hisself was one of your relations,' he told her, kissing her cheek and making her blush pink. 'And don't you forget it.'

'Ay, speaking of the slasher, my granny met him once, you know. What, she did, no word of a lie!' Morris added when the others began to laugh. 'What's so amusing?'

'You are, you owd goat,' Madge told him. 'Your

tales are that tall they make Blackpool Tower look like a gatepost.'

Livvy and Clifford slid their gazes to one another at the mention of the resort and shared a secret smile.

'Aye, well, you tell me this, then, know all: how, if it's nobbut tosh, did she know the colour of his eyes?'

'Who? What eyes?'

'My granny! She knew the colour of the Ripper's eyes! Bright green, she said they were, like a dragon's hide. So there.'

Madge was wiping tears of mirth from her eyes and shaking her head. 'Eeh, I don't know. I'm certain of one thing, now, all right, and that's for sure: I can see who you take after. Dragon's hide indeed. The pair of you ought to have wrote novels.'

Rather than be offended, he appeared pleased at this. 'Aye, happen we should, and bestsellers they'd have been, too.'

'Oh, I don't doubt it forra minute!'

All the while that this was going on, Livvy had been watching her sister through the corner of her eye. Joan, her head swinging back and forth between her grandparents as though watching a tennis match, was grinning, seemingly without a care in the world – certainly, it really did appear she was none the worse for her break-up. It puzzled Livvy no end. Tapping the girl on the shoulder, she motioned to the kitchen and when Joan nodded led the way to the adjoining room.

'Shut that door, lass, give our ears a break forra few minutes. By, they go on, them two.'

'Tell me about it. They can be funny, though.'

Smiling, Livvy busied herself with the kettle. 'So,' she remarked after a while, keeping her tone light, 'it's really all over then between you and . . .' She pulled an apologetic face. 'Sorry, I never even asked you his name.'

'Harry. And it don't much matter that you didn't, for aye it is over.'

'I thought you said you were daft about each other?'

'We were.' She shrugged. 'Things change.'

'Things or people?' Livvy pressed, and was vindicated when her sister flashed a coy smile. She'd had a sneaking feeling there was more to this. 'There's another lad involved. Am I right?'

'Maybe. I'd *like* there to be. It's the one what asked me to dance when Harry got mad,' she revealed, resting her chin in her hand, her eyes dreamy. 'By, he's handsome, Livvy.'

Livvy couldn't contain a chuckle. 'You said that about the last chap.'

'I know, but this one's even handsomer! Tall and tanned, an' all, to boot. Eeh, you should see him.'

'Happen you could fetch him home some time

247

and then I will,' she said, lifting the tea tray. She felt much more reassured now that they had had a chat. Their Joan was a fickle piece, that was the top and bottom of it. Nor was there any harm in it, young as she was. 'Come on, we'd best get back in. Poor Clifford's probably had his lugholes chewed off by now.'

'I knew you'd wed eventually.' Joan was smiling smugly.

'Oh, did you indeed?'

'Course. You two were just too daft to see it!'

'Aye, happen we were,' Livvy laughed.

'Be happy, eh, sis.'

Choked at the sincerity in the girl's tone, she nodded. 'Right you, give over, else you'll have me bawling. Go on, get the door, good lass.'

Livvy watched from the opposite side of the road at least a dozen customers come and go before she could muster up enough pluck to approach the chip shop.

When eventually she entered, it was with a hangdog expression and a ready apology on her lips, however she didn't get the chance to speak it; looking up and spotting her, Bertha rushed from behind the counter to envelop her in a sturdy hug.

'Eeh, you're all right – you had me that worried!'

'I . . . did?'

'Aye. When you never showed on Saturday, I

imagined all sorts. Had she fallen poorly? I asked myself. Been knocked down by a bus? But nay, here you are, in the flesh and looking none the worse into the bargain, glory be.'

'Oh, Bertha.' Livvy was shame-faced. Yet, although on the one hand she was filled with guilt, quickly beginning to override it was a sense of quiet joy that the woman cared so much. 'I never meant to worry you. Aye, nor let you down. I could stand here and tell you that I *was* ill or some such, but it'd be a bare-faced lie. Truth is, I got a bit of bad news and went off my rocker a bit on the ale. I'm that sorry, love.'

The woman chuckled. 'You're honest, I'll give you that, and that's why I like you. No harm done, I suppose – don't we all get a touch of the madness sometimes?'

'You mean I've still got my position?'

'Course you have! Anyroad, you're a sound little worker.'

Thank God. 'I've been dreading facing you. It'll not happen again, I swear it. Ta, thanks, Bertha.'

'That's all right. But hey, get cracking. As much as I like you, I'm not so doolally yet that I'd pay you for standing there looking pretty. Hop to your duties, lass.'

Laughing, Livvy made off for the back room to don her white coat and hat.

At the end of her shift, she emerged into the street

and made not for the bus stop but Vera's rooms. She'd been fizzing with anticipation all day, could hardly wait to tell her friend the good news regarding her and Clifford.

'Hiya, love!' she trilled when Vera opened the door – then, doing a double take, she gasped. 'Eeh, you look bloody awful. Love, what's wrong?' she cried when the woman crumpled to her knees against the wall and began to sob. 'Ay now, come on, come inside.'

After making a pot of tea and pressing a cup into a still weeping Vera's hands, she sat and waited for her to talk.

'It's all right, you take your time,' she soothed.

'Livvy, what the friggin' hell am I going to do,' she managed to choke out at last. 'And to think I used to reckon I were ruined before – ha!'

'What's happened?'

'I'm expecting.'

Livvy's jaw almost hit the tabletop. '*What?*'

'You heard me! I ain't felt right for weeks and knew I had to swallow my pride and go and see the doctor. He confirmed it this afternoon.'

Stunned to the marrow, Livvy could only stare agog.

'D'you know the irony, though, love?' Vera went on in sheer misery. 'Shall I tell you what this shitshow of a life of mine did? It had me get the job at

Burton's first – my sister let me know this morning. There was I, over t' moon thinking this is it, girl, you begin a fresh start here, and then a few hours later it all went to pot and disappeared in a puff of smoke. God, I hate myself, *hate* being me. I hate it!'

'But how?' Livvy was swinging her head. 'We never took the risk, never did nowt with no customer unsheathed. We always used French letters.'

'Customers, aye.' Vera's words were little above a whisper. 'Not boyfriends.'

As realisation dawned, a groan escaped Livvy; she put her face in her hands. 'Lord, no. Carl . . . Oh, *Vera.*'

'I'm a brainless bitch, I know – trust me, I don't need you to say it. I'd convinced myself he was the one, hadn't I. It didn't even enter my head to use owt. Livvy, just what in God's name am I going to do?'

'You'll not consider . . . you know? Getting rid, will you? Please don't say you would.'

'No, no. But oh Christ, Livvy, what a mess!'

Taking in her friend's devastation, etched in every line of her face, Livvy's heart broke for her. She groped for Vera's hands and squeezed them, desperate to instil some strength into her and have her know she wasn't on her own in this, never. 'You've been sat in here all on your lonesome all day, stewing? Love, why didn't you come to Top o'th' Brow, come to see me? Eeh, I do wish you had.'

'How will I cope, Livvy?' Vera's face had gone as grey as putty and her eyes had turned wild. 'This is one step too far – my family shan't support me in this. I've got no one. A babby, here, in these poky little rooms – there's barely enough space to swing a kitten. And brass! What will I do for brass – who'd mind the child? Oh God. Oh God!'

'Sshhh, now. First thing's first.' She rose and, placing her hands on her hips, glanced around. 'Do you have a suitcase, some mode of bag?'

'Aye, but—'

'Fetch it.'

'Love, I don't understand.'

Stooping and taking her friend's face in her hands, Livvy smiled. 'It's simple, Vera. You're coming home with me.'

'What?'

'You heard. Now come on, shape yourself.'

'But I can't . . .'

'Aye you can, love, and you are. You're my mate, and mates stick together. And I'll tell you this much for nowt: that bastard might have tried ruining my life, but he'll not do the same with you. I'm going to be here for you, Vera – me and my family, we all will. We'll make this work, you just see if we don't.'

'I don't know what . . . what to say, I . . .'

'Say nowt – less talky, more movey! Pack up all the things you need and to hell with the rest – this furniture's falling to bits, anyroad; sod it and leave it here. Go and fetch your case.'

Ten minutes later, the women left the rooms for the last time.

Pausing in tandem a short distance away, they each glanced back over their shoulder. So many memories hid behind those walls. Countless men had come and gone from there; plenty of fun and laughter, too. And memories not so good, none more so than those made when Carl Rivera came on the scene . . .

Livvy took a deep breath, and Vera did the same. Nodding, they turned their backs and set forth for the bus stop.

'This is nice.'

Snuggled side by side with Livvy in her bed, a plate of toast on the counterpane between them and cups of cocoa in their hands, Vera smiled. 'I can't thank you enough for this, you know. You are sure, ain't you, that your family don't mind?'

Letting out a loud yawn, Livvy shook her head. 'No, do they heck. You're my friend, and that makes you theirs, too. The white lie I told, about you having weakened with some bloke you were engaged to and who recently perished in the war, halted any misgivings. Besides, you know our Joan's fond of you. What's more, believe me, Grandad would have made it known had he disapproved of you being here for whatever reason. Oh, we'd have known it, all right!'

Vera grinned. 'He's a bit of a tartar, in't he?'

'A bit? Huh!'

'Nah, I love him, mind. He reminds me of my own grandad. Eeh, I'm that happy to be here, love.'

The women had had a long chat earlier about the future and how best to proceed from hereon in. Livvy had told Vera she must take the job at Burton's, that when the time came they would all chip in and work around the childminding – somehow, they would manage. They had spoken at length about Clifford and the betrothal, and Vera had been over the moon and stars for her friend that everything had at last worked out. And that revenge in at least some form had been meted out, and Carl had got the stuffing knocked out of him and was gone from their lives for good was the icing on the cake – and that went for both women. Vera wanted him nowhere near her, and especially to have nothing to do with the baby.

'Everything's going to work out just fine, you'll see,' Livvy told her, and was gratified to see her friend's smile of this indeed now being a likelihood. 'I'm only thankful you don't snore, girl.'

Jabbing Livvy in the ribs and making her half choke on her drink, Vera giggled. 'No, but you do! God help me. 'Ere, I wonder if Clifford snores? You'll soon find out. I hope he snuffs and snorts like a ruddy steam train.'

'Oh, ta very much, I don't think!' Livvy laughed. 'Eeh, I still can't believe it's happening, you know, love. Me, wed.' She shook her head in wonder. 'He's made me the happiest lass in Lancashire.'

'He's the lucky one, bagging you. You're a good egg, Livvy Bryant.'

'New beginnings, eh, girl?'

'New beginnings.'

They chinked mugs. Smiling and leaning their heads against one another's, they reached for another slice of toast.

Chapter Twelve

On a chill, mid-March morning, Livvy and Clifford exchanged vows at the local registry office.

As the new Mr and Mrs Bamford emerged into the frost-stroked street, their two bridesmaids following behind, the small waiting party assembled erupted into cheers. Their family and friends, including Ned, Bertha and Gwen, and several of Clifford's closest chums, were all there. Livvy doubted that even if she lived to be ninety, she'd ever know a level of happiness like this again.

Clifford had both astonished and delighted Morris by asking him to be his best man. Now, the old fellow puffed out his chest and, when he thought no one was watching, wiped a rogue tear from his eye.

'My congratulations to youse both and more,' Madge said thickly to her granddaughter, crushing her to her gigantic bosom in a suffocating embrace, which was swiftly followed up by one from Celia.

'You look smashing, Livvy,' Joan said, kissing her sister's cheek, then her brother-in-law's.

'Aye, now ain't you glad you listened to me?' Vera asked, cradling her large bump. Common as undernourishment was amongst the working class, introductions during this war had gone some way in improving the health of the most vulnerable. Children and babies, as well as expectant and nursing mothers, were now issued with free milk, orange juice and cod liver oil, and were faring better than they ever had. Vera, it was plain to see, was testament to that. The pregnancy bloom had well and truly reached her, and she glowed. 'Go on, admit it, it's much nicer than that drab owd thing you were going to wear.'

Poking out her tongue and making the woman laugh, Livvy was forced to concede.

Due to the rationing constraints, she'd opted to wear a dark brown skirt suit and hat, which had been hanging in her wardrobe for several years, for the ceremony. However, Vera had been horrified when she'd shown her the outfit and was having none of it. She'd returned to Glaister Lane a few days later with a fine wool gabardine suit in pine green. Her knowing look when Livvy had questioned her on where on earth it had come from had been answer enough. She may well have left her old profession behind her, but not all connections relating to her past lifestyle

– namely those of the black-market variety – had been severed.

The magic wrought by the hourglass fit and square shoulder pads when Livvy tried it on had brought forth gasps of approval from her friend and sister – each agreed that it was as though it had been tailor-made for her. And Clifford's face as he'd watched her walking towards him that morning had sealed the opinion.

'I still say we ought to have honeymooned at Clark House,' he said later, nuzzling her neck in the privacy of the kitchen back at the housing estate. 'I wanted you so badly that night as we stood on the landing. It would feel like a dream come true to have you in my bed at last beneath that roof.'

Wrapping her arms around him, Livvy hooted with laughter. 'Oh aye, yes, and I can just picture now the boarding-house keeper's face when we came to book in. She thinks we're ruddy siblings, remember?'

'Well, no matter where we stay in Blackpool, it'll be special with you by my side,' he murmured. 'Ta, lass, for making my day, my month, my whole life.'

'Come on, you two.' Joan's voice filtered through to them from the living room, interrupting their kiss and making them smile. 'You're missing all the fun!'

That night, leaving her grandad, sister and friend behind at number twenty-two to join her husband over the road, Livvy was in floods of tears. 'I can't believe we'll not all be living together no more,' she cried, drawing each of them to her in a hug.

'Bloody women,' Morris muttered, raising his eyes to the heavens. 'You're only going all of twenty bleedin' steps away up the street.'

'Aye, well, it's still sad!'

'You can always stop on here, lass, and I'll take your place the night by Clifford's side?' Madge piped up, bringing roars of laughter from the gathering – all but her husband and Clifford himself, that was. Whilst the new groom pulled a mock horrified face and fell to his knees begging Livvy not to do it, earning him a clip round the earhole from Madge, Morris folded his arms in a huff.

'Don't be getting your long johns in a twist, you, I were only kidding,' Madge said. Then to everyone's delight she clutched her husband's shirt front, pulled him towards her and planted a smacking kiss on his lips, which immediately cheered him up no end. 'I love you, you owd bugger.'

That night after their lovemaking, as she lay in the unfamiliar bed, watching the unfamiliar shadows play along the unfamiliar ceiling, Livvy cuddled up closer to the man she knew inside out and back to front, and smiled. And all was well with the world.

Twirling on the spot outside Celia's front gate, Joan's skills of persuasion were out in full force. She batted her long eyelashes and turned large pleading eyes on to her sister, knowing full well it would work, just as it had always done since she was a small child. 'You don't mind me borrowing your frock, do you, Livvy? Only nowt I own is anywhere as nice as your gear is, and I want to look extra special tonight. Pleeease?'

'I knew I shouldn't have left some of my stuff behind with you in the house . . . Go on, you young minx, you can wear it.'

'Ay, ta, Livvy! You're the best, you are.'

'A ruddy fool, more like, where you're concerned,' she shot back, however there was no anger in the words. Truth was, the lass looked smashing. She'd certainly filled out in all the right places these past months. 'Where are you and Doris off to, anyroad?' she went on. She could just imagine it now, the eyes popping from every lad's head when this one walked in the room. 'Or do I even need to ask?'

'Aye, the Palais,' Joan confirmed, her pretty face alight. 'You should see me dancing, now, Livvy. I knock spots off every last girl there when I get on that floor.'

'Eeh, there's no danger of you coming down with a dose of false modesty, is there?' Livvy laughed. 'And will a certain young pup be there, an' all . . . I thought so,' she added at the look that crept over her sister's face. 'That's what the frock's really about, in't it: it's for his sake alone.'

'Leonard likes this one, says I look nice in it—' Joan slapped a hand to her mouth.

'You mean you've worn it before and I didn't know? By, you're a cheeky article, you!'

'Sorry.'

'Aye? Well, your grin says otherwise!'

'I will fetch him home to meet you all soon, honest,' Joan said when their chuckles had subsided. 'Only as I said, he's shy and ain't reet comfortable around strangers. And then there's the other thing.'

Frowning, Livvy shook her head.

'Grandad! Eeh, he'll eat the poor beggar alive.'

'Fair point,' Livvy laughed. 'Mind you, he'll have to face the music sometime the way you're both going.' Joan had successfully bagged the dancing partner who had wrought an end to her and Harry's relationship, and the pair had been going steady ever since. 'It's been a good few months now since you started seeing him. And aye, I know you said you wanted to make sure he was definitely the one for you before you introduced him to everyone, but well . . . From where I'm standing, it looks as if he might well be, eh? So you'd best not leave it for too much longer.'

'I'll not. I'll speak to him about it tonight.'

Livvy waved her off shortly afterwards and returned indoors to begin preparing the evening meal, and as she worked, her sister and this Leonard chap remained firmly on her mind. If she didn't know any better, she'd bet that another wedding would be on the cards by next year. Her little sister getting wed and starting a family of her own, though. It didn't seem two minutes since she was playing skip rope in the street with her frock tucked into her knickers and her dirty knees on show for all the world to see. A nostalgic lump filled Livvy's throat. By, but the years didn't half speed along, that they did.

Married life was matching up to every expectation Livvy had had and more. A fortnight in, they were still enjoying their honeymoon period and had only yesterday returned from a week's cold and blustery holiday in their favourite resort. Not that the weather had dampened their spirits, far from it. Blazing sunshine or snow blizzards, it wouldn't have made a difference, for the pair had barely left the bed.

That evening, it was coming on for ten thirty, and Livvy and Clifford were snuggling on the sofa, Madge and Celia having already retired for the night, when she put to him her thoughts on Joan. 'She seems smitten, you know, with this one. I want to meet him.'

Tired after a hard day's toil, Clifford had his eyes closed. 'Tell her to fetch Leonard home, then.'

'Oh, I have done, but apparently he's the bashful type around them he don't know, and sounds reluctant.' She chuckled. 'Talk about chalk and cheese – our Joan couldn't be more different.'

'Aye, well. They do say opposites attract.'

At his weary tone, her face softened. Leaning over, she kissed him gently. 'Sorry, love, am I keeping you up, nattering on? Let's away to our bed, eh?'

'That's the best thing you've said all night – and ay, be warned, for I'm not so tired forra bit of the other.'

He wiggled his eyebrows, and laughing Livvy made a dash for the door, with Clifford hot on her heels. 'Stop it, you swine,' she whispered, clapping a hand to her mouth so as not to waken the others as he tickled her. 'My grandma will have your guts for garters if— Oh.' Her brow furrowing, she shushed him. 'Did you hear that?'

Clifford had just shaken his head when the noise reached Livvy again.

'It's someone tapping at the window – who the devil can that be at this time?'

Sharing a frown, they crossed together to the door.

'Joan! What's wrong, has summat happened? Is everything all right?'

'Aye, aye.' Grinning from the front step, she flapped a hand to ease her sister's concerns. 'Sorry, I know it's late, and I did try to knock quietly, only I had to come and tell you.'

'Tell me what?'

'Leonard's agreed to meet youse all. He's picking me up to go dancing from home tomorrow. In't that gradely?'

'Gradely, aye,' Livvy said, still holding a hand to her heart. 'By gum, though, you could have mentioned it in the morning. Gave me the fright of my life, you did; I thought summat terrible had occurred.'

'Nowt terrible, only wonderful,' she gushed, hugging herself. 'You're going to just love him, I know it. Well, ta-ra for now.'

Sighing and shaking her head when the girl had walked away, Livvy shut the door and turned to Clifford with a crooked smile. 'Well, that's that sorted, eh?'

'Aye. Now, Mrs Bamford . . .' He motioned to the stairs.

'Lead the way, lover boy!'

Joan was on pins. 'What time is it now, Grandad?'

'That's the umpteenth time you've asked me that – there's a ruddy clock there, is there not? See for yourself!'

'When Leonard gets here, you will behave yourself, won't you?' Clasping her hands together, her wide stare was beseeching. 'Just do this one thing for me and I promise I'll never wind you up ever again.'

'Behave myself? Me?' Morris sat forward in his chair.

'Aye. Please.'

'Not on your nelly!'

'Aw, Livvy, tell him! He's going to spoil it, I know it!'

'He'll not spoilt nowt, he's having you on,' she assured the girl over their grandfather's impish crows. 'Give over, you,' she added to him with a grin. 'The poor lass is nervous enough.'

'Well, all this ruddy bother over some lad.'

'He's not "some lad". He's more than that to me – I really like him, Grandad.'

Morris was about to respond, but a knock sounded before he had the chance – Joan went into full panic mode and leapt to her feet:

'He's here. Oh God, oh God, oh God . . .'

'Calm *down*. Bloomin' 'eck.' Livvy, along with Vera seated on the sofa beside her, could hardly contain her laughter. 'Go and let him in, lass, before he catches his death of cold.'

The three of them listened with craned necks at the hushed tones coming from the hallway and shared amused glances. When the living room door finally opened and Joan breezed back in, they sat up straight, ready smiles in place.

'Everybody, this is Leonard.'

'How do you do? It sure is nice to meet y'all.'

Livvy was rooted to the spot, could neither move nor utter a thing. She was vaguely aware of Vera's ragged gasp and her snatching up a cushion to conceal her swollen stomach, however it hadn't the power to snap her from her stupefaction. She gawped dumbly. *This couldn't be happening . . .*

'A Yank?' Unaware that anything was amiss, Morris nudged Livvy none too gently. 'He's a bleedin' Yank!'

'And you must be Mr Tattersall.' Carl's long legs closed the space between them in two strides. He bowed slightly from the waist and held out his hand to the old man. 'Leonard Rivera, sir. It's a pleasure to make your acquaintance.'

Morris scrutinised the hand for several seconds, then at Joan's soft cough thrust out one of his own. 'Nice to meet thee, lad.'

'That's Vera, a family friend,' Joan said, pointing, to which Carl nodded politely to the dumbstruck woman. 'And this is Livvy.'

He turned his head and brought his gaze up slowly to greet hers. When it locked with her own, she felt the world shudder on its axis; she shook her head.

'I can see where your sister gets her looks from,' Carl drawled. His eyes, however, belied the silky tone; they were as hard as ice. 'It's very nice meeting you at last.'

'I . . . I can't . . .'

'Livvy? Livvy, what is it?'

'Shift from my path, Joan, I'm going to be—' Slapping a hand to her mouth, she bowled past the bemused girl and into the kitchen.

Livvy brought up what felt like her soul into the

266

sink. Shaking from head to toe, she clung to the draining board by her fingertips and took some strangled breaths.

'Are you all right?' It was Joan. She came towards her and laid a palm against her sister's forehead. 'By, you're burning up! Have I to fetch Clifford—'

'No!' *Good God no, not that. Anything but that!* She dragged herself upright and dabbed at her mouth. 'No,' she repeated, quieter now. 'I'll be all right . . . just give me a minute.'

'Well, me and Leonard are going to get going now, if you're sure . . .'

'I'm sure,' she rasped.

'I'll see you tomorrow, then? Ta-ra for now.'

When she'd gone, Livvy closed her eyes. She heard the girl bid farewell to Morris and Vera, followed by *his* voice doing the same. Then:

'Bye, Livvy,' Carl called through to her. 'Hope you're feeling better soon, honey!'

Her guts leapt to meet her throat once more. Scrambling back to the sink, she heaved up the remainder of her stomach.

'What the hell . . . What the *hell*?'

'I don't know, Vera,' Livvy croaked. 'I don't understand.'

They had slipped outside to the back garden to speak without fear of Morris overhearing.

'Bastard. Rotten, stinking, evil, awful bastard!' Vera raged, pacing up and down the strip of flagstones. 'He's planned this. Oh, has he. It'll be when he dropped that package off – you know, the first one? You said Joan arrived home not long after, didn't yer? He were hiding nearby still, I bet, saw her and made sure to remember her face. I bet he thought all his Christmases had come at once when she started going dancing not long after and he clocked eyes on her. Oh aye, that's what's happened here. I mean, he weren't shocked, was he, when he saw us just now? No. He's set the whole godforsaken thing up!'

'Calm yourself, love,' Livvy soothed. She felt anything but herself, could never be again, not after this, but she had to be practical. 'Think of the babby.'

'His babby, you mean? Christ, Livvy, what if he saw?' The woman clutched at the hair above her temple in sheer panic. 'He can't know, he can't – he'll hound me, the both of us, 'til our dying days!'

'Vera, please. This ain't helping.'

She let out a long sigh and it seemed to deflate her; she dropped on to the back doorstep beside Livvy. 'How can you be so collected?' she whispered, hugging her knees.

'I'm not. Far from it. But squalling and flapping about like a headless chicken ain't going to solve owt, is it? I need to think.'

'Leonard – huh. Bloody Leonard, I ask you!'

'Joan still referred to him as such whilst they were here: she clearly don't know he's give her a false name.'

'Mebbe not, but what about the rest? A local lad, she's always said he was.'

'Aye.'

'Claimed he dwelled up Tonge Moor.'

'Aye,' Livvy murmured again.

'The barefaced liar!'

Rising, Livvy folded her arms and walked to the bottom of the garden, skirting past the mangle and abandoned Anderson shelter on her way. 'Joan had to have had her reasons. He must have made her spout them untruths.'

'Well, of course he has, but still it's riling, Livvy, that she lied. My God, the shock! I thought I was about to keel over when he walked in, give birth to the child then and there.'

'How you feeling? Is the little one all right?'

'I think so. You?'

She shrugged. 'Throat's a bit sore, but I'll live.'

'Livvy, what in the world are we going to do?'

'I don't know, Vera. I just don't know.' And to think she'd believed him gone for good . . . What bloody fools they had all been.

For a handful of glorious months, she'd seen neither hide nor hair of Carl Rivera. No visits to the chippy or the Red Cross selling centre. No suddenly appearing in the street or following her home. No parcels, either. Not one single, solitary word or sighting. None. Nothing. She'd truly thought that Clifford's visit had worked and that at long last they had seen the last of him. *Clifford*. Lord, how could she tell him?

'You can't keep summat like this from your husband, Livvy. He'll have to know,' Vera was saying now, as though reading her mind.

'I know, but how . . . I'm so frightened of how he'll react. He'll kill him this time, I'm sure.'

'Good, and may he rot in hell,' was the woman's muttered response.

'Then there's the lass. How I kept my gob shut just now and not blurt to her the full horrible story is beyond me. But I couldn't. I *couldn't*. A pound to a penny he'd have denied to the hilt all knowledge of me and you. And lovestruck as Joan is, she'd have likely took his word for it. Either that or else he'd have taken great pleasure in revealing all my business, and then what would my family do? Perhaps Joan – all of them – disown me? I wouldn't bear it. I don't want them to be ashamed of me, Vera.'

'Your sister might well be in danger, though; has to know the truth.'

'No.' Livvy was steadfast on this. 'She's a pawn in his game. An important one, aye, to get to me – he needs her. He'll not harm her. It's with me his warped designs lie. Joan don't even come into it.'

'You'll not even try to put an end to this?'

'How, Vera?' Livvy cried, her wrought nerves snapping. 'Just what excuse would I make? That girl's as hot-headed as they come. She'll not thank me for bad-mouthing him or trying to split them apart; will likely cling to him all the more tightly just to prove me wrong. The poor cow's besotted. Oh, damn and blast that swine of Satan!'

Vera, her own tears flowing freely, held her as she cried; they clung to each other.

'We need to come up with a plan, Livvy,' she said finally. 'Come on, girl, we can do this.'

'But how?'

'I don't know, but we will. Let's put our thinking caps on, eh, and figure out a way to get rid of that sod for good. Together.'

'Together,' she agreed.

The women were waiting and ready to confront Joan when she returned later that night from the Palais. Having persuaded Morris to go out for a couple of hours and enjoy a few games of dominoes with Ned, it was just Livvy and Vera sitting by the fire when the girl entered the house.

'All right, you two?' Rose-cheeked and starry-eyed, Joan breezed into the living room and flopped with a heady sigh on to the sofa. 'By, I've had a gradely evening.'

Dropping her gaze to the dress Joan wore – her dress – and knowing what she now did made Livvy's stomach turn over. *Leonard likes me in this one* . . . He'd seen Livvy herself in it, that was why. She shuddered.

'So? What did youse think of him, then, Leonard?' Joan wanted to know, sitting forward with her elbows on her knees. 'In't he the most handsome, polite and all-round smashing fella that you ever did see?'

'A Tonge Moor lad, eh?' Vera said.

Joan's smile slipped a fraction. She glanced away. 'Aye. Sorry about that. Only Leonard reckoned it best in the beginning to say he were local; some folk can be funny about lasses taking up with the Yanks. He didn't want me having the stigma of Spam Bag. That's what they call English girls, you know, what go about with GIs. Not that I'd have been mithered, like, but he were worried my family mightn't approve. He were just thinking of me.'

No, as with the ridiculous pseudonym he'd concocted, he wanted the rest of us in the dark for as long as possible, no distractions or suspicions, to give him ample time to work his nasty magic on you, Livvy screamed silently with her eyes. Reel you in, have you fall head over heels, so that by the time we discovered the truth of who he really was you'd be too far into him that nothing we might say would have you think bad of him, leave him. That's what it's all about. Silly, poor naïve girl . . .

'Grandad took it better than I thought he might,' Joan continued with high laughter. 'You two, though, I thought the pair of you were about to flake out cold, going by the looks on your phizzogs. What occurred? Did youse both come down with the same sickness, or summat?'

'Something like that,' Livvy murmured. 'But we're fine now.'

'Gawd, I hope it ain't catching. I'm meeting Leonard again next week and I can't miss that – I'd sooner die!'

'Don't be so stupid,' she snapped to her sister. All this dramatic talk was beginning to get on her wick. 'It wouldn't be the end of the world.'

'You don't get it, do you?' Her large eyes were deep with conviction. 'I love the absolute bones of him. What's more, he feels the same about me. You might as well know now, for it'll have to be aired at some point, but me and Leonard are to be wed. And, when the war's over, I'll be heading off to live with him in America.'

Livvy and Vera gazed back at her mutely.

'Well, say summat then! Bloody hell, I drop a bombshell like that and youse just sit there like dummies?'

273

At last, Livvy spoke. Her tone was low. 'He's asked you, has he? To marry him?'

'Aye, he has. This very night, as a matter of fact.'

'And you've said aye?'

'Of course!'

'Right. Right.' Livvy rose to her feet. How she ever managed to squeeze past her lips the next words, she would never know: 'Well, congratulations, Joan.'

'Aye? You really mean it? Eeh, Livvy, thanks.' She threw her arms around her in a quick hug. 'I always knew you were smashing! I knew you'd understand, would just want me to be happy. Course, I'll come back to England and visit you all when I can. Here, you could all even come over to us! Fancy it, eh: holidays in Chicago! We'll all have such a great time.'

Livvy forced out a smile. 'Perhaps. Now, I'd best be across the way home. Clifford will be wondering where I've got to.'

'Goodnight, God bless, Livvy.'

'Night, God bless, lass,' she returned thickly, her heart breaking for her sister. What she wouldn't have given to snatch the girl into her arms and hug her to her breast, keep her safe for ever and never let go . . . But she couldn't. She couldn't. Not yet at least. 'See you in the morning,' she added to Vera, who nodded understandingly.

Tomorrow was the day she and her friend would decide how best to tackle this and get rid of Carl Rivera once and for all. Walking the short distance to her door, Livvy offered up a heartfelt plea for help. For if there was one thing she was certain of then it was this: boy, would the scheme have to be something good.

Chapter Thirteen

'SO WHAT'S HE like, then?'

'Eh?'

'This Leonard lad of our Joan's. I were sorry to miss him on Saturday, but it couldn't be helped: me and Celia had a hot date with Gary Cooper at the pictures.'

Avoiding Madge's eye, Livvy kept her full attentions directed at the canned goods on the grocer's shop shelves. 'Oh, you know,' she replied noncommittally.

'Our Joan seems daft about him. Mind you, your grandad were saying he's a Yank? I didn't know that.'

'None of us did,' she murmured.

'So d'you reckon when this lot's over with, and all the "over here" Americans return over there, she'll be going with him? Fancy.'

No, she didn't fancy it, not by a long chalk. Come hell or high water, Joan wasn't going anywhere. *Not if the idea she and Vera had cooked up together yesterday panned out as they wanted it to.*

'Huh!'

'What's wrong?' asked Livvy, turning her head to frown at the split and faded poster affixed to the shop wall that her grandmother was now pointing at.

Britain had launched an anti-gossip campaign several months after the outbreak of war, and slogans such as the one they were looking at began to appear everywhere, warning the public to keep mum as spies could be walking amongst you in plain sight and you never knew who was listening.

'We ought to ask the grocer if we can have that and stick it up above your grandad's chair at home. Careless Talk Costs Lives – it will in Morris's case, all right, if he carries on. "Take heed, lad," I'd be able to warn him when he starts up with one of his tall tales, "for I'll ruddy do you in if you don't shut it!"'

The ghost of a smile stroked Livvy's lips. 'You know you'd not be without him, Grandma, really – stories and all. You can't fool me.'

'Aye,' she admitted. 'He's norra bad owd boot – deep, deep down, that is. I suppose I could have done worse. Aye, there's fellas aplenty a hell of a lot badder than him.'

With this, Livvy wholeheartedly agreed.

And some were far too good for their wives . . . Clifford, she felt, was surely testament to that.

The crippling guilt, which had been gnawing at her insides since the discovery, was worsening by the hour. Still, she'd revealed to her husband nothing of what she and her friend had learned.

Vera's urging that she must tell him was increasing, too, and though Livvy knew at the back of her mind that the woman was right, she was loath to speak the words to him. Should Clifford go berserk, which was an almost certain possibility, he might well go too far with the American this time and do something he might regret. She just couldn't risk that. She wouldn't see him locked away – or worse, swing from the rope – for that monster. So long as it remained within her power to protect Clifford from himself, then she would do it. Her deception was for his sake alone.

Brains were what was needed to tackle this, not brawn. And by God would she put her all into this; was absolutely determined to pull it off. Carl could well be gone – no, he would be gone – by this time next week. Maybe, just maybe, Clifford need never find out.

'Are you all right?' the man himself asked later as Livvy was clearing away the dirty dishes from their meal. 'You've hardly touched your grub again.'

'Course, why wouldn't I be?' she shot back, her

heart beginning to drum. 'I'm just not hungry, that's all.'

'Ruddy hell, all right, snappy.' Grinning, he held up his hands.

'I'm sorry, love.' Depositing the plates on to the table, she slithered into his lap and rested her cheek against his. The shame was almost unbearable. 'I don't deserve you, you know,' she whispered.

'Ay, now. What's all this?'

'Nowt. It's nowt.'

'Is it your Joan? Is that what's bothering you?'

'Eeh, lad . . .'

'I thought so. You've been a bit off ever since you met her beau. Does he not meet with your approval?'

'I . . .' She scrambled round inside her head for a suitable response. 'I do worry somewhat that he's not good for her, aye,' she said carefully. 'Oh, but it's no big deal, really: I'm sure everything will work itself out. It always does, eh?'

Nodding agreement, appearing relieved that her mind was apparently eased by getting the words off her chest, Clifford reached for his cup and drained the remainder of his tea. 'Right, I might go up for a bath.'

'Aye, go on,' she said, smiling, relieved to have the conversation over with. 'Leave me in peace to wash these pots.'

When he'd gone, she made no attempt to head for

the kitchen. Instead, she took herself across to the sofa to go over in her mind yet again every last detail of the plan.

'Can you believe that miserable manager won't allow jitterbugging or lindy-hopping at the Palais? A reet killjoy, he is – swing bands are my favourites, an' all. Leonard swept me up forra turn last week and the manager asked us to leave the floor. Them kind of dances take up too much room, he said. I reckon he's just jealous 'cause *he* can't do it – probably got two left feet.'

Livvy offered nods in what she hoped were the right places, but her mind was far from her sister's ramblings.

'Aye well, we'll have another go at it this evening, whether the manager likes it or not! I don't care what he says, I intend on enjoying myself, and he can like it or lump it.'

'What time's he coming here to pick you up?' she asked as casually as she could, purposely avoiding Joan's eye lest she saw reflected within her own the sheer importance of her question.

'Who, Leonard?'

Bloody Leonard . . . 'Aye.'

'Six. Why?'

'No reason. Just wondering, that's all.'

The girl nodded, smiled and returned her gaze to

the magazine in her lap. Letting out air slowly, Livvy closed her eyes briefly in relief then trained them across the room to keep them rooted on the clock.

'Now you're sure about this,' Vera whispered later as Livvy prepared to leave. 'You'll be all right?'

Glancing to the foot of the stairs, beyond which Joan could be heard humming to herself as she got herself ready for her night out, Livvy mouthed back, 'I'll have to be, won't I? This has to be done.'

'Good luck, love. And please, be careful.'

A quick hug and the friends parted ways.

Shaking like a leaf at the magnitude of what she was about to do – so very much depended on the first part of this going well – Livvy left the house and turned right, in the direction of Winchester Way.

Keeping her head lowered when she approached Thicketford Brow and Doris's home – the last thing she wanted was for her sister's friend to catch a sighting of her and make mention of it to Joan – Livvy scurried onwards towards the squat building of the Independent Methodist Church.

A light drizzle began to fall as she took up watch; pulling the collar of her coat around her chin and thrusting her hands into her pockets, she narrowed her eyes and waited on.

As she knew it would, Carl's lanky figure appeared at last over the dip in the distance. Hatred like no other burst like an inferno through her body. He was getting closer, closer . . . With every vestige of effort she could summon forth, she banked down her rage. She took a series of steadying breaths, nodded to herself and set off to catch up with him.

'Livvy!' His surprise when he spotted her was evident. 'Hey, baby. What are you doing here?'

'Don't you "hey baby" me,' she told him. However, her voice was far from angry. Instead, she'd delivered the words on a sulky girlish note – she shot him a pout for good measure. 'I can't believe you've done this to me.'

Blinking in clear confusion, he took another step towards her. 'Done what?'

'You know darn well what, Carl Rivera!'

'Livvy, baby . . .' Wiping away with a finger the lone tear she'd squeezed out to plop to her cheek, he asked, tone high with concern now, 'You're talking about Joan? Is that it?'

'Well, of course it is. Why lie, eh? Why tell me for all that time that you loved me, when all along you were just using me to get to *her*. How could you?'

'I wasn't. I didn't. All this, it's not what you think—'

'Oh no? Then you tell me this: how come Joan reckons you're going to get married, hm?'

He blanched. 'She told you that? I said she wasn't to – sure, it was only a passing comment I made to please her—'

'Aye, she told me, all right. You've broken my heart, Carl.'

'So let me get this straight.' His gaze was wide with expectancy. 'You're telling me you actually *do* love me, after all? As I love you? Is that true, Livvy?'

'Of course it is!' Doing her best not to grimace when her skin met his, she touched his cheek in a gentle stroke.

'I knew it.' His face was one large smile. 'I knew you did really, were just playing hard to get. Oh, honey!'

Livvy was almost knocked from her feet as he grabbed her in an iron hold and kissed her full on the lips. She snatched her body back, couldn't help herself, before quickly stuttering at his expression of hurt, 'Not here, love. Folk will talk!'

'Oh, of course. Sorry, baby, I didn't think. I just can't resist you – *God*, you're beautiful.'

She giggled shyly. 'And you, Mr Rivera, are a silver-tongued charmer.'

'Hang on,' he said suddenly – Livvy held her breath. 'If you do love me, and were resisting me for so long because you needed me to prove to you just how serious I was, then what's changed, huh?'

Lord, but he really was the queerest, most delusional person she'd ever had the misfortune to meet. 'Seeing you with our Joan. Hearing her going on about you two all the time . . . it's killing me, Carl. I just can't pretend any longer. I want you to be mine, not hers!'

'And your good friend Clifford who beat me up—'

'He did what?' She put a hand to her mouth. 'I didn't know about that, honest. Eeh, the swine!'

'Yes, well, he did. He warned me to stay away from you, accused me of some terrible things . . . Did you tell him? About our night together?'

'No, no. Besides, it's none of his business.' Thinking quickly, she nodded. 'I'll bet it was Vera, the silly mare. She never could keep her trap shut. Anyroad, I certainly shan't be having owt more to do with Clifford after what you've told me. He had no right to harm you.' She crossed her fingers and apologised to her beloved in her mind, then, 'He means nowt to me.'

'You went away with him; that day I saw you both, you were catching a train together—'

'Oh that! No, love, you misunderstood: we were meeting a mutual friend at the station who was arriving in Bolton.'

He gasped, smiled. 'You were? But I thought—'

'Oh, now hang about – you didn't think me and him . . .'

'Yes.'

'What? No! No, Carl.'

'Livvy. Oh, Livvy.' He moved in for another kiss, then when she dodged it settled for an embrace instead. 'You do believe it was just play-acting with your sister?'

'Was it?'

'Baby, of course. I have a confession to make,' he added, sighing deeply. 'I planned on using Joan to bribe you into being with me.'

Tell me something I don't already know. Bastard, bastard . . . 'Oh?'

'I was going to sort of . . . threaten you a little bit. But only because I love you – you understand, right?'

'Sure I do,' she chirped. 'Leonard.'

'Ah. Yes.' He gave a half-sheepish, half-self-satisfied grin. 'That came to me in a flash of genius. Well, you'd have grown wise right away had your sister started bleating on about meeting a Carl. Leonard was my father's name.'

'Was?'

'He's dead, along with my mother. There's no one.'

'But by the way you've spoke in the past, you've gorra big family what meet up for loud dos with plenty of food, your parents alive still—'

'Perhaps I bent the truth a little. Fact is, Livvy, I've got not a single soul to call my own but you. Do you see now why I won't let you go? I was going to tell you that if you didn't agree to be my girl then I'd marry Joan and take her away to America with me, away from you. I just, I didn't know what else to do, I—'

'Shh, it's all right. It's all right.' She smiled. 'Well, your plan worked, Carl, you clever thing. Here I am.'

'You really mean it, don't you? Gee, Livvy, we're going to have such a swell time! You and I, together for ever—'

'There is one little fly in the ointment, love.' She nodded sadly. 'Our Joan.'

'What about her?'

'Well, she needs to know the truth about our love.'

He bobbed his head. 'You're right.'

'So you'll tell her how you really feel about her?' Livvy's heart had begun to thud.

'Yes.'

Got you, you swine. 'But here's the thing: you can't mention anything about us.'

He frowned. 'Why not?'

'If you do, it will ruin everything. We shan't be able to be together.' Seeing his face fall, she went in for the kill. 'My family, they're very unforgiving, Carl. They don't understand love like we do. If they were to discover I'd stolen my sister's beau away from under her nose—'

'But you wouldn't be! We loved each other way before Joan came along.'

'*We* know that,' she said patiently, 'but they wouldn't see it that way. They'd go berserk, might well harm you, even me—'

'They wouldn't.' His eyes had turned to steel. 'No one will touch a hair on your head while I'm around.'

'But it's norra risk we can take, love. Now, here's what I propose instead that we do. You tell Joan whilst you're out with her tonight that you've met another lass – not mentioning no names, of course – and that you want to be with her. Let the girl down gently, though, won't you?' Tears were threatening at the prospect of her dear sister hearing it and having her heart shattered in two, but for God's sake, what was the alternative? One must be cruel to be kind – it had to be done.

'When it's done with,' she went on, 'I'll slip from the house one night when they're all abed and go to another town – somewhere far away where no one will find me. I'll look for some rooms to rent, aye, and after the war we can finally be together.' She searched his face for any sign of disbelief. 'What d'you reckon?'

'You really will wait for me?'

'Aye, love, of course.'

'But the war . . . It might not end for years and years—'

'Oh, I'm sure it'll finish soon. Anyroad, a special love like ours will endure, won't it? What we've got, nothing can tear it asunder, not even time.'

Carl nodded thoughtfully. Then laughter burst

from him and he lifted her from her feet and twirled her around. 'Oh, honey. We'll be so happy together.'

'Course we will. I'll write to you, you know, whilst I'm away.'

'You better,' he grinned. Then his face turned sombre and he glanced around before saying in lowered tones, 'Everyone's working flat out now back at Burtonwood. There are rumours buzzing that something real big is coming, that the invasion to liberate France and so begin the Allied victory on the Western Front is about to get under way. Things sure are hotting up.'

'You'll be on my mind morning, noon and night, love, I swear. Right, well, we'd best get going, start the ball rolling.' She motioned towards the estate. 'Oh, and Carl?'

'Yes, baby?'

'After tonight, I don't want you visiting the Palais.' *She had to keep him away from her sister.* She stuck her bottom lip out in perfect imitation of a jealous moue. 'All them lasses parading themselves there every evening . . . I don't want you being tempted away.'

'Come on, now! As if I would. Sure, you've nothing to worry about—'

'Even so,' she said firmly. 'I've almost lost you to one woman, I'll not take the risk of it happening again. You must promise me.'

Taking her cheek in one of his hands, he nodded solemnly. 'I promise, Livvy.'

'Good. Now, we really had better be making a move. Joan will be waiting for you. I'll go on ahead, and you follow in a few minutes, so they don't grow suspicious. All right?'

'Kiss me before you go.'

She made a show of giggling and batting at his hands, which had begun to rove. 'There's no time. We must act now.'

'There's always time for kissing. Come on. Leave me with something to keep me going until we meet again. Please, Livvy.'

Christ's sake. 'All right, love. Just a quick one, mind.'

Scrunching shut her eyes, she held her breath and tolerated with rising bile the crush of his lips and taste of his tongue. When at long last he drew his head back and she was able to escape a few steps away from him, her palms felt wet with blood caused by her nails digging into her palms, so tightly had she been clenching her fists.

'I have to hurry now, Carl.'

'Okay. I love you, baby.'

'Aye, and me you. Ta-ra.'

She half ran the short stretch up Winchester Way and turned left into Blair Lane. Immediately that she was out of sight, she paused to scrub a sleeve across her mouth and spit several times on the ground.

Then she was off again, sprinting now, along New Lane and down Bridson Lane, and on to her street and the square.

Joan looked up as she entered the house: 'Where did you get to?'

'Oh, I just had to nip back home for summat,' she answered, smiling, ignoring a desperate-to-know-what-had-happened Vera, who was boring a hole into the side of her head with her gaze. She couldn't chance looking her way, must concentrate on acting natural. The woman would know the lie of the land soon enough.

'You didn't see Leonard, did you, outside? He's late.'

Doing her utmost to retain eye contact, Livvy shook her head. 'Sorry, lass, I didn't.'

'I were just saying to Vera, did you know that some soldiers remove their dog tags on the battlefield just in case they're killed, to delay identification? They do it for the money, so the army won't stop their wives and kiddies dependants' allowances right away. I reckon that's really romantic. It's summat Leonard would do, that. He'd not be thinking of hisself neither; so long as I'm all right, he'd be happy. He's a gem, you know, Livvy.'

Oh lass, lass.

'Ah, speak of the devil and he shall appear!' Joan added seconds later, oblivious to the accuracy of her passing comment, jumping to her feet. 'This'll be him, now. Well, ta-ra, you two.'

'Bye, lass,' Livvy murmured. And knowing what was to come, she just didn't have it in her to wish her a good night as she normally would have, irrespective of whether it might evoke possible suspicion. 'You look after yourself.'

The moment the front door closed behind the girl, Vera was out of her seat: 'Well, love? What occurred? Did he swallow it?'

'He did.'

'The whole thing?'

'Hook, line and sinker.'

Heaving a long breath, the woman pressed Livvy's shoulder. 'Well bloody done, girl.'

'Vera, what about Joan? Lord, I feel wretched just thinking about it . . . Her heart's going to shatter.'

'Aye, and believe me, Livvy, she'd be feeling a lot worse later when she learned the real truth of things, for it would have been bound to come out. This is the kindest thing all round. Besides, she's young yet. She'll get over it.'

Hugging herself, Livvy bit her lip. 'I do hope you're right.'

'Trust me. Now, where d'you keep your pencil and paper? It's time to drop my sister in Worcestershire a line.'

'She'll definitely agree to receive letters there for

me from Carl, won't she, love, to uphold the pretence? And reply to any what he sends as though they were from me?'

'We'll soon find out.'

An hour elapsed, then two, and still Joan hadn't returned.

Seated either side of Morris, who was chattering nineteen to the dozen about something or other – the women were not listening – Livvy and Vera remained on tenterhooks, awaiting the rattle of the front door.

Livvy had told Clifford that she was spending the evening at number twenty-two to enjoy a bit of time with her friend and grandfather playing cards, and that he needn't wait up for her. And being the man he was, he'd believed her without a single shred of doubt, increasing her levels of guilt ever more and proving to her further still that he didn't deserve a scheming cow like her for a wife.

'Where the hell is she?' Livvy hissed, rushing to the window to scour the street the moment that Morris left the room to go to bed. 'She ought surely to have been back by now.'

'Aye.' Vera's brow was lined with shared worry. 'Time is getting on a bit, I must admit. Let's just give her a little longer.'

Another hour passed. Livvy, having reached the

end of her endurance and imagining all sorts, was preparing to put her coat on and go out to look for the girl when Vera held up a hand: 'I'm sure that was the gate ... Aye, there you see,' she added as the door opening sounded. 'Now, love, act natural.'

Nodding and returning to her seat, Livvy held her breath.

'All right, Joan?' Vera asked when she entered the living room.

'You all right, lass?' Livvy mimicked.

'Aye.'

'You're sure?' Livvy whispered, moving to the end of the sofa to look properly into her sister's face. There was a definite puffiness to her red-rimmed eyes; it was evident she'd been crying. 'Lass?'

'No! No, I'm not, as it goes. I've been walking the streets for hours, just trying to make sense of it ... Leonard's ended it!'

The women exhaled simultaneously.

'Oh, he never has,' Livvy managed, rushing to grip Joan's hand.

'Eeh, the swine,' threw in Vera.

'He says he's met someone else and that he loves her. I've lost him, Livvy. What will I do? I love him!'

'Lass, lass ...' Tears wobbled on her own lashes; she dabbed at them quickly. 'My poor little love.'

'He can't do this, you know; he'll have to come back to me.'

Vera knelt by the girl's feet beside Livvy and took her other hand. 'Let him go, love. It's for the best, and you deserve better.'

'She's right,' Livvy said, however Joan continued to shake her head.

'Youse don't understand. He'll have to come back. He'll *have* to, for he must marry me. I'm carrying his child.'

Chapter Fourteen

'YOUNG YET, IS she? Soon get over it, will she, Vera?'

'Eeh, what a bloody mess.'

Having spent the past hour holding and rocking a weeping Joan until she finally fell to sleep through pure exhaustion, Livvy was wrung dry both emotionally and physically. Never, *never* would she have seen this coming. What the hell were they meant to do now?

'He's gorra knack for it, I'll give him that.'

'What?'

'Ruining females' lives. First you, then me, now your Joan – and we'll not be the only ones, I'll be bound. Oh no. Carl Rivera causes nowt but destruction at every which way he turns. He's a master at it.'

'He cajoled the lass into it, seduced her, aye. Worked his horrible, oily charm on her and won his prize. She's always been reet against messing around outside of wedlock. She certainly weren't considering it with Harry, her last beau, vowed to me she wasn't that stupid. I hate him, Vera. I hate that bastard with every fibre of my being and more besides. May the Lord strike me down, and I never thought I'd wish this on any of the military boys, but I hope he's killed. I hope to God he gets wiped off the face of this earth – for all our sakes.'

'For the sake of womankind in general,' her friend agreed grimly. 'But 'tain't likely, though, is it, more's the pity. Burtonwood's a maintenance base – its men work on aircraft and the like only, to keep the pilots supplied. No operational missions fly from there.'

'Well . . . some accident or other, then, perhaps! Surely they must occur sometimes in an environment such as that?' She sighed. 'Do you know what really sticks in my craw, though, shall I tell you? When all this is over, and the war is no more, he'll be paraded about like a sodding hero. A brave serviceman, done his bit for his country – aye, and crushed the lives of who knows how many in *our* country in the process. Whilst my darling husband, he'll be remembered amongst most as nobbut a coward. Now where's the justice in that?'

Vera hadn't the answer.

'Oh, how will I break the news of Joan to Grandma and Grandad? They'll hit the roof. The girl shan't get much sympathy from that quarter, oh no, not if I know them. "The only place you'll find sympathy is in the dictionary between shit and syphilis" is one of the owd man's favourite sayings, after all.'

'He's a card, Morris.' Vera laughed softly. 'But you know, Livvy, him and Madge love the bones of you and Joan; I reckon they just might surprise you.'

'We'll see.' Yes, they would, for there was no concealing this, no coming up with some grand plan to make this go away. God help them. 'I'll sit them down tomorrow with the lass and put them in the picture.'

'Joan sounded dead set on Carl marrying her, love, didn't she? What if she'll not listen to reason, that he's a bad bugger and that she'd be better off without him – and what if your grandparents agree with her, take the fight to the American authorities?'

'I don't know,' Livvy whispered. 'I'm just too tired with it all to think straight.'

'Just as everything was working out, too; it's bloody unfair. Your meeting with him earlier couldn't have gone any better – for all the good it did. Now look where we are.'

'I'll stop over here tonight in case Joan wakens and needs me – Clifford will understand. Why don't you go up, love, get some shut-eye? You look all in.'

'I am a bit, aye.' Vera confirmed her admission with a mammoth yawn. The child was overdue and the pregnancy beginning to take its toll on the expectant mother. 'I don't blame this mite not wanting to be born – it likely senses the state the world's in and is thinking sod that, I'm stopping put! I tell you summat, though, I'll be glad when he or she does arrive. I'm worn out all the time lately.'

'And then the real work begins,' Livvy told her with a small smile. 'Just remember, though, you'll not be alone.'

The woman dropped a kiss on to Livvy's head. 'May God bless you, love, for now me and Joan both need you more than ever before. These children shall be lucky to have you.'

Two children. The reality struck Livvy later when she was lying beside Joan in the small bed. For years, she'd yearned for just one child to fill the void, and now two had come along at once. Not her own, of course, but close enough. And by God, she'd love them with all that she was. *Both begot by the same man, siblings. Products of her rapist's seeds.* Oh, but what a bloody mess indeed.

'I'm going whether youse lot like it or not.'

It was the following morning and the family were assembled in the living room of number twenty-two.

Madge and Morris had been made aware of their youngest granddaughter's predicament and, as Livvy had suspected, were far from pleased with the matter. There had been no shouting, however, for which she was grateful; she doubted whether her shattered nerves would have withstood it. The deed was done, so to speak – where would have been the point in letting their tempers explode? Husband and wife had simply exclaimed a few colourful choice words and let it be known their disappointment, and now sat sullenly wearing matching grim expressions.

'He's no good, Joan,' Livvy tried again now, whilst Madge and Morris nodded their agreement. They had been informed of Carl's desertion and wanted him nowhere near the girl. 'He dumped you only last night for another lass! Let him be, forget all about him, and allow your family to help you instead. I'll do everything I can for you and the child; you're not alone.'

'And let the swine get away with his responsibilities? No chance! He'll put a ring on my finger and give this baby a name, whether he wants to or no.'

'You'll shackle yourself to a no-good wastrel like that?' Madge said. 'No, Livvy's right. Don't get me wrong, the situation's far from ideal, but the alternative's a far worse fate. He clearly don't love thee – what sort of basis is that forra marriage? You'd be chaining yourself to a man through duty alone, and believe me when I say it, that shan't bode well. I've seen it happen countless times afore, and not once did it have a happy ending. You'll grow to resent one another, and no one more than that poor babe stuck between the two of you will suffer for it. Just let the low-down dog go. It's the best thing all round.'

The obstinacy in Joan's gaze hadn't wavered an

inch. She flicked her head in dismissal. 'I'm going to Burtonwood to confront him,' she persisted, eyes ablaze with dogged determination, 'and there's nowt youse can do to stop me.'

'Bloody GIs,' Clifford muttered beneath his breath – and turning the blood in his wife's veins to ice.

Still her husband was none the wiser concerning events. Livvy just didn't have the courage to tell him – and especially so now. As each hour then day had passed, the thought of doing so had become infinitely more difficult; he would never forgive her for lying to him. She could only be thankful that all mention of Joan's lost love throughout this was still of 'Leonard' and not his real identity. Thus far, Clifford had no cause to suspect anything was amiss, and for that Livvy remained truly thankful.

'I'll go alone, you know, if I have to,' Joan threatened, shrugging on her coat. 'I ain't much fussed either way.'

Silence hung in the air as thick as porridge. It was Clifford who broke it:

'I'll come with you.'

'No.' Livvy shook her head at him fiercely. '*No.*'

'The lass will do this whether you want her to or not, Livvy, and she shouldn't face it on her own. Someone has to go with her.'

'Then I'll go,' she heard herself say. What option had she? Rather that than her husband be confronted with the facts.

'You will, Livvy? Really?' Joan asked tearfully.

A quick glance to Vera, who raised her shoulders in a helpless motion, and Livvy nodded. 'I'll fetch my coat.'

The sisters left the house. Shoulders hunched, head down, Livvy turned her thoughts in on themselves and prayed for all she was worth that when they reached the base, their request to see Carl would be refused. If he should see them, let slip to Joan about anything . . . the ramifications didn't bear thinking about. *Please, please.*

They were midway up the street when Morris's yells, calling out their names, reached their ears.

Slowing, they shared a frown then hurried to retrace their steps.

'Grandad?' Joan asked as they approached the gate, however he appeared incapable of further speech.

'Tell us, what's wrong,' Livvy urged.

Hopping from foot to foot on the step, his face white, he thumbed towards the living room beyond. 'The lass . . . The babby!'

'Vera's gone into labour?' Livvy whispered.

'No sooner had the front door closed behind youse both than she let out a cry, and a dam burst from beneath her ruddy skirt! Quick, now. Come on!'

'Calm down,' Madge ordered her husband when

he re-entered the room, his granddaughters hot on his heels. 'Flapping shan't help none. You,' she added to Clifford, 'take yourself across the road home with Morris here; youse'll only get in the way. Joan,' she went on, 'you'll go with them.'

'But I need to see Leonard! He has to know—'

'Not now, for Christ's sake,' Livvy snapped at her. As excited as she was that the baby was soon to be here, she couldn't help being equally as thankful for the incredible timing and didn't intend on squandering this opportunity to delay her sister's plans. 'It'll have to wait. Right now, this is more important.'

'I'm scared, Livvy,' Vera whimpered when it was just the two of them and Madge. Livvy rushed to squat by her side.

'I know, love, but I'll be here, and so will Grandma. We'll not leave your side. Eeh, Vera . . .' She stroked her hair and grinned. 'You're going to be a mummy!'

'Let's get you upstairs, lass.' Madge helped Vera to stand and guided her to the door. 'Livvy, fetch newspapers to cover the mattress. And for God's sake get the kettle on for some tea.'

'Well, would you look at her.' Madge's voice was filled with wonder. 'She's perfect, lass. Perfect.'

Propped up on the pillows in the remade bed, washed and dressed in fresh clothing and her hair

302

tidied, Vera gazed down at the being she'd not once took her eyes from.

'You were brilliant, love.' Livvy wiped away a tear. 'Just over three hours in labour – by, that's fast, in't it, Grandma?'

'It is, especially for your first. You got off lightly there, lass!'

'I'd do it all again ten times over if I had to,' the woman murmured. 'I just can't believe she's mine.'

'*All* yours,' Livvy said meaningfully, and they shared a nod.

'I'm going to call her Enid, after my mam. Enid Olive.' She smiled. 'If that's all right with you, Livvy?'

'Of course, I . . . Oh, love.' Dissolving into joyous tears, she put her arms around mother and child and hugged them gently.

'I'd best nip across the road, fill the others in on the good tidings,' Madge said. 'They'll be that pleased, 'specially poor Morris – by, I thought *he* were about to have kittens!'

'Aye, go on, Grandma, and I'll brew a fresh pot. Sod the rationing, we're celebrating.'

Livvy was loading the tea tray and humming happily to herself when Madge returned, Morris and Celia in tow. She glanced behind them for Clifford and Joan, but there was no sign of them. 'Where's t' other two?'

'You'll not believe it – by, she will have her own way, that girl.'

Dread trickling through her, Livvy asked, 'What d'you mean?'

'They've gone to Burtonwood. Joan refused to wait and wouldn't let up; Clifford's gone with her.'

No. 'When?'

'Oh, not long after they left here, apparently. They ought to have been back by now, surely – unless summat's afoot.' Shaking her head, Madge clicked her tongue, adding wearily, 'D'you know, if it's not one thing it's another.'

'I, just have to . . .' Passing the tray across to the woman, Livvy escaped from the room and made for the solitude of the bathroom.

Trembling, she perched on the side of the tub. Carl had revealed all. He had, it was true. Joan and Clifford knew, about everything – the pair would never forgive her. What was she going to do? Where the hell were they? Please don't let Clifford have done something foolish. Oh please, she couldn't lose him . . . *Why* weren't they back yet?

'Livvy?'

Blinking back to the present, she glanced around the space in puzzlement for a moment, wondering where she was; so consumed with her thoughts, she could barely recall coming up here.

'Livvy!' Madge called again. 'Have you got stuck in the bowl?'

'No, Grandma. I'm, I'm coming . . .'

'Good, for the wanderers have returned, just come round the corner, and your husband don't look best pleased to say the least. Summat's occurred, you best come down.'

'What's happened?' Livvy asked fearfully halfway down the stairs, as Clifford and Joan entered, having forced herself from the bathroom on legs that felt like wax. Their faces were stiff and unyielding, giving nothing away. 'Lass? Love?' she whispered.

'Leonard don't exist,' her sister stated at last.

'What?'

'Eh!'

Madge and Morris stared at her in bemusement.

Livvy, meanwhile, had dragged her gaze to Clifford, where it remained locked. The enmity pouring from his eyes told her all she needed to know. He'd found out, he had. He knew.

'I gave his details at the base camp and were told there were no one there by that name. Not Leonard Rivera, anyroad. There was a *Carl* Rivera there, though. I asked to see him instead and when I told them who I was, they refused. Turns out he's put a block on me, said that if I should ever show up, I was to be sent away, that he doesn't want to see me. All this time . . . it were nobbut lies. He used me to have his wicked way – none of it's been real. I only gave in to him because he swore to me he'd asked his

305

commanding officer for permission to marry me, and was just waiting for the go-ahead. He duped me. And now he's left me in t' lurch; it's over. How could he do it? The rotten swine – I wish I were dead!'

Dumbfounded, the elder members of the gathering rallied round the distraught girl to offer support. Clifford, his gaze never once having left his wife, flicked his chin for her to follow and left the house. And with her heart like a stone and her stomach in knots, she did.

Inside number nineteen, Livvy waited in silence. Her husband was standing by the fire with his back to her and she watched the back of his head, dreading what must come but yet just wanting it to be over with. The stress of all this was too much; it was killing her.

'What the hell's going on, Livvy?' he asked at last.

'Lad . . .'

'I know that you know.' His words were flat. 'I saw it, in your eyes, when we got back just now. What have you done?'

'Carl planned it from the off. He had the lass fall for him to get to me; he was going to use her to bribe me into being with him. I met up with him. I tricked him into thinking I loved him after all, convinced him to leave Joan be. Then she dropped the bombshell that she was in the family way, and she just wouldn't forget him – and now you're going to leave

306

me, ain't you?' She'd spoken the entirety in one long rush. Taking a deep breath, she finished with, 'Please don't.'

'You lied to me.'

'No, love, I didn't. I just didn't tell you.'

'It amounts to the same thing, Livvy! It's your past profession all over again. You swore to never keep things from me any more, said you'd always be honest from now on. For God's sake, why do this?'

'Because I was afraid! I was afraid of how you'd react if you learned he was back on the scene, of what you'd do . . . I'm so sorry, Clifford. I was just trying to protect you. Protect Joan – even Vera.'

'Vera?'

She closed her eyes. 'Her child, too, is Carl's.'

'I don't believe I'm hearing all this . . .'

'I'm sorry.'

'Anything else I should know? Hm? Any more lies you've fed to me?'

'No, honest!'

'I trusted you. A great way to begin married life, this is, keeping things from one another.'

Closing the space between them, she laid a tentative hand on his arm, but he moved away from her reach. She let it fall back to her side.

'When did you meet him?' her husband asked suddenly.

'Yesterday.'

'Oh yes. When you told me you were going out to keep Vera and Morris company across the way.'

'Aye,' she whispered, cringing.

'Where?'

'Where . . . what?'

'Where did you meet him, the Yank?'

'On the brow, by the church. He was due to pick Joan up; I lay in wait for him, to speak to him in private.'

Clifford released an incredulous snort. 'So let me just see if I've got this right. You went out – alone – to meet up with a man who once raped you, in a place bordered on either side with secluded fields and woodland? Really? Can you actually hear yourself? What if he'd have got it into his head to drag you into the bushes – I mean, it's not like he ain't already got form, is it? What if he'd have attacked you again, eh, with no one around to hear your screams? Why would you do it, put yourself in danger like that? Why?'

Now that he put it like that, it did sound incredibly risky. 'At the time, I honestly didn't think, wasn't thinking soundly, I . . . I just needed rid of him! He might have told our Joan at any moment, about me, the prostitution—'

'You told him you loved him? Is that what you said?'

'But only so's he'd believe me. Of course, I never meant it. It were just words—'

'Happen it's just words with me? Aye, mebbe I'm right. *May*be you've just been telling me what I wanted to hear all along as well.'

'What? No, don't talk so daft! You're just twisting what I'm saying, now.'

'Did he touch you?' Clifford's eyes bore into her soul. 'Did he?' he repeated lowly.

'No. Well aye, he sort of did – but I had to go along with it, I—'

'What the hell d'you mean, sort of?' he whispered. His stare was wide. 'What was it?'

'Love, *please*.'

'I need to hear it, Livvy.'

'He . . . held me. In his arms. And he . . . he . . .'

'Tell me.'

'Clifford . . .'

'Say it!'

'He kissed me! He kissed me, aye! Right here,' she cried, stabbing at her lips with her finger, 'full on the mouth – tongues, the lot! Is that what you want to hear? Is it? And I hated it, hatcd it!' She held out her palms to reveal the marks scoring the flesh there from her fingernails. 'The sheer strength it took to endure it . . . But I did it. I did it for them that I love, nothing more. You must believe me.'

Her husband stumbled past her to the door. 'I can't . . .'

'No, don't go – Clifford, please. You're letting Carl win by doing this, don't you see it?' she howled to his retreating back, scuttling after him into the street. 'This is just what he wants – don't give him the satisfaction!'

'You said once, Livvy, that I shouldn't wed you. That I deserved better. Well, d'you know what? Happen I should have heeded your words. Happen I should, for I reckon you were right.'

'No. No, no, wait I . . . Clifford!' she cried out tearfully as he strode down the garden path. 'I love you. Clifford, don't go!'

'Goodbye, Livvy.'

No.

He disappeared around the corner from view and her legs buckled beneath her. She fell to her knees on the hard road.

'Livvy? Eeh, love.'

'Bertha. I'm sorry, I didn't know where else to go. I couldn't face my family, I couldn't . . . Oh, Bertha, what am I going to do?'

The woman ushered her inside, up the back stairs and into her private sitting room. 'Now, sit, whilst I brew a sup of tea. Then you can tell me everything.'

And Livvy did. In imitation of last time during

their first meeting, she poured out her heart, told Bertha every last sorry detail; she left nothing out. Afterwards, eyes red raw from crying and her chest aching from the heaviness of her heart, she rested her head on the woman's shoulder and released a long sigh. 'I've only ever wanted what's best for them I love. I just seem to keep getting it wrong.'

'That's some tale. D'you know, you never seem to catch a break, you, do yer, poor lass.'

'I'm tired, Bertha. So very tired.'

'And no wonder. I'm giving you a week off to sort your home life out – and no arguments.'

'Eeh, Bertha. Ta, thanks.'

'As for this Yank fella: shall I give you my take on it, lass?'

Raising her head to look into her eyes, Livvy nodded eagerly.

'Ignore him.'

She blinked. 'That's it?'

'That's it,' she confirmed firmly. 'He's done the worst to you now that he possibly could – there's nothing left for him to spoil, no one to corrupt. If he comes sniffing around again, trying to get you to be with him, say no. Just no – and keep on saying it until he grows bored.'

'And what if he never does?'

'He will.'

'You don't know him like I do. He's not one for letting go.'

'What's he going to do? Drag you from the bosom of your family by the scruff of your neck? Tell him to take a running jump! If all else fails, summon the police, get him done for harassment. Happen a stint in t' clink will make him see the error of his ways.'

Bertha made it all sound so simple. Nevertheless, she'd tried every other option, had she not? Perhaps this was worth a shot. What had she to lose? 'And Clifford?' Livvy murmured after a while.

'His pride's dented and he's hurt. If I know men, he'll come round before too long. Give him time.'

'Oh, here she comes, look.'

Having left Bertha's chip shop an hour or so later, Livvy was feeling far more reassured about the future and had been all fired up to offer support to her family and make things up with her husband. Now, seeing the two women who resided at the bottom end of her street up ahead, gossiping by their gates as per usual, and hearing the scathing comment, her chest tightened in weary dread. She wasn't a fan of confrontation at the best of times; right now, even more so. She hadn't the strength for this after every-thing else. *Please, just leave me be.*

'That husband of yours seen the light, has he? Didn't take long, did it?'

Eyes straight in front, Livvy had taken several steps past them and was about to heave a sigh of relief when those next words hit her full around the face. She juddered to a halt. Slowly, she turned back around to face them. 'What did you say?'

'You heard,' the taller of the women retorted. 'Aye, and if you don't want folk having an opinion on your business, then here's a tip for you: keep it private, eh! Caterwauling in t' street like a ruddy fishwife – aye, we saw you earlier. So, the man's gone, has he? Well, that were a blinkin' short marriage!'

'Clifford's not gone. He just . . . he needed time to cool off, and—'

'Mind you, I ain't even surprised that he were daft enough to take a tart like you on, nay. That coward wouldn't know good sense if it jumped out and bit him square on the arse. He ain't got all his marbles, neither, for if he did, he'd be away helping our boys fight this war.'

This proved too much for Livvy. Bad-mouthing her was one thing – blimey, it wasn't as though she wasn't used to it, was it? – but ripping chunks out of her husband? Oh no. She wasn't standing for that. Striding forward, she thrust her face into the bullish one and curled her lip.

'Just who the frig do you think you are, eh?' she snarled, looking the dowdy pair up and down. 'Sad, sad bitches, youse are, the pair. Your lives are that dull you have nowt better to do but tear other people apart. Well, I'm telling you here and now, missis' – Livvy prodded the speaker hard in the shoulder, making her stagger back – 'spout whatever poison you fancy about me; I ain't much mithered no more. But Clifford? If I ever hear another word against him from that disgusting tongue of yours, I'll rip the thing clean from your head and shove it down your throat! He's worth a hundred of youse, you know that? A more kind, decent and upstanding fella you're never likely to meet, so just you think on.'

Evidently surprised at being tackled like this – Livvy normally ignored all vitriol thrown her way by the estate's residents – the neighbours' mouths were flapping.

'Huh – hark at her!' one managed to choke out at last, just as Livvy was about to continue on for home. 'Miss High and bloody Mighty! Say what you like: you're a rotten whore, Livvy Bryant, and always shall be. It's alone you'll be now – and it's nowt less than you deserve. That husband of yourn shan't be back, you just wait and see!'

'Well, that's where you're wrong.'

All three women whipped their heads around at the male voice that had called out from across the road – and gasped in tandem. Clifford was standing viewing them.

As though in a dream, Livvy watched him walk the short distance to her side. He put his capable arms around her, and she huddled into his chest with a soft sob.

'She's Livvy Bamford now. And my wife is no whore.' He threw the words at the neighbours like blades, making them wince. 'Nor will she ever be alone. Here I am, in the flesh – and what's more, I ain't going nowhere.'

'Lad?' Raising her face, Livvy gazed into his eyes in wonderment.

'Nowhere,' he repeated. He pressed his lips to hers. 'Let's go home.'

Not a further peep was heard from the women as, backs straight and heads held high, the married couple marched away.

Chapter Fifteen

'WELL, LASS?' HER employer asked Livvy on the Saturday when she returned to work after her break. 'How're things with you?'

'Good, Bertha. Reet good.'

'And I can tell – aye, that smile of yours says it well enough.'

She and Clifford had spoken well into the late evening upon their return home that day. Just as she'd done months before, when relaying to him her life story and reasons behind her more disastrous decisions, so she did again with regards to this most recent debacle with Carl.

Calmly and with patience, they had begun to understand one another's actions, had aired every aspect of their feud, however uncomfortable, and, mercifully, managed to work it out. Apologies from both sides – Clifford had insisted upon this, regretted some of the things he'd uttered in anger, although Livvy thought and told him so that they were well justified – and a long night of slow lovemaking had soon brought them back together, exactly where they belonged. Never would anything, anyone, put a road through them again.

'So your husband's all right, now?'

'He is.'

'And the others?'

'Vera and her daughter are doing just gradely. As for Joan . . . she lost the baby.'

'Eeh, has she? Perhaps it's for the best, you know, all things considered?'

Livvy nodded with a small sigh.

'How's she doing?'

'She's getting there, bless her, and coming to terms with things. She blasts Carl more often now than she spills tears for him at any rate, which we can at least be glad about. The rose-tinted specs have fallen from her eyes good and proper, glory be. He used to mock our town, you know, so she's told me, reckoned Bolton's nobbut a dirty, black hole and the folk what dwell in it little better than savages. She put his arrogance and brashness down to it just being the American way, told herself he just made gaffes sometimes, but that no harm were intended. She's so mad about that, now, you know: that she sat there and let him lambast her home like that. Proud of her roots is our lass.'

Bertha nodded approvingly. 'Sounds like she's grown up some from all of this.'

'Oh, she'll not be swayed with sweet talk as she has been, not by any fella again. Aye, matured she has. Well, she's had to, eh? This is a second chance she's been given, a fresh start, and she knows it. There's lasses aplenty what don't get so lucky.'

'Will you ever tell her the true facts of things, do you think?'

'Mebbe. One day. Her and Vera's children would have been siblings, after all. Aye, when Joan's strong enough, happen I might. As for Carl Rivera . . . We've agreed, me and Clifford and Vera, to give what you suggested a go and ignore him. We can but try.'

At that point, a group of customers entered the shop, bringing their conversation to an end – with a nod and a wink, the women rolled up their sleeves and got to work.

Livvy was almost midway through her shift when a good-looking red-haired fellow appeared and approached the counter. Turning her attentions to him, she smiled: 'Yes, love, what can I get you?'

'Am I speaking with Bertha?'

He talked with a deep American drawl; Livvy shook her head. 'No, lad, but I can fetch her for you?'

'I'd appreciate that if it's not too much trouble, ma'am, thank you.'

318

'No trouble at all,' she responded lightly – though inside, she was itching with curiosity.

She summoned Bertha from the back room and watched her exchange with the GI discreetly. He spoke at length, although Livvy wasn't close enough to hear what it was about, then Bertha's face cleared and she beckoned to her employee. Livvy blinked in surprise.

'You want me, Bertha?'

'I do, lass. Come over here a minute, would you? This young man here would like a word.'

A word with me? What on earth could he want with her? Brow creased, she made her way across.

'Now before you hear what he's got to say, I have a confession to make,' Bertha announced. 'The advice I gave you on ignoring the queer one? Just to be on t' safe side, I also had a whisper in a few yankee-doodle-dandy ears belonging to some of my regular customers. I asked them to put Carl straight, you know, when they saw him at base? Well, it seems that they did.' With that, Bertha motioned for the man to continue where she'd left off and returned to her duties.

'Ma'am, I'd like to apologise to you for Carl Rivera's conduct. The servicemen who Bertha spoke to in here told me he's been harassing you? Is this correct?'

So Bertha had mentioned only the basics. That

much was clear, for what she'd suffered at that animal's hands would certainly need a stronger description than that. She nodded.

'I don't know what must have been going through his head to act as he did, but I can assure you he won't be bothering you any more. Not since our little . . . chat. You have my word on it.'

'Sorry, who are you?'

'Marvin, ma'am. I'm Carl's brother-in-law.'

Livvy raised her eyebrows. 'You're wed to his sister? But I thought . . . he told me he had no family.'

'Oh, he has family, all right – a whole bunch of them.'

She shook her head slowly. What was *wrong* with him, at all? Talk about compulsive liar, it wasn't in it.

'But that's beside the point – you misunderstand me,' the American went on. 'I'm not married to his sister. Carl is married to mine.'

'What . . .?' All this time. All this time, he'd had a poor wife waiting for him back home? 'I don't believe this.'

'It's true. She gave birth to his child just before we left for England.'

'He has kiddies?'

'Four, as a matter of fact.'

'Four!' *Oh, ruddy hell.*

'Listen, I have to dash, but please, allow me to say once again that I'm sorry for how he's treated you.

You'll hear no more from Carl Rivera. Goodbye, ma'am.'

Marvin's prediction proved false three days later. Livvy did hear from Carl after all.

It came in the form of a letter through the post at number twenty-two. A letter addressed to herself, Vera and Joan.

Reading and re-reading the scrawl on the envelope numerous times, she knew instinctively who it was from. There was no one else it could be but the person who had wronged all three of the addressees.

Hesitantly, Livvy tore it open and scanned the sheet contained within.

It held no explanation, logical or otherwise. Instead, a singular word stared back at her.

Just one, written in bold capitals in the centre of the paper:

SORRY.

Livvy carried it and the envelope to the fire and dropped them on to the flames.

When only ash remained, she straightened, took a deep breath and carried on with the rest of her life.

Chapter Sixteen

25 December 1944

'WHAT TIME ARE we on, now? Twelve p.m.? Let's have a look-see . . . Reginald Foort at the theatre organ: "A Musical Christmas Stocking". By, I like the sound of that.' Tossing the Christmas week edition of the *Radio Times* on to the floor, leaving the drawing of the tired and homesick Tommy on the front cover to keep up his forlorn stare at the paperchain-festooned ceiling, Morris flapped a hand to Vera, sitting closest to the wireless set. ''Ere, you lass, turn that on! Ay, make us feel all nice and festive, it will.'

Looking down at the cherry-cheeked child slumbering contentedly in her arms, she asked, 'What am I meant to turn the knob with? My nose?'

'It's all right, it's all right.' He rose reluctantly. 'Don't trouble yourself none, I'll see to it myself.'

'Cheek!' Vera, who had more than established

herself as one of the family, hooted with laughter. 'Anyroad, I wouldn't bother if I were you.'

Tongue poking out of the side of his mouth in concentration, he twiddled through the stations, becoming increasingly irate. 'Why can't I find the bleedin' thing?'

'That's what I was trying to tell you. Did you not hear me say—'

'I heard. Aye, and why shouldn't I be bothering, like?'

'Because, Morris, you were looking at the Christmas Eve broadcasting, not Christmas Day.'

'Oh, hell's teeth. The wrong page; was I really?'

'Aye. And another thing.' Vera's eyes shone with mirth. 'That issue itself, what you've just been reading for the past twenty minutes? It's twelve months old.'

'Eh!'

'See for yourself.' Vera pushed the magazine along the floor towards him with her foot. 'It says so there, in t' top corner: December 1943.'

'Well, where's this week's? And where's that thing even come from! See, you see, youse lot don't pull your weight enough around here. Last year's, I ask you!'

'Well, that's rich, I must say.' Having entered the room, Livvy stared down at him in mock severity, hands on hips. 'Grandad, d'you reckon there might be any danger of you actually helping out today? You've not done a hand's turn since you got up – we're up to our bloomin' eyes in it, here.'

'Eh? Me? This house is bursting at the seams with a whole ruddy army of wenches, and you expect me to step in and risk getting in your road? Not likely! I'm stopping well out of the way, I ain't that daft.'

'Look, Clifford's doing summat, and he's not getting an ear-bashing, is he?' She nodded to the space beneath the window, where her husband was on his knees busy decorating the Christmas tree with glass baubles. 'So come on, shape yourself.' Nudging Morris, she encouraged him up from his chair again. 'Don't you fret, I'll soon find summat for you to do.'

Grunting and grumbling, he stood facing her in his slippers. 'I'm not doing no women's work, so just you think on.'

'Huh, would you listen to it!' Madge's voice filtered through from the kitchen. 'King of the bloody castle, he favours hisself!'

'Right,' Livvy intervened before Morris could yell back a retort, 'here's the deal. You can either mind little Enid in Vera's place so she can come and lend a hand in the kitchen, or you can peel some spuds. What's it to be?'

'Not much of a choice, is it?'

'Well, it's one or t' other, so make up your mind.'

Rubbing his gums along his lips in contemplation,

Morris finally threw up his hands. 'Pass me the blasted tatties. It's the lesser of two evils, I suppose – babbies don't half wear me out.'

Livvy went to do his bidding, then, holding in laughter, returned to the bustling kitchen. 'He's gorra face like thunder, him, in there.'

'He will have,' her grandmother snorted. 'Glass back owd swine, he's nowt else.'

'How's the grub coming along?' Livvy asked her sister and Celia. 'By, it smells good, anyroad.'

This sixth Christmas of the war was proving an even more austere event than those before it. The main dish on today's menu was mock goose, a form of potato casserole. Though the family – the whole country, for that matter – would have loved to have had turkey with all the trimmings, it just wasn't possible. However, the fare did show some hope of being at least an adequate feast, and for this they were truly thankful.

Months ago, Glaister Lane's residents had got together and decided to purchase between them all a sow. Housed in the back garden of the man who had first suggested the idea, Peggy the Piggy had gorged on all of the neighbours' kitchen scraps, which they had collected in a joint bin at the end of the road. Yesterday, Peggy had faced her fate and the meat had been distributed equally between the whole street.

Numbers nineteen and twenty-two had decided to pool their pork rations and treat themselves to a banquet; the women had been planning and preparing since early morning. Each was determined to make this a wonderful Yuletide get-together that would be enjoyed by all.

'By, that were marvellous,' Morris announced later that afternoon, rubbing his pot belly as confirmation of a job well done. 'Them tatties turned out gradely, didn't they? I reckon they were the best part of the meal. Aye, the best part by a long chalk.'

'Here we go . . .' Madge rolled her eyes. 'He peels a handful of potatoes and fancies himself a cordon bleu chef.'

'Speaking of the French . . .'

'Who was?' Madge demanded.

'You was! Cordon bleu – 'tis France language, that.'

His wife was frowning in confusion. 'All right, well, what about it?'

'There was this one time, at Passchendaele—'

'Now come on, I'm not having this,' she insisted, folding her arms. 'Ypres is in bloomin' Belgium, so what the devil has this story got to do with France?'

'France, Belgium – it makes no odds, 'tis all the same to me. A trench is a trench, you know, whatever country you're fighting in! Anyroad, as I were saying: Passchendaele—'

'Oh, please, no more talk of it . . .'

'No, no, you'll like this one. Easter Monday, it were. Eeh, what a dark one it was, an' all—'

'It's cosy in here, in't it, with the lights from the tree and the fire burning, like a scene from a Christmas card,' Livvy intervened before her grandmother blew her top. Cuddling baby Enid Olive – what a gift that had been to her, her friend naming the child after her, and amazed her still to think on it – she sighed happily. 'I wonder what life will be like by next Christmas? Eeh, I do hope it'll all be over. Surely the climax to this war ain't far off, now.'

'I'll not hold my breath after the other night's antics,' Morris declared grimly. 'Half five in the bloody morn of a Christmas Eve and the sirens go off. Near leapt clean from my skin, I did, hearing that Moaning Minnie after all that time.'

Clifford murmured agreement. 'Almost two and a half years since the last time it sounded. Even the air-raid wardens have been disbanded since last month – our own, Ralph Robertson, were telling me. He had no post to report to when it started up, wasn't sure what to do. Strange, it is, aye. I only hope it won't mean the start of further things to come.'

'I were frickened,' Madge announced suddenly, taking them all by surprise. 'I were, I admit it. I thought no, this ain't normal after so long, summat's not right. I expected a bomb through the roof at any second.'

This show of open vulnerability from their stoic and feisty matriarch subdued them. They glanced around at each other, not quite knowing what to say.

'I've been thinking about things, for quite a bit now, and . . . Tell us a story, lad,' she suggested all at once to her husband, shocking the party. She had a look in her eye that no one could ascertain. 'Go on, it's what you do best,' she urged, and her lips moved upwards in a half smile.

'A story? Well . . . what about?'

She pretended to think for a moment, then: 'How about a tale of someone moving house?'

'Eh?'

'Come along, lad. You can do it.'

Narrowing his eyes, Morris seemed to take himself off into the recesses of his mind to revisit the many, *many* tales residing there. At last, he clicked his fingers: 'I've got it!'

'Aye?' Madge murmured expectantly.

'Picture this: it were a cold and foggy day at the end of Queen Victoria's reign. My parents had just moved house, and though they liked the place, they'd found a pot doll sitting on the windowsill in the kitchen on the first day, and that they soon discovered they couldn't get rid of.'

'Oh, Morris . . .' Rolling her eyes, Madge folded her arms.

'No, listen, you'll like this one. This pot doll was cursed, they reckoned. As my mam hadn't liked the look of it, my father threw it out with the rubbish. And what occurred? Next morning, it was back – found it sitting on the doorstep, he did! Well, he thought, I'm not having this, so he took it out back and burnt it. And what occurred then? Next morning, it was back again – sitting there aye, normal as you like, not a char or scratch on it, on the bottom of the ruddy bed—!'

'Grandad, stop.' Having realised by now what her grandmother had been trying to tell him, Livvy reached for his hand. Eyes shining, she nodded encouragingly. 'Another story. *Think*. About someone moving house? *Someone* sitting not a million miles away from you?'

'You mean?' He blinked to his wife in wonder. 'Wench, is it true?'

'Aye, Morris. I want to come back.'

As man and wife hugged, Clifford and Livvy grinned, and Vera and Celia shared a smile, Joan flapped a hand:

'Hang on, hang on.'

'What?' the room asked in unison.

'So how *did* they get rid of the doll?'

'Eeh, daft lass.' Adding her laughter to the room, Madge wrapped her and Livvy in her arms. 'By, it's good to be home.'

Epilogue

'Ooh, d'you know, I could just eat you, yer little love. I could really,' Livvy cooed.

From the cosy cocoon of her pram, baby Enid bestowed upon her a shiny-gummed grin and gurgled in response.

'She's an absolute credit to you, Vera,' Livvy told her friend, walking beside her. 'She's set to be a little stunner, an' all, I'll be bound. Just like her mam,' she added, and they shared a meaningful smile.

'She's a little guzzle guts, I know that much.' Glancing down at her chest, Vera chuckled. 'Mind you, she's gorra new tooth coming through – God help me!'

'Ouch – I don't envy you there. All the same, you just enjoy these early years, love, for they're gone in the blink of an eye,' was Livvy's sage advice, with her sister in mind.

The atmosphere, when they reached the small parade of shops, almost crackled with quiet anticipation. Warsaw, the first European capital seized by the Nazis, and in all probability the city to have suffered the worst during this conflict, had been liberated by the Red Army the previous day. People milled about discussing the developments, and the general mood was one of guarded hope. Surely other places would continue to follow, become free from German control, and the war would soon be over with? Could they really allow themselves to believe that the end of this whole hellish nightmare was in sight? It was a tantalising prospect.

'We'll try the butcher's first, shall we?' Vera suggested, nodding ahead. 'See if they've owt nice in for Joan? She's that desperate to make a good impression this evening, poor lass – a nice bit of ham to offer to her visitor with their cups of tea will cheer her up no end.'

Livvy was touched by her thoughtfulness. Vera had displayed not a trace of envy upon learning that Joan's former beau Harry was coming round later to see the girl. The two of them had begun speaking in recent weeks and had quickly grown close again – a fact that delighted all of the family, and none more so than Joan herself. That she was being given the chance to start a new chapter, go forward with her life on a clean path, free from all traces of Carl Rivera, was a miracle that she certainly wasn't taking for granted. Vera, despite her circumstances having turned out wholly differently, would have been well within her rights to harbour some bitterness, however she didn't. She couldn't have been happier for the girl. 'That's a good idea, love, aye. Come on, let's hurry, before a queue forms.'

As they were entering the shop, a couple of customers were just leaving – Livvy and Vera stepped aside to allow them to pass. Yet the polite smile soon slipped from Livvy's face when she registered who they were. *Oh, here we go.* It was the viper-tongued pair from her street, who had bad-mouthed her and her marriage publicly before Clifford had come to her rescue. Not wanting further ruckus but refusing to be cowed, she retained eye contact and stared them out in dignified silence.

'Bold floozies,' one muttered as they brushed past, whilst her companion followed up the scathing remark with a loud sniff of agreement.

Livvy and Vera exchanged no words between themselves when the women had gone. It was how it was – they were more than used to it by now. They merely shot one another a weary look and, after depositing the pram beside the door, continued on inside the butcher's.

'Ignore them two. They're never happier than when they're ripping others to bits.'

At the kindly-spoken statement, Livvy glanced around in surprise. The voice, she discovered, belonged to an attractive blonde woman. Her friend, standing beside her, was taller, plumper and as dark-featured as the other was fair, and she too was regarding Livvy and Vera with open amiableness. Livvy would have placed them both in their thirties. She hazarded a smile.

'Eeh, she's a bonny mite,' the blonde woman went on, inclining her head to Enid outside beyond the glass pane. 'Your first, is she, lass?'

'Oh, she's not mine,' Livvy, who had been pushing the pram when they arrived and so understood the woman's assumption, told her. 'Enid is my mate here's daughter.'

'I'm Janie, Janie Hudson. And this is my mate, Lynn Ball. We dwell at Padbury Way, there, just facing the shops.'

Livvy and Vera nodded to them in turn, with the former saying warmly, 'I'm Livvy, and this is Vera. We're on Glaister Lane.'

'Hello, Renee, lass!' Lynn called out suddenly as the door opened and a pretty young woman with rich chestnut curls entered. Her companion, who followed her in, was much older, and both looked pleasant enough. 'Baby Ruby outside, is she?' Lynn went on, and at Renee's nod: 'I'll have to slip out forra cuddle in a minute.'

'You will not, you bugger, yer,' Renee's friend told her. Then, putting back her scarf-covered head, she chuckled heartily. 'It's taken us all ruddy morn to get her down – leave her be, for she'll soon be up and shouting her little head off. Renee here's all in.'

'Renee Wallace, the butcher's daughter-in-law,' Lynn introduced Livvy and Vera. 'And *her* mate, Mrs Gob-on-Legs, there, is Iris Flynn. The pair live on Monks Lane.'

'Huh! You, my lass, would give me a run for my money any day of the week,' threw back the elder woman good-naturedly. 'Nice to meet youse,' she continued to Livvy and Vera – although it was clear by her expression, and Renee's, however much they tried to mask it, that they knew of their past reputation. Nonetheless, both women were smiling, and Livvy and Vera returned them gratefully.

'You know I love you really, wench.' Lynn blew Iris a kiss. 'It is taxing, though, in't it. By, it is. I've got twin boys, you know – try that for size then, if you reckon one kiddy's hard work,' Lynn informed Vera and Livvy, grinning.

'Aye, and then they start toddling, and the real work begins!' piped up Janie, laughing. 'My youngest, by he's a handful and a half.'

The six of them were chattering merrily when the mountain of a man behind the counter called out, 'Right then, you fine and beautiful specimens, who's next?'

'Gordon, lad, you don't half spout some rot,' Iris

told him, looking down at herself. 'These here young 'uns might deserve such compliments but not I, so don't you try none of your soft-soaping with me!'

He let out a bellow of laughter. 'Now would I lie to you? You make coming to work a pleasure, and that's the God's honest – my life would certainly be a lot duller without you in it, my darling.'

'The blockhead,' Iris said to the other women minutes later, making them laugh as, their purchases made, they each bade one another goodbye outside the shop. 'He's norra bad egg, though, I suppose.'

For their parts, Livvy and Vera had thoroughly enjoyed the exchange and the conversations with these lovely residents. Still, they were unsure whether they ought to pinch themselves to check for certain that this was real. Each one had been so accepting that it was difficult to believe, and definitely not something they were used to.

'Happen we'll see youse tomorrow, Livvy, Vera,' Janie said as she and her friend turned for home.

'Aye, ta-ra for now,' put in Lynn, flashing a smile.

'I second that,' Renee told them. She too smiled to Livvy and Vera.

'And I third it!' Iris announced with a firm nod. 'We'll be seeing youse, lasses. Ta-ra.'

'Eeh, Livvy,' Vera breathed when they were alone.

'Weren't they nice?' she answered, equally as stupefied.

'I reckon we just might have made some mates for life, there, girl.' Vera nodded to confirm it, adding on a whisper, 'A fresh start all round, eh, love?'

'A fresh start,' Livvy echoed with a sense of completion, and there were tears in her eyes.

ABOUT THE AUTHOR

Emma Hornby lives on a tight-knit working-class estate in Bolton and has read sagas all her life. Before pursuing her career as a novelist, she had a variety of jobs, from care assistant for the elderly, to working in a Blackpool rock factory. She was inspired to write after researching her family history; like the characters in her books, many generations of her family eked out life amidst the squalor and poverty of Lancashire's slums.

You can follow her on
X @EmmaHornbyBooks and on
Facebook at www.facebook.com/
emmahornbyauthor

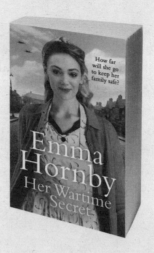

**In the depths of war, can she survive
her father's cruelty?**

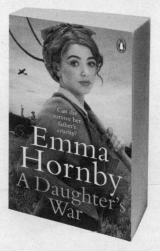

Worktown Girls at War: Book 2

Bolton, Lancashire: 1939. At seventeen, Renee Rushmore lives at home
with her father Ivan – a cruel man who rules the house with an iron fist
and keeps Renee isolated and alone. She is desperate to escape him,
but with no friends to help her, what hope does she have?

Then war breaks out. With factories and farms looking to take on
female workers, Renee dares to hope that her freedom might be within
grasp. And when she hears through a kindly local farmhand named
Jimmy that Oak Valley Farm is in need of help, she might just have
found her chance.

**But her father's eyes are on her day and night. With the help of Jimmy,
will Renee be able to escape Ivan's cruelty and find
happiness at last?**

AVAILABLE NOW

How will she choose between following her dreams and protecting her brother?

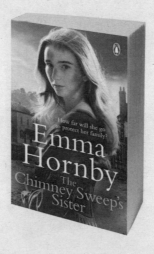

Jenny and her little brother Noah are orphans, living hand to mouth in a cellar dwelling in the heart of the Manchester slums.

At the tender age of nine, Noah is a chimney sweep's boy: a dangerous job, where he's wickedly mistreated. But they survive on his earnings, for which his older sister Jenny feels terrible guilt. It's only her fiery temper that's prevented her keeping down a job herself. With her brother's safety – his life – on the line, Jenny resolves to try and control herself, and put her talent for singing to good use. Can she earn a crust by entertaining the punters at the taverns and inns around town?

It seems like a dream come true when she catches the attention of a music hall manager and is offered a spot on a bigger stage, along with an enviable wage. But there's a darker bargain to be struck in return for their new riches . . .

How far will Jenny go to protect her brother, and will they ever find the security they crave?

AVAILABLE NOW

She only wanted what was best for her family . . .

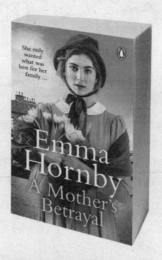

Manchester, 1867

Mara longs for a peaceful life free of violence and poverty.
But she has married into the O'Hara family, who have a
reputation for drunkenness and quick tempers. Her eldest
stepson Conrad is the worst of them all – a brute and a
criminal who makes Mara's life a misery.

But when Conrad is accused of a crime he didn't commit,
Mara is the only one who can prove his innocence. Perhaps
this is her chance to finally free her family from
his toxic influence . . .

**Will Mara clear Conrad's name, or will she have the courage
to break away from her stepson's villainy?**

AVAILABLE NOW